SILENT CITY

ALSO BY CARRIE SMITH

Forget Harry

SILENT CITY

A Claire Codella Mystery

Carrie Smith

CROOKED
LANE

NEW YORK

Published in the United States by Crooked Lane Books, an imprint of The Quick Brown Fox & Company LLC.

Crooked Lane Books and its logo are trademarks of The Quick Brown Fox & Company LLC.

The Library of Congress Cataloging-in-Publication Data is available upon request.

ISBN (hardcover): 978-1-62953-310-0
ISBN (paperback): 978-1-62953-374-2
e-ISBN: 978-1-62953-311-7

Cover design by Lori Palmer
Book design by Jennifer Canzone

Printed in the United States.

www.crookedlanebooks.com

Crooked Lane Books
2 Park Avenue, 10th Floor
New York, NY 10016

First Edition: October 2015

10 9 8 7 6 5 4 3 2 1

To Cynthia, the courageous one,
and to our beautiful children, Cameron and Matthew

TUESDAY

CHAPTER 1

The ringing of her cell phone ruptured the early morning silence. McGowan cleared his throat right in her ear. "Reilly's got a body in his precinct and only a rookie detective to catch it. Some guy named Muñoz. It's your old stomping ground, Codella. Why don't you skip the morning briefing and give him a hand? Nothing like hitting the ground running, right?"

No *hello*. No *how you doing?* No *good to have you on board again.* Was he happy to have a body to keep her out of his morning meeting so he wouldn't have to rally the team for a big welcome back? Well, she didn't want one any more than he wanted to give one. "Sure. I'll head right over."

Claire Codella swung her feet off the bed, skipped the shower, and stepped in front of the sink. *Who would she see at the scene*, she wondered, *and what would they say when they saw her?* She stared into the medicine cabinet mirror and imagined what the CSU guys would notice. The hair, of course. The hair was the dead giveaway. It was still so goddamn short. But at least it was black again. The first growths sprouting from the damaged follicles had been rusty colored, coarse, and kinky. They had capped her scalp like the tight ringlets on the sculpted bust of an ancient Roman emperor. At least the ringlets had relaxed, and now with a little styling gel, she could make her hair look spiky. Maybe she would even fool a few people into thinking she was some wannabe punk rocker instead of a cancer victim.

She splashed cold water over her face. Her eyes were as blue as ever, and her skin still as pale and smooth as bone china, but she knew she wasn't exactly attractive with hair like this. Attractiveness had been irrelevant for the past ten months, of course.

During her illness, she had not given one thought to looking good, and she had not once thought about sex except as something distant and abstract, something that existed in the world but didn't directly touch her daily life, like the Taliban, the state of the economy, poverty, or famine. Even now, she felt no sexual desire. Like her extremities, that ultimate private zone of her body was numb. Months of vincristine—one of the six toxic chemicals making up the hyper-CVAD chemotherapy cocktail—had deadened her nerve endings. The tips of her fingers now tingled morning, noon, and night as if she had recently suffered frostbite and were still—and perpetually—in a state of partial thaw.

"How long will this numbness last?" she had asked her oncologist, Dr. Abrams, at her first posttreatment exam.

He had shrugged. "It could last several months, or it could never go away," he'd conceded matter-of-factly. He was a say-it-like-it-is-but-don't-panic-about-things-you-can't-change guy, and she liked that about him. She preferred the truth to gentle fantasy landings. During investigations, she always gave the truth—as sensitively as possible, of course—to the families of the violently murdered. She could deal with lifelong neuropathy, she supposed, so long as it didn't prevent her from pulling the trigger and passing her periodic shooting exams. She could endure the lack of interest from the opposite sex right now, too. And she had even suspended her vanity for months. But apparently, that was now returning.

Twenty minutes later, she stepped out of a taxi on West 112th Street. "Hey, where ya been, Detective?" the skinny uniform in front of the building called out. "And where's your latté? You always have a latté."

"Not anymore." Codella's eyes darted up the treeless block of grimy tenement buildings. In the pre-rush-hour calm of early morning, she could feel the nervous pulse at her neck as she ducked under the crime scene tape. Everything about this scene felt familiar and yet it was different too—or maybe *she* was just different.

"You must be Muñoz," she said to the towering dark-skinned detective who approached her.

"Eduardo Muñoz." He smiled.

"Follow me, Detective," she said, and he fell into step behind her like a six-foot-five lost dog. At least he wasn't Brian Haggerty. At least she didn't have to face *him* yet.

They entered the lobby of the yellow brick walk-up, and the heel of her left boot landed in a sticky spill in front of the aluminum mailboxes. It made a crackling sound as she peeled it off the tiles. She took the stairs two at a time, just in case Muñoz or anybody on the landing above doubted her stamina, and the movement of her arms made her shoulder holster jiggle uncomfortably. She hadn't adjusted it properly to her new weight, and the Glock pounded annoyingly against her ribcage.

On the fourth floor, her lungs were screaming, and she had to will herself to take even breaths as she approached the familiar, smiling uniform outside the apartment.

The reddish-haired officer stared at her intently as he held out a clipboard and a pen. "Nice to see you, Detective."

Her foggy brain wouldn't cough up his name so she glanced surreptitiously at his nameplate. O'Donnell. Then she remembered. "Good to see you too, Joe." She took the pen and signed in. Then she handed it to Muñoz. As he signed his name, she slipped on Tyvek booties. "How long you been in the 171st, Detective?"

"Four days."

"Before that?"

"Narcotics. Undercover."

"So this is your first homicide case?"

He nodded.

"Here, put these on." She handed him booties like a mother dressing a small child. A year ago she might have been annoyed having to do this, but now she found she didn't mind. Playing mother was a far better alternative than playing the child, and she had been the dependent one far too often recently. She watched Muñoz stretch the booties around his very long leather shoes. Surely this big guy who looked like a Knicks guard had been to death scenes before. He must have seen ODs and stabbings and shootings, she thought. But that didn't mean he knew what to look for.

"Stand here," she ordered as she stepped through the door. "Right against the wall. I'll call you when I want you."

The clapping began with one pair of nitrile-gloved hands, slow and deliberate. Then the other crime scene investigators joined in. It took Codella a few seconds to realize they were applauding her.

"Our genius returns!" announced Banks, the lead investigator. He was a thin, gangly man, with arms and legs that looked disproportionately long for his torso, and apparently, he still wasn't letting her live down the *New York* magazine article that had called her a "genius of deductive reasoning" after the Wainright Blake case last year.

"Fuck off." She smiled good-naturedly.

"You're the one who's been fucking off."

They all laughed.

"Oh, right. That's what I was doing."

Muñoz waited and watched by the door as she turned her attention to the body on the living room floor. "How'd he go down?"

"No blood. No marks on the body," said Banks. "The medical examiner's on his way."

Codella studied the corpse like a masterpiece at the Met. The victim's neck tilted unnaturally to the left so that his chin touched his left shoulder. His arms were outstretched at ninety-degree angles from his body and his palms were facing up in what could only be a deliberate pose. He was wearing a pair of cotton boxers—a muted blue-and-green-plaid version of a loincloth—and his torso was bare. As in most depictions of Christ, he had scant chest hair. But the ripple of well-toned arm and stomach muscles made him conspicuously more buff than a medieval Christ. The placement of his legs confirmed the intentional symbolism. They were bare, bent slightly at the knees, and the right foot had been carefully placed over the left. Only nails piercing flesh were missing—and a crown of thorns and cross. Now, due to the muscular contraction of rigor mortis, this man was frozen into a Christlike statue, and he would remain this way until putrefaction freed him from his virtual cross.

She stared at his thick hair, as coal-black as her own. She noted his refined Latin features, his five o'clock shadow, his prominent Adam's apple. She snapped his photo with her iPhone. *Who are you?* she wondered silently. *What the hell happened to you?*

Banks's eyes were on her as she lowered her phone. She could read his mind like a tabloid headline. *Genius Cop Sees First Corpse After Cancer. Can She Take It?* And now she wondered if she could. Having focused so intently on eluding her own death for the last ten months, did she still have the unwavering resoluteness and cool rationality required to focus on someone else's?

She wondered if Banks or any of these other crime scene detectives ever stopped to analyze why they had chosen their particular vocation. Before now, she hadn't dwelled on the deeper implications of her work either. But sitting hour after hour in a hospital bed and walking the halls attached to an IV pole had provided her with abundant time to reflect on all the unpleasantness of her childhood. She didn't need anyone's help to see that choosing a career in law enforcement was her antidote to growing up with a violent and abusive father. A religious person might conclude that she was doing penance for the damage he had caused in the lives of the people around him. A psychologist might conjecture that she was still trying to save others from violence because she had not been able to protect her own mother. But even if those assumptions had once been true, did they still apply? Doctors had just saved *her*. And maybe it was time to move on in her life. Maybe it was a mistake to have come back for more of this grisly business.

Her mouth was dry. She unwrapped a piece of the Biotene gum a chemo nurse had told her would help relieve her dry mouth, one of the lingering effects of so many toxic chemicals in her system. She kept her eyes down. She knew she was doing the worst possible thing, giving into self-doubt in front of others, and if she didn't find her footing fast, they would all smell her insecurity. Of course it wasn't a mistake to be here, she told herself. This was her life. Getting back to her life necessarily meant getting back to other people's deaths.

She gripped the sleeves of her soft leather jacket, hoping that this prized possession she'd bought on the day she'd joined the detective ranks could bring back all the confidence she'd had before she'd been tethered to a chemo pole so many times that it had begun to feel like another—albeit unwanted—appendage. She took a deep breath, raised her eyes, and turned to O'Donnell. "What do we know?"

"Not much. The dog was howling all night. The neighbor," he motioned toward a door on the opposite side of the tiled, five-by-five-foot hallway, "called the super and the super came up early this morning. This is what he found."

"Where's the dog now?"

"With the super."

"What about him?" She gestured to the body.

"His name's Hector Sanchez. Lived alone. He's a public school principal."

She turned back to the dead man. *Okay, Hector Sanchez. You're the dead one, not me.* She moved farther into the apartment and snapped several more photos.

"Hey, we already got him from every angle, Detective," one investigator assured her.

"Don't waste your breath," Banks told him. "She always takes her own." Then he looked at Muñoz. "Good luck with her. You're about to get a real education."

Codella stopped snapping. "Ignore him, Detective. Get over here and take photographs. Your camera. Your eyes. Never rely on someone else."

The body lay sprawled on a deep-crimson faux-oriental rug. The room's ceiling was high, and the crown molding was intricate though not well preserved. Deep fissures in the plaster cried out for skim coating. New York public school principals, she observed, apparently couldn't afford to renovate their apartments any more than NYPD detectives could. The radiator below the windows was hissing and clanking, and the windows were cracked open to let in the bracing November air.

The victim's flat-screen TV, mounted on the wall above a non-working fireplace, was on, though the volume had been muted. "Did anyone here mute this TV?" she called out.

Two investigators simultaneously shook their heads. Everything was as it had been, they assured her.

The victim's laptop rested on a brown leather hassock in front of a matching leather chair facing the flat-screen TV. Codella moved to where she could see the laptop screen, but it was black.

"Have you lifted prints and checked for DNA on this?"

Banks nodded.

"Okay if I have a look?"

"Be my guest."

She found gloves and put them on. The laptop was plugged into a socket in the wall where a table lamp also drew its power. She pressed return and the screen blinked back to life, revealing an open Internet browser. The computer's cursor was poised in a blank text box in the browser. Hector Sanchez, it appeared, had been about to compose a message before his murder.

She scrolled up in the window and discovered that the victim had been reading a thread of postings initiated by a blogger named Helen C. Her initial message had been posted at 3:48 PM the day before.

My son was BRUTALLY attacked in the boy's room of PS 777 this morning. An older student forced him into a bathroom stall and pushed his head into a toilet bowl full of urine. And the attacker's punishment? An in-school suspension so he "isn't out there on the streets." I'm sorry, but since when does the perpetrator get the protection instead of the victim? There's no such thing as "public education" in this country anymore. Our taxes pay for PUBLIC INDIFFERENCE. We're forced to share the burden of each other's dysfunction and violence. I didn't come to PS 777 for this. I came because the principal promised my son the special services he needs. SO MUCH FOR PROMISES!

Muñoz had come close and was reading over her shoulder as she scrolled down to the responses this post had provoked.

You're an idiot if you think anybody keeps promises . . .

It's even worse in middle school. A SIXTH GRADER threatened my son at knifepoint!!

Take heart. Remember, blessed are the meek . . .

Why are you people always shoving your biblical shit down people's throats?!!! Urine wasn't enough for her son?

A little advice from the wise . . . Get a FAKE ADDRESS!! Register your kid in a BETTER CATCHMENT. Nothing's equal—even in the public school system. The poor kids get poor schools and the rich kids get the bells and whistles.

All those principals and teachers care about is their union-negotiated salaries, benefits, retirement packages, and tenure. Thank the unions for what happened to your son.

If you're pushing a classmate into a toilet bowl at the age of
12, just imagine what you'll be doing when you're 18.

No shit, Dr. Freud!!

She turned to Muñoz. "Interesting. He comes home, peels
down to his boxers, and keeps up with the school message boards."

"You think this Helen C. has something to do with his murder?"

"Too early to tell. Let's not skip ahead. Let's get all the details
first." She turned to Banks. "This computer goes to the precinct."

"Yes, ma'am."

"Any evidence the murderer stripped the victim?"

Banks shook his head. "There's a suit jacket neatly draped on
a chair by his bed, matching pants on a hanger on the closet door,
and a pair of jeans and a T-shirt hanging on the handlebars of his
spin bike. I'd say he undressed himself."

"But was he wearing the suit or the jeans and T-shirt?"

Banks shrugged. "The suit, I'm guessing. The jeans could have
been there for days—like mine always are."

"And you think he undressed himself why? Because murderers
don't know how to drape jackets neatly? If the victim went to the
trouble of hanging his pants on a hanger, why didn't he go the extra
distance and put the hanger in the closet?"

Banks shrugged. "You're the genius, not me."

She turned back to Muñoz. "Are you a boxers or briefs guy?"

Muñoz's eyes got wide.

Banks snickered. "Uh-oh. The cougar's been caged up too long."

She rolled her eyes.

Muñoz grinned with impressively white teeth. "Boxers," he
said. "Why?"

"And you live alone?"

"Hear that guys? She's looking for some action," said Banks.

She flipped him a lethargic bird and turned to Muñoz. "How
often you hang out in your boxers?"

He shrugged. "Pretty often. My apartment gets hot. Like
this one."

"And if someone rang your bell, you'd open the door in your
boxers?"

"Depends who was at my door."

"Let's say it's a guy you know."

"Sure."

"A guy you don't know?"

"Probably."

"A woman?"

He considered. "I'd probably throw on pants."

"Not me," said Banks.

She turned to him. "Was the entry forced?"

"Nope."

Her eyes shifted to the flickering flat-screen, which was tuned to MSNBC. *If* Banks was right about Sanchez undressing himself, then the murdered principal had been sitting here in his boxers, and at some point his doorbell must have rung or someone had knocked and maybe that was when he'd muted the TV, set his laptop on the hassock for the last time in his life, and opened the door. But who was at that door?

Muñoz moved toward the windows and stooped to examine something on the bottom shelf of an end table. "Check this out, Detective Codella."

She stepped over. With her gloved hands, she picked up a *New York Times Magazine*. "Is This Man the Savior of PS 777?" asked the headline from last June, and below that question was a photo of Sanchez standing on the front steps of a school, arms crossed over a suit jacket, black eyes facing the camera.

"Well, well, well. We've got ourselves a celebrity." She opened to the five-month-old article.

It's a typical Monday morning at PS 777 on Manhattan's Upper West Side. I'm five minutes early, and principal Hector Sanchez is still outside greeting children as they climb the front steps of the school. Students line up patiently to shake hands with the man who has made it clear they are his number one priority. Welcoming children into the building is Sanchez's favorite part of the day. "You look into those eyes," he tells me, "and you still see excitement. The desire to learn hasn't been extinguished yet. And I don't want to let them down."

Fear of letting the children down is what keeps Sanchez up at night, and it's what drives him all day as he applies for grants, makes daily classroom visits to monitor the quality of instruction, and enforces new codes of behavior intended to build respect among students and end misconduct.

Five months ago, Sanchez inherited a school in crisis. And like any leader promoted on a battlefield, he has improvised. "When I got here," he tells me as we tour the now clean, well-lighted campus that serves 608 students in kindergarten through grade 5, "the bathrooms reeked. The halls were dark. The PA system was broken. How can you expect good behavior and high achievement in a place like that? The first thing we did was paint and clean and screw in light bulbs."

The new principal got a slap on the wrist for his trouble—he didn't fill out the required paperwork and use custodial union labor (which might have delayed the paint job and the light bulbs for months). Instead, he charged the paint on his credit card, picked up a paintbrush, and enlisted willing parents and children to help. Needless to say, this maverick has his critics within the Department of Education, but the parents of PS 777 are solidly in his corner. In a school where more than 80 percent of third graders have failed the state reading and math assessments for five consecutive years, they believe Hector Sanchez is the school's best and last hope. But does he face an impossible challenge?

She returned the magazine to the shelf. "E-mail me a copy of that article, Muñoz."

Muñoz nodded. "What do you make of it?"

"He was a savior and now he's been crucified. Hard to miss the connection. Keep looking around, but put some gloves on first."

Beside the end table was a gold couch with crimson throw pillows. The wall above the couch was bare. "Do we know how long this guy was living here?" she asked no one in particular.

"According to the super, about two years," said Officer O'Donnell at the door.

"Own or rent?"

"It's a co-op building."

"Anybody find his cell phone?"

"No," said a CSU investigator, "but there's an iPhone charger on the kitchen counter."

"I want that phone. Find me that phone. It goes to the precinct along with the computer, any bills, and that *New York* magazine."

Her eyes settled on a framed photograph on the bookshelf. She moved closer, and the image surprised her. She'd seen it many times before, on a billboard mounted on the side of the bus stop shelter at West Eighty-Eighth Street and Broadway.

Two Caucasian women and their young African American daughter smiled into the camera above a caption that read, *We're a Proud PS 777 Family.* One of the women had neck-length, blond-streaked hair; high cheekbones; brilliant green eyes; a silky complexion; and sumptuous lips. "Look familiar?" she asked Muñoz.

"Isn't she that actress?"

"That's right. Dana Drew. She's on Broadway right now. You ever see her on those billboards all over the Upper West Side?"

"I live in Chelsea. I see them there, too."

Banks came over. "Lemme see. She was hot in *Time's Up!* Did you see that?"

"She's a lesbian," said one of his team.

"Yeah, a really *hot* lesbian," said Banks.

Codella tuned out the predictable conversation that followed as she studied the photograph. The woman beside Drew could not have looked more different from the actress. Her brown hair was as short as Codella's postchemo hair. Her expensive-looking button-down shirt could have belonged to a male hedge fund manager dressed for a night out in Tribeca. Whenever Codella passed that billboard, it was difficult not to wonder how the chemistry between the beautiful actress and her stylishly butch partner played out in private. What, she wondered now, was the photograph doing here? "This goes into evidence," she told Banks.

Fifteen minutes later, Rudolph Gambarin stepped through the door in a full Tyvek coverall and signed O'Donnell's clipboard. "You're back," he observed matter-of-factly when Codella greeted him.

"I'm back."

"I wasn't sure you would be."

"No?"

"I looked up your lymphoma. Burkitt's. B-cell. Extremely aggressive." It was the kind of tactlessly truthful statement few people would say to a cancer survivor, but Codella didn't take offense. She had long ago concluded that Gambarin was a very high-functioning member of the Autism Spectrum Club. The need for tact never occurred to him, which made it fortunate that most of his so-called patients were dead.

"Lucky for me the more aggressive the lymphoma, the more responsive it is to chemo." She smiled blandly, but behind the smile and the casual answer was a tsunami of bad memories. She remembered the day last April when she had checked into the hospital for her first treatment. She had waited almost two hours in admissions for her bed to become available. When she finally got upstairs, she had quickly learned that her roommate was an anorexic woman of about fifty.

The roommate had no visitors. Instead, she used her call button frequently to summon nurses' aides, nurses, and doctors using a variety of pretexts like the need for a blanket, a question about her medications, or a complaint about the treatment she had received from a different aide, nurse, technician, or doctor. She spoke to each caregiver in a high, quavering child's voice that had gotten under Codella's skin even before she was hooked to her first IV bag. Codella had watched the chemotherapy drugs in that first bag drip down in evenly spaced intervals, slowly slide through the clear plastic tube, and enter her body to do their work while her fifty-year-old regressed anorexic roommate went on and on like a helpless child to whomever would listen.

Codella had expected the chemo drugs to make her nauseous right away—everyone knew that chemotherapy made you throw up—but she hadn't felt queasy at all that first night, which gave her a false sense of optimism. She must be stronger than other cancer patients, she had naïvely concluded, and her optimism had grown as each bag was finished and each new bag was hung from her chemo pole and hooked to her newly installed port.

After five days of the twenty-four-hour drip, she walked out of the hospital, rode home with her neighbor Jean, and felt relatively normal for two more days—until her white blood count crashed to, as her doctor put it, "impressively low single digits," and she spiked a one hundred and two fever and ended up back in the emergency room. And then she began to learn what "aggressive" chemo was all about.

"CODOX-M/IVAC regimen?" Gambarin was asking now.

"Hyper-CVAD. I wouldn't wish it on anyone." *Well, almost anyone*, she amended, considering that repeated rounds of multiagent chemotherapy might be a fitting form of punishment for brutal killers of women and children.

Gambarin nodded. "What have we got here?"

"No blood. No weapon. No obvious contusions. No signs of a struggle. Just a curious New Testament tableau." She gestured toward their Latino Jesus on the carpet.

Gambarin pulled on nitrile gloves, moved closer to the body, and stooped. He didn't speak or move for several seconds. Then he finally announced, "Judging from the position of his head, I'd say his neck was broken." He pointed. "Third or fourth cervical vertebrae, I'm guessing. In which case, he probably died of asphyxiation, but I'll have to confirm that." He rose. He was thin and his knees were agile for a man in his midfifties. "I'll be able to give you more information tomorrow. I'll call you when I have something."

With that, he turned his full attention to his "patient," clearly dismissing her.

Codella stepped past O'Donnell into the fourth-floor lobby, ducked into the fire stairwell, and speed-dialed the head of her old department, Captain Matthew Reilly of the 171st Precinct.

"Thanks for getting there so soon, Claire," he said.

"Who's the new guy?" she asked.

"Muñoz? He's not really ready to catch a homicide, but Schugren and Blackstone were at a break-in and Murphy has a hit and run on West End and Ninety-Sixth. Fucking bad corner. Nothing they do on that corner makes it better. Portino wasn't here yet. It's been a helluva twenty-four hours. Muñoz was all I had."

What about Brian, she wanted to ask. *Where was he?* In the not so distant past, Brian Haggerty was the one Reilly would usually call on a case like this if she were not available. He was the best detective Reilly had now that she had moved to Homicide. But she stopped herself from asking. What did she care anymore? Better for her that he wasn't here.

Reilly seemed to read her mind. "Haggerty's got a dead baby. He's chasing down the mother's boyfriend."

"Jesus."

"So I had to call McGowan, get him to loan you back."

"Don't worry. Muñoz will be fine." She stared through the open apartment door at the victim's ribcage where she had observed dark curls of hair just below his navel. "But this situation is anything but fine," she told her former commander. "Somebody decided to make a public school principal look like Jesus on the cross."

"Shit. What do you make of it?"

"I don't know yet. I'll keep you posted. For now, send more uniforms to help Muñoz with the canvass. I'm going over to the school. Given what's here, I think we should investigate on both fronts. We'll need a lot of background checks, and I think we should put some low-profile security in place at the school—just on the off chance we've got a crazy teacher over there." She didn't mention Sandy Hook, the school in Newtown, Connecticut, where a single gunman with a thirty-round magazine had mowed down twenty children and six teachers. She didn't have to. Now everyone thought about Sandy Hook when schoolchildren were involved.

Reilly said, "I'll send two officers, more if I can spare them. Portino can be your contact here. Ragavan will meet you at the school. He's stepped up a lot, you know. You'd be proud of how he's coming along since you left."

"Ragavan's perfect," she said. Anyone but Brian was perfect, she told herself, and now she recognized the futile overcompensation in her thoughts. She did want to see him. She wanted to hear his voice. She could see him now in her head passing her a Starbucks cup and saying, "Your daily latté, Detective." Despite everything that had happened and although she wasn't happy to admit it, the simple truth was that she missed him. "I'll be in touch," she told Reilly and hung up.

When she reentered the apartment, Gambarin was measuring the victim's core temperature. She waved Muñoz into the lobby. "You ever run a canvass, Detective?"

"Sure." He smiled. "In Narc you're always looking for someone."

"Okay, but you never ran one for me, so let's get a few things straight. I don't tolerate sloppiness. I don't leave stones unturned. Your team does it by the book. They record everything. You aren't done until they've spoken to every human being in this building. And everything gets documented. Names, addresses, contact information. I want to know where they were, who they were with, and exactly who they saw come and go between yesterday afternoon and this morning. And I want a phone call the minute you find something that could possibly help us. Your team will be here soon. Spell out your expectations and make sure they're addressed, because I'm holding *you* completely responsible for what happens here. Understood?"

"Perfectly," he said.

"Good."

They went downstairs and traded cell numbers.

CHAPTER 2

Muñoz watched Codella head toward Frederick Douglass Boulevard. Then he sat on the front steps of Sanchez's apartment to wait for his canvass team, closed his eyes, and expelled a long sigh of relief. Somehow the morning had not turned out as awful as he had expected. No one had called him New Dick this morning.

"New Dick" was the nickname Detective Blackstone had christened him with four days ago. For three mornings in a row, Blackstone had greeted him with "Hey, New Dick" or "Look, New Dick's here" in front of the other detectives. Muñoz had hoped the nickname would eventually be forgotten, and when Blackstone had patted his back yesterday afternoon and said, "Have a drink with us, Muñoz," he had assumed it was finally a relic of the past.

"Sure, why not," he had said, even though it meant delaying his other plans.

At six thirty, he had pulled open the front door of the bar, inhaled the familiar odor of stale alcohol, and waited for his eyes to adjust. He had frequented more than his share of dark neighborhood bars, but neighborhood bars in Chelsea were very different from the St. James Pub. Here he felt no welcoming, interested stares. He felt no sense of relief. *Why had he agreed to this?* was his first thought as the door had closed behind him.

Muñoz hadn't seen the ambush coming until he heard Blackstone's bombastic voice bellow, "New Dick!" above the music, the five sports channels on flat-screens, and the chatter of patrons well on their way to weeknight inebriation.

In a schoolyard, Muñoz realized now, Blackstone would have been the boy with social aggression issues. In a street gang, he would

have been the most violent gang leader. In a wolf pack, he would
be constantly fighting to maintain the role of alpha male. He was a
bully, and if you tried to fight a bully, you just gave him the satisfaction of knowing he'd gotten under your skin. If you pretended
you didn't care what your bully said, there was no guarantee he'd
cease and desist either. Aggressors could smell fear and anxiety in
their prey.

Blackstone and his posse—Murphy, Schugren, Aceveda—were
sitting at a table across from the bar. Muñoz took the empty chair
next to Blackstone who immediately slapped his back and said,
"What'll it be?"

"Heineken."

Blackstone made a dramatic show of snapping his finger at the
bartender. Then he leaned closer to Muñoz and said, "So what do
you think of our tame little precinct?"

"It's great."

"Better than cruising crack houses?"

The odd choice of words caused Muñoz to look up. He met
Blackstone's eyes and the other detective didn't look away, so he did.

Then Blackstone asked, "Was there a lot of *action* for you in
those crack houses?" and Muñoz thought he saw him wink at the
other cops.

"Not sure what you mean," said Muñoz. But he had a terrible
feeling he knew *exactly* what Blackstone meant.

"Oh, I think you do," said Blackstone quietly.

The Heineken came. Muñoz sipped it. Murphy cried out when
the Knicks scored on a breakaway slam dunk. All around the bar,
people were cheering, but Muñoz felt as if he were sitting in an
isolation bubble. He was trapped, and he wasn't sure how to escape
before a fatal shot was fired.

Blackstone leaned toward him and sniffed the air. "Is that after-
shave you're wearing?" he asked in a loud voice. Then he sniffed
again, more dramatically. "Or is that," he paused for effect, "*perfume?*"

Muñoz sipped his beer. "What's your problem, man?"

"No problem, New Dick," Blackstone responded. "It's just,
well, I've been meaning to ask you all day because—don't be
offended, I'm just being honest—ever since you joined the precinct,
the detective pool smells," he paused for effect again, "a little *girlie.*"

He chugged his beer. "Hey, guys, is it just me or do you think Muñoz smells a little girlie, too? Have a sniff."

Murphy leaned in, then Schugren and Aceveda. They were like classic stooges. Muñoz jerked away and stood.

"That's enough," he said.

"We getting you all hot and bothered?"

"Hardly." He pulled on his jacket.

"But you're not denying you're a fag?"

There it was, Muñoz thought. The deathblow. The two sudden adversaries looked at each other. This time Muñoz was determined not to look away first.

"Well?" Blackstone pressed. "It's okay. It's a new world, right? But we wanna know if it's a fag who's got our back." And then all four men were waiting for his response.

There was only one path to salvation in that moment, Muñoz realized. He would have to punch Blackstone in the gut so hard that the beer in his belly erupted from his mouth like lava. So why was he waiting? He was no coward. He'd just spent almost two years of his life getting guns pointed in his face on a regular basis, and he hadn't panicked then. He was stronger, taller, and fitter than Blackstone and every other detective at their table. But he couldn't bring himself to do it. Despite his size and strength, he wasn't wiping the floor with their asses. Apparently, he was as *girlie* as he smelled.

"Jesus Christ," Blackstone exploded with glee. "He's a fuckin' fag. We got ourselves a fuckin' fag in the unit."

Muñoz turned. "So long, guys."

"That's right. *Guys.*" Blackstone repeated the word as Muñoz walked toward the door. Blackstone's grating, triumphant voice somehow carried over all the ambient noise. It was like a guided missile aimed directly at his ears. "We're guys, all right. *Real* guys. Not *your* kind of guys." He heard the four men laugh as he pushed open the door and stepped out into the chill night.

What had he done or not done? he wondered. How had he given himself away? What had Blackstone seen that he didn't even know he had shown? How was it that this overblown asshole could nail him to the wall? Muñoz had heard their laughter in his head all the way home.

He pushed it as far from his mind as he could when his team arrived ten minutes later, two uniforms with pounds of paraphernalia hanging off their belts. They stood in front of the apartment building while Muñoz briefed them on the situation.

"We've got a school principal in there who was murdered sometime last evening. There was no forced entry. Whoever did it must have come in and gone out through that front door." He pointed. "Either the victim let him in or someone else did. And we're gonna talk to everyone in there. We need to know who entered and left the building yesterday afternoon and evening. We need times, details, descriptions. I want everything on paper. And remember, you could be talking to the killer. Keep your eyes and ears open."

The officer named Caputo paid careful attention. He was the kind of young, enthusiastic cop Muñoz himself had been a couple years out of the academy. He obviously had big plans for himself, and helping out on a murder investigation instead of cruising the blocks between Amsterdam and Manhattan Avenues in a cramped patrol car was an opportunity to prove his usefulness. Muñoz sensed he could count on this man.

The officer named Garcia was older and less moved by the urgency of the situation. "Eight doors a floor. Fourteen floors." He stopped short of doing the math. "This'll take forever with just three of us, Detective." His tone challenged Muñoz's right to ask so much of them.

Muñoz remembered Codella's words as he stared into the man's passive-aggressive eyes. *Let's get a few things straight. I don't tolerate sloppiness. I don't leave stones unturned.* "Then I guess we won't have to figure out what to do with the rest of our lives," he told Garcia, and he held Garcia's stare until the officer averted his eyes. Being six foot six had plenty of disadvantages when it came to riding in compact cars, flying coach, and buying beds. But height had an upside, too. People usually backed down when Muñoz confronted them.

He pointed to Caputo. "Start on fourteen and work down to eight. And you," he turned back to Garcia, "start with the ground floor apartments and move up. The victim lived on six. I'll take five and seven. No one goes anywhere near the crime scene. If you come across anyone who saw the victim yesterday or saw someone strange in the building, call me on my cell right away." Then Muñoz climbed the fire stairs to seven feeling like a detective for the first time since his official promotion. *Fuck Blackstone*, he thought. *Fuck them all.*

There was no answer at the first two doors he knocked on, but when he rapped on the third one, a dog barked and a delicate female voice on the other side said, "Shhhhhh, Carter. Stop. It's okay."

The door opened and a woman, maybe twenty-five, looked up at him. She had long, wavy hair with natural bronze highlights, and the eyes behind her glasses were yellowish green, like cat eyes. They were bright and intelligent. He pulled open his blazer to show her his shiny new shield.

"What's going on?" she asked. "They wouldn't let me leave. Is it true Hector's dead?"

Muñoz nodded. "You knew him?"

"I walk his dog every day. Charlie."

"When was the last time?"

"Yesterday. One o'clock. I do it every day while Hector's gone. What happened to him?"

"We're trying to find that out. Does he keep his door locked while he's at work?"

"Always. Top and bottom. Two different keys. I keep a set in my apartment."

"Did you see him yesterday or just his dog?"

"I saw him, too."

"What time was that?"

She thought for an instant. "A little after five, I think." She leaned down to scratch her dog's ears. "I dropped off some doggie treats I forgot to leave earlier. There's a pet food store I go to. Carter and Charlie went with me. They have organic dog treats."

"People buy organic treats for their dogs?"

She smiled.

"Do you remember what Sanchez was wearing when you saw him just after five?"

"Jeans. A short-sleeved shirt. Yellow or tan, I think."

"What sort of mood was he in?"

"Cheerful. Same as always." She shook her head. "How could something like this have happened?"

"That's what we have to find out. Did he say anything about his plans for the night?"

She shook her head and curled her index finger around some strands of hair.

"Was anyone else in his apartment when you saw him?"

"No." She paused and considered. "I mean, I don't think so. I'm pretty sure I would have noticed."

"Did you stand at his door or go inside?"

"I went into the living room. I was there for three or four minutes. I petted Charlie. Where's Charlie now?"

"With the super."

"I'd take him, you know. I'd give him a home." She was still curling her finger around the strands of hair.

She was very pretty, he thought, and very kind. The antithesis of a bully. And how different his position would be right now with Blackstone if he were the kind of guy who'd look at her and think, *I'd like to take you home.* He could sit with Blackstone's posse and shove back beers and shots and be one of them. But that thought was even more unappealing than being their victim.

"What did you talk about while you were in his apartment?" he asked the young woman.

"Charlie's walk." She smiled. "Hector always liked to hear what Charlie had done. Yesterday I let him off his leash in Riverside Park, and he ran after some teenagers playing Frisbee and caught it midair. They started throwing the Frisbee for him over and over. I told Hector he needed to get a Frisbee and play with Charlie."

"What did you notice in the apartment?"

"Nothing unusual." She winced apologetically.

"What was he doing?"

Her brow furrowed as she thought. "He was holding his phone," she remembered.

"Cell phone or landline?"

"Cell phone."

"And did you happen to see his laptop anywhere?"

"As a matter of fact, I did. The case was next to the door."

"You're sure about that?"

She nodded. "Carter was sniffing at it. I had to pull him off."

"Was it open?"

"Partly. It was crammed with stuff."

"You're sure the laptop was in it?"

She nodded again.

"Sanchez has a footstool in his living room. Was there anything on the footstool?"

She frowned. "I don't think so. Why?"

He ignored her question. "Did you see anyone enter the building yesterday who you didn't recognize?"

She thought for several seconds. "The FreshDirect guy was hauling boxes in as I left with the dogs."

"Anyone else? Anyone later in the day?"

"Not that I saw."

"Where were you last night?"

"Out with friends. I left around seven, I think."

"All right, Miss—"

"Swain. Cameron Swain."

He wrote down her name and phone number. He gave her his card. "Call me if you think of any other details that might help us."

She took the card and closed her door. He walked to the far end of the corridor that led to the other wing of the building. Then he stopped and turned back. He knocked on her door again. She hadn't retreated yet and she opened almost immediately. "More questions?"

"Just one. Sorry. Did Hector Sanchez ever greet you at the door in his boxer shorts?"

She was obviously surprised by the question. "Hector? He'd never do that."

"Why not?"

"He just wouldn't," she said. "Trust me. He wasn't that kind of guy."

CHAPTER 3

Codella stood on the sidewalk and stared at the façade of Manhattan North. Ten months had passed since she had last entered this unattractive glass building where her new homicide unit was stationed. She took a deep breath and held it in for several seconds. She had to face Dennis McGowan sooner or later. During her leave of absence, he would have shut her out of his mind completely, she was certain, and he would not be happy to have her back in his squad. For all she knew, he had even secretly hoped she would die. He would be looking for ways to discredit her, and she couldn't let that happen. She had to play the good subordinate and update him on everything.

She gripped the door handle and stared at her reflection in the glass. She certainly looked tough enough to hold her own, she thought. Someone seeing her for the first time might mistake her for a military recruit at the end of basic training. She could imagine her new homicide colleagues making cracks behind her back or taking surreptitious cell phone photos and texting them to each other.

She pulled open the door. Just inside was the Plexiglas-partitioned area where uniformed desk cops were stationed. These officers were the first line of defense between this fortress and the general public. They deflected the onslaught of Harlem's men and women with anger issues, outraged recipients of misdemeanor violations, hysterical victims of muggers or pickpockets, drunks and homeless people with nowhere else to go, and the occasional curious reporters doing research for a crime blog.

As she entered, these officers looked toward her and then quickly away assuming she was just the latest petitioner who would demand, complain, excoriate, or vomit on the tile. She recognized all of them and reached through her foggy brain to recall their names: Andy Vaccaro, the desk sergeant whose family came from the same part of Italy as her father's family; Paterson, who was manning the phone line; and Kevin Hernandez, who was processing a patrol officer's arrest. She didn't feel up to greeting them, and she was relieved by her anonymity.

It was just before nine when she reached McGowan's second-floor office. His door was open and he was leaning back in his swivel chair, his big puffy hands knitted together behind his neck. He didn't hear her arrival. He seemed to be focusing on something outside his window, perhaps the ominous, bulging cloud formations in the direction of Fordham Road or the crane two blocks north, perched precariously atop the skeleton of a high-rise ascending out of the rubble of leveled warehouses. Maybe she had underestimated his capacity for introspection, it occurred to her. Was he perhaps sitting there debating his future—whether to give up the paid overtime he enjoyed as a lieutenant and finally take the captain's exam and join the next generation of NYPD police leaders? Was he feeling dismissed and undervalued by one of his superiors at One Police Plaza the way she was by him? She felt an unexpected flicker of compassion for him, and in the very next instance she told herself, *What the fuck are you thinking, Codella? He is after you. He'd love nothing better than to drum you out.*

She rapped on his open door. He swiveled around and his hands came down as he stood. His bristly reddish-brown hair was sculpted into a flat mesa on the top of his head. He was over six feet tall—towering next to her five-foot-two-inch frame, but short, she thought with private enjoyment, compared to the detective she'd just met, Eduardo Muñoz. She observed that he was still a little thick around the belt, although she recalled him telling other detectives last year that he had joined a gym. "So you're back," he said.

His lack of enthusiasm wasn't lost on her.

"That body you sent me to see? It wasn't just a body. It was a body laid out like Jesus Christ on the cross. A public school principal."

"Homicide?"

"No doubt about it. Crime scene is finishing up. Gambarin is there. I've got a canvass started. I'm going to head over to his school right now. Just wanted you to know. I'll keep you posted on developments." She took a step back, toward the door.

"Wait." He came around his desk. "Let's give this to Fisk and Nichols."

"What?"

"You heard me."

"Why?"

"Because you're just getting back on your feet."

"I'm *on* my feet, sir." She pointed down, and then met his stare.

"The media will be all over this," he finally said.

"I'm used to the media."

He raised his brows, and she knew at once that her words had been a mistake. Now he was remembering the Wainright Blake case. Solving that case had gotten her more media attention than she had ever wanted, and because of that case she had been promoted to his unit. She had been forced onto him. And now he was undoubtedly regretting his early morning call to her. Better to have given her a rousing welcome back at the morning briefing than hand her another case that she could run away with. But he had handed it to her, and she wasn't about to give it up. He was still staring at her. He was waiting for her to look away first, and she did. She had to give him something. "I'll keep you in the loop on everything, Lieutenant," she assured him in her most respectful voice.

"See that you do." He turned his back to her.

CHAPTER 4

Codella showed her shield to the school safety officer, a woman named Rivera. Then she entered the main office in time to hear an agitated woman saying, "Where's the sub, Janisa? I need her here now. Why wasn't this handled?"

"It *was*," said Janisa, a younger Hispanic woman behind a waist-high counter. "I called the sub on Friday. It's not my fault she didn't show up."

"Well, get us someone else *now*. I've got twenty-seven kids in that room with no teacher." The agitated woman sideswiped Codella on her way out the door.

"Can I help you?" asked Janisa.

"Who's in charge when your principal isn't here?"

"Marva Thomas. That was her." She pointed to the door where the woman had just disappeared. "She'll be back."

Janisa got on the phone, and Codella surveyed the office. Opposite the counter were beat-up wooden inboxes of the PS 777 teachers. A nicked wooden bench, which fifty years ago must have shined with a high-gloss varnish, was built into the wall perpendicular to the door. Above the bench was a long cork bulletin board with school announcements. The school's chess team had qualified for a regional tournament and was having a bake sale to raise money. Someone named Sofia Reyes had posted a sign-up sheet for an after-school workshop on differentiated instruction strategies, but so far only one name had signed up: Vickie Berrard. On the other hand, several names had signed up to hear a representative from the McFlieger-Walsh School Publishing Company give a "Sneak Preview of iAchieve" on Wednesday at 3:45 PM Codella scanned the handwritten names on that sign-up sheet. Christine Donohue. Anna Masoutis. Kristin DeMarco. Jenny Bernstein. Eugene Bosco. Natalie Rapinoe. Roz Porter.

Then she retreated to the hallway outside the office. Twenty feet to her left, a student-created banner mounted near the front doors read, "Welcome to PS 777—Explore! Learn! Grow!" On the wall above the school safety officer were hundreds of photographs below the headline "We're the Proud Families at PS 777." Codella approached the wall, and her eyes fell on the placid image of a mother in a black chador embracing a thin, almost frail-looking son. In the photo next to that one, a Hispanic father, mother, and three young children had been caught by the camera's lens in an instant of raucous family glee. Another photo showed a single black mother and two children, girl and boy, sitting erect and staring into the camera with uncertain smiles. The mother's solid torso, high African cheekbones, and turban made her look dignified but uneasy, as if a semiautomatic rifle were pointed at her head.

These were not amateur snapshots, Codella observed. Rather, they were carefully composed, professionally lighted portraits, each capturing a singular mood and family character. They reminded her of the photo she had seen in Hector Sanchez's apartment, and she scanned the faces until she found the photo of Dana Drew and her family. She followed Dana Drew's pale left arm around the shoulder of her attractively androgynous partner. She studied the actress's right hand resting delicately on the shoulder of her smiling honey-skinned child. Why had a copy of this portrait been in the principal's apartment? Why this one and none of these others?

While she stood there, Detective Sunil Ragavan, a short, slightly built man with thick black hair, arrived. "We have an unmarked car in front of the school, Detective Codella."

"Good. I want it there during school hours until further notice. And you're going to be my eyes and ears in here."

Ragavan nodded.

"I see you've found our Wall of Pride." Marva Thomas was suddenly standing behind them.

Codella thought she detected a wisp of sarcasm in the woman's reference to the photos. She turned to face her. "I'm Detective Codella. And this is Detective Ragavan."

Marva Thomas shook their hands. "How can I help you?"

"May we speak privately?"

Thomas's office was smaller than a walk-in closet at the stately Beresford on Central Park West, the crime scene of Codella's last murder investigation as a precinct detective in the 171st. Marva Thomas closed the door behind them and gestured toward two straight-backed chairs. "Please, have a seat." She was a light-skinned African American woman with delicate features. Codella judged her to be in her early to midforties. Her hair was combed tightly back in a bun, and her facial makeup was subtle and flattering. Her nails were polished in a muted shade of red, and she wore no wedding band. A handwritten note on an index card taped to the side of her computer read, *Be kind to one another, tenderhearted, forgiving one another, as God in Christ forgave you. Ephesians 4:32.* "What can I do for you?" she asked.

"I'm sorry to have to tell you this, Ms. Thomas, but Hector Sanchez died last night."

The woman's gasp seemed genuine, as did the tightening of the facial muscles around her mouth and eyes into an expression of confusion. "How? I don't get it. He's in excellent health. He's a runner. He runs marathons, I think. He—"

Codella cut her off. "He was murdered."

In the silence, Thomas shook her head in tight little movements. "By whom?"

"We don't know."

"How?"

"I can't discuss that. How well did you know him?"

"He became principal here last winter."

"What was he like?"

Thomas paused before answering. "Hardworking. Demanding. He definitely had a vision for the school."

It was a diplomatic answer, Codella decided. "What did you think of his vision?"

"There were good and bad parts."

"How did the staff feel about him?"

Thomas squinted. "Why? Do you think someone here might have murdered him?"

"I don't think anything yet. All I know is a school official has been killed and until we know why, we'll err on the side of safety and take every precaution necessary to ensure the protection of your staff and students."

"What kind of precautions?"

"We've posted an officer outside the building, and Detective Ragavan here will be stationed inside to assist with our investigation and provide an additional layer of security. That said, keep in mind that we have no indication there's a risk to anyone. There's no need for panic, and you can help us by not discussing our security concerns and measures with *anyone* else on your staff."

"Of course. But I do need to inform my district superintendent."

Thomas's gaze shifted repeatedly from Codella to the three-inch-long scar bisecting Detective Ragavan's right cheek. By now, Codella thought, the assistant principal was probably wondering if he had acquired the scar in a rough Mumbai slum or in a fight with a crazy knife-wielding addict. People couldn't conceal their fascination with human imperfections. Codella had experienced their fascination firsthand during the long months of strangers staring at her bald scalp and gaunt cheeks. Ragavan's real story was far less dramatic than anything Marva Thomas was imagining, of course. As a three-year-old in Montclair, New Jersey, he had fallen under a neighbor's backyard swing and sliced his face on a rusty nail.

Codella repeated her earlier question. "How did the staff here feel about Sanchez?"

"Hector liked things his way. If you followed his rules, you had no problems."

"But?"

"Sometimes his rules conflicted with union rules."

"Would you say he had enemies?"

Thomas chuckled. "This is the New York public school system. A principal *always* has enemies."

"Who?"

"Annoyed parents, disgruntled teachers, controlling administrators."

"Who were Sanchez's enemies?"

"That I can't say."

Can't or won't? Codella wondered. She wasn't naïve enough to believe that a woman who taped scripture to the side of her computer couldn't be a liar. "Tell me about yesterday. Was it a typical day?"

"Around here, not much is typical." Thomas paused. "But we did have an incident."

"Go on."

"One of our fifth graders attacked another student in the first-floor boy's restroom."

"His head was pushed into a toilet bowl."

"Then you know about it."

"Tell me about the student who got attacked."

"He's a fourth grader. John Chambers. He has sensory integration issues and OCD. He's mainstreamed."

"What does that mean—*mainstreamed*?"

"He's special ed. He has an IEP—an Individualized Education Plan—but he spends most of his school day in a general education classroom. It's hard for him. He gets teased a lot. He has some noticeable compulsions, one being that he insists on washing his hands every hour. If he doesn't, he has a meltdown. Jenny Bernstein lets him leave the classroom when he starts to feel agitated."

"Tell me about this other student."

"Miguel Espina. He's almost twelve. He's been held back twice. Very intelligent. Extremely troubled. Bad home situation. The mother's an *exotic dancer*." She raised her eyebrows.

"You mean a prostitute?"

She nodded. "He was transferred here this year."

"Why wasn't he in his classroom?"

"He slipped out."

"Where was Sanchez when this was happening?"

"At the district office."

"Why?"

"Margery Barton had called a principal's meeting."

"Who's she?"

"The district superintendent."

Codella touch-typed names into the notes app on her iPhone. Marva Thomas. John Chambers. Miguel Sanchez. Jenny Bernstein. Margery Barton. "Sanchez reported to this Barton woman?"

"Yes."

"Where were you when the attack occurred?"

"In the library. We had a parent workshop going on."

"What parent workshop?"

"A Title I family involvement program Hector started. Twice a week we bring in family members and teach them basic literacy skills," she explained with more enthusiasm. "More than half our parents don't speak any English."

"How many parents would you say were in the building?"

"More than thirty."

"I'll need their names. Who else was there?"

"Carole Berger, one of our special ed teachers, and Sofia Reyes, the literacy consultant."

Codella typed these names into her iPhone. "Did anything unusual happen?"

"No, except that we ran out of donuts. If it weren't for the donuts, maybe the attack wouldn't have occurred."

"How do you figure?"

"Ordinarily, I'd notice a student wandering the halls. I was too busy tracking down Mr. Jancek, our custodian, to make a Dunkin' Donuts run."

"When did you find out what happened?"

"Delia—Delia Rivera, the security officer—came up and told me."

"And then?"

"I called Hector's cell. He didn't pick up so I texted him, but he didn't respond to the text either, and I knew he'd be upset if he wasn't informed immediately, so I called Dr. Barton's office and had her receptionist deliver a message to him in the meeting. Then I called Yolanda Espina, Miguel's mother, to get over to the school. I knew he'd want to speak with her."

Codella added Yolanda Espina's name to her list. "Sanchez gave the Espina boy an in-school suspension," she said remembering Helen Chamber's angry post. "Did you agree with his decision?"

Thomas made a tight smile. "He's the principal, not me. He *was*, I mean."

Codella allowed the woman's answer to swell and take shape in the silence that followed. Was it contempt she heard in that voice or merely resignation? She glanced at Ragavan before she said, "We're going to need a complete list of the school staff and parents with addresses and telephone numbers. Can you get on that right away?"

"Of course."

"And I'd like to speak with some of your staff."

"The teachers can't leave their classrooms unattended."

"I understand. I'll speak with teachers later, but I'd like to speak with some other staff members, starting with your school safety officer, Delia Rivera."

Thomas nodded. "I'll send her in. You can use Hector's office."

CHAPTER 5

Haggerty's head was still pounding as he stepped off the elevator on the fifth floor. Three Advil were never a match for too much vodka and too little sleep. He found Muñoz standing in front of the fire exit writing in his notebook. Haggerty hadn't said more than twenty words to Muñoz since the tall detective had transferred to the precinct—Reilly had assigned Portino to be his mother hen—but his presence had certainly caused a lot of talk at this morning's briefing. "How's it going?" he said.

Muñoz stopped writing and looked up with a wince, as if he expected Haggerty to address him as New Dick. The poor bastard probably didn't know yet that Blackstone had changed his nickname this morning. Now he was Rainbow Dick, because of last night. It was the talk of the squad room.

Muñoz said, "Morning, Detective Haggerty. I didn't expect to see you here."

Haggerty took a few steps back so their height differential wouldn't mean he had to crane his neck. He smiled. "Get me up to speed."

"Detective Codella put me in charge of the canvass."

"How many guys you got on the vertical?" He pulled out a cigarette.

"Two. That's all Captain Reilly could spare. One's working his way down, the other up. Detective Codella gave me detailed orders. To be honest, she scared the shit out of me."

Haggerty twirled the filter end of the cigarette between his fingers. Detailed orders. That was Claire, he thought. She always gave agonizingly meticulous instructions. When they'd been partners, he had stood beside her many times while she had spelled out her expectations to junior detectives and uniforms.

"Let's avoid any misunderstandings here," she would say at a crime scene if she hadn't worked with a detective before. "If I tell you to stand by the door and don't move, that means you don't pace around in front of it like you're waiting for your kid to be born, and you don't step across the threshold even one centimeter and contaminate the evidence. And if I tell you, 'Don't let anyone pass by you without my permission,' that includes CSU, the chief of police, and the mayor. You ask them to wait, politely, of course, and you call me. You don't come in to get me. You *call* me."

Claire's obsession with little contingencies had rubbed off on him. At some point, he'd started to give those meticulous orders, too. She made anyone who worked with her a better detective, so he understood why Muñoz didn't want to disappoint her. But Haggerty half-wished he would so that he could step in and run the case. He would be running it right now, he thought, if he hadn't left his cell phone in his jacket pocket last night and missed the 6:00 AM call. How many chances was he going to get to work with Claire again now that she had left the precinct? If they worked a case together, maybe she'd forget all the shit that had happened between them. Maybe they could work themselves back into their old comfortable rhythm and everything would be fine again, just like before.

He struck a match, lighted his cigarette, and blew a stream of smoke past Muñoz's left shoulder. "What have you learned so far?"

Muñoz seemed to consider. Finally, he said, "Not much. We still have a lot of doors to knock on."

Haggerty pushed open the door to the fire stairs. "All right. Keep knocking, then."

He climbed a flight to the crime scene. The body was still on the floor when he stepped into the room. Banks nodded tersely, but he was bent over something and turned his attention back to that. Haggerty got the details from O'Donnell instead. Then he went downstairs and stood on the front steps and lighted another cigarette to take his mind off his head. He was thirsty, and his stomach was churning.

He watched the patrol cops in front of the building drink their Dunkin' Donuts coffee. He studied three workmen across the street erecting a scaffold. Half a block down, two Spanish-speaking building porters wearing work gloves were shouting back and forth as they carried industrial-sized garbage bags out to the street for pick up.

He sat on the steps, finished the cigarette, and flicked it skillfully into the street between two parallel-parked cars. A familiar number popped up on his phone. "Quit calling me."

"I hear there's a body," said the nasal voice.

Haggerty stood and walked up the street toward Morningside Park out of range of the uniforms. "There's a body all right. A really interesting body."

"You're on it, then?"

"Of course I'm on it." He lighted another cigarette.

"What can you tell me?"

"Lots." *But that doesn't mean I'm going to,* his tone implied.

"Who was he?"

"A school principal, and everyone will know that before you file any story. Whoever gets the inside scoop on this will have a very juicy front page, that's for sure."

"Help me out here."

"I told you, you're wasting your time calling me."

"I'll make it worth your while."

Haggerty turned back toward the other end of the block and smiled at the north- and southbound cars on Frederick Douglass Boulevard as if they were a fan club. One or two little tips could wipe out a lot of credit card debt, and although he had never succumbed to that temptation, he knew plenty of cops who had, including his old man.

"Go to the press conference like everyone else," he said and ended the call.

He returned to the steps in front of the building and closed his eyes because the sunlight was making his head feel like a geological hot spot about to erupt. He pictured himself this morning, in that woman's bed—what was her name?—while his phone sat in his jacket pocket in her living room with the ringer off while Reilly was trying to hand him this lovely opportunity to work side by side with Claire.

He wished more than anything that he hadn't gone with the woman. But it was either follow her home or go home alone and think about Queen Smith's baby all night, and he had to get the baby out of his mind. He could still see her now, small and irrevocably silent, the way she had looked yesterday morning lying like a discarded doll on a filthy throw rug in the bathroom of an under-heated, roach-infested apartment in the Coretta Scott King housing project. He could still hear Queen Smith's deafening primal howls within the narrow crumbling plaster walls. She had been so out of her mind when he got to the scene that the first responders were physically restraining her as the EMTs tried and tried to revive the little body with no success. He could still hear her weeping and screaming, "My baby, my little baby," and then he had spent the day tracking down the crackhead boyfriend who apparently couldn't stand a baby crying while he wanted to sleep.

Now he could think about Claire instead of the baby. He pictured her face—the flawless skin, blue eyes, coal black hair, perfect lips. And even in his hungover, sleep-deprived state, he felt a terrible combustion of desire and dread in his gut, and he knew that he didn't just want his old partner back, he still wanted all of her, and he was desperate to see her again but unsure he was *ready* to see her, to come face to face with that night when everything had gone terribly wrong.

By now, he figured, he must have replayed that night—the night of Portino's fiftieth birthday—a thousand times. He could still see Claire walking into the bar in her black leather jacket an hour after everyone else. She had taken a seat at the opposite end of the table from him. For seven years, they had spent so much time together that he'd assumed he knew everything there was to know about her. He knew her shoe size, her favorite NBA players, her food cravings, her Starbucks order. He knew from the way she sometimes checked her hair in the side mirror of a cruiser that she had a secret hair vanity. He could tell when to shut up so she could think and when to tell a joke so she would relax. He knew all her facial expressions and what each of them meant. But he had never seen her look at him the way she had looked at him that night, across the table, as if just the two of them existed, while Blackstone was busy making one of his garrulous toasts, and in the next moment, when she had abruptly stood and left the bar with no explanation, his desire for her had surfaced like some primordial sea monster that wasn't even supposed to exist, and he had realized instinctively that his desire for her was different, that it had absolutely nothing in common with the desire he felt for the women he charmed in bars and got into bed.

He had examined that night in his mind from every conceivable angle, and he recognized now what he hadn't known then—that he had made a fatal mistake when he had followed her out of the bar. She had left because she was as terrified of her feelings as he had been of his. She had not been ready to face them, and he should have let her escape. He should have waited for her to come back to him—because whether or not she ever had, at least they would still be friends today.

He had been too drunk for that kind of wisdom. Instead, he had caught up with her outside, turned her around, pressed his hand into the small of her back, and pulled her close, expecting her to relax in his arms. She hadn't relaxed. She'd said, "What the fuck are you doing?" and tried to push him off, but he had held her even tighter.

You couldn't hold on to someone like Codella. She had to choose you, and in that moment, she hadn't. And was that so surprising? He could only imagine how bad he must have smelled and tasted as he'd tried to kiss her. He still didn't know how long he'd pressed himself against her, murmuring whatever it was he'd said about his feelings until Reilly and Portino had come out of the bar and pulled him off her and told him to go home. The rest was history. Two weeks later she'd accepted the Manhattan North homicide post and two months after that she was in the hospital, and now their seven-year partnership seemed like a distant memory of better times.

He opened his eyes and let the pounding between his temples obscure her image in his mind. "What the fuck!" he mumbled.

CHAPTER 6

Marva Thomas led the detectives into Hector Sanchez's office. "I'll send in Delia Rivera, and I'll be next door if you need me," she said in her most professional voice. Then she retreated.

"Your mother just called," Janisa told her as she passed the front desk toward her own small office. "I put her through to your voice mail."

"Thanks," Thomas said grudgingly. Despite Janisa's earlier protests, Marva was still convinced the receptionist had failed to line up a substitute for Roz Porter's second grade, and she wasn't about to forget it. If Hector weren't dead, he would have skewered her for the lack of coverage. She would have gotten an F for the day on his infamous grading scale. She shut her office door and whispered a perfunctory prayer for his soul. Then she concentrated on the fact that two NYPD detectives were sitting on the other side of the wall to her right, but the red message light on her phone kept blinking as if to say, *Notice me.*

She listened to the succinct message in a voice exacting and oppressive. "I can't get myself to the bathroom. I'm shutting down." She heard the unstated command. *Come home. Take care of me. You exist for me. Don't keep me waiting.*

She dialed.

"How soon will you be here?"

"I'm still in my office."

"Didn't you get my message?" Her mother's irritation was palpable.

"Yes, Ma. Just now."

"Well, what's taking you so long?"

"I've got a crisis. I can't come home right now."

"What kind of crisis could you have?"

In a clinical way, Marva registered her mother's absolute narcissism. Her eyes found the Post-it note taped to her computer and she quickly read the verse from Ephesians. She stared at the word *compassionate*. She did not feel compassionate. "I'll call Carla for you," she said calmly.

"No!" came the impatient reply.

"Why not?" But she already knew the answer.

"She's busy. She's got the boys. You know that."

The silent insult roared in Marva's ear—*your sister's obligations, her whole existence, are more important than yours*—and Marva wanted to crush the receiver under her sensible SAS work shoes. She didn't respond.

"I'm going to have an accident soon."

Have one, Marva wanted to say. *Just not on my couch.* She breathed deeply and tried to resurrect the calm she'd felt two mornings ago during the 10:00 AM service at St. Michael's when the choir had sung "Abide in Me" as she had stared at the vibrant Tiffany stained glass behind the altar. Something in the hymn's melody always released her deep sadness and made her cry and left her feeling serene and purified. Now she was able to keep the anger out of her voice when she said, "Then I'll call Mrs. Sucek to come and help you."

"I don't like it when she comes over. She always looks so put upon."

Marva closed her eyes and counted to ten. She had ceased to feel true Christian empathy toward her mother long ago. She only felt obligation and resentment. "It's going to have to be the neighbor if you won't let me call Carla." She waited. Her mother waited. Marva was not going to break the silent standoff this time.

"Okay," her mother finally conceded. "Call the neighbor." Then she hung up on Marva.

Marva called Mrs. Sucek, the building super's wife. Then she replaced the phone in its cradle and let out a deep sigh. She felt suddenly bilious and bloated, as if she'd been slammed by a killer period. She pushed out her chair and lowered her head. She took several deep breaths. Then she picked up the phone again and dialed the district office. "Dr. Barton, please. Right away."

"She's busy," said Karen Babb, Barton's new receptionist. Apparently Babb was quickly learning that the best way to keep her job was to shield her boss from as many callers as possible.

"You have to interrupt her, Karen. This is Marva Thomas at 777. She needs to take this call."

"I'll see what I can do."

A minute later, Barton was on the line. "What is it, Marva?"

"It's Hector. He's *dead*. He was *murdered*. Two detectives are here right now. They just found his body."

"At the school?" Barton's digitized panic was deafening through the receiver.

"No, no, no. At his *apartment*."

"Oh, thank God for that." Barton sighed, and Thomas guessed what the administrator was thinking: A principal murdered at home was bad enough. A principal murdered on school premises was an absolute disaster. "Do they know who did it?"

"Not yet. They're posting security in front of the school. They say it's just precautionary, but who knows." Thomas steadied her voice. She wanted to blurt out, *What should I do?* She wanted to say, *I'm not ready for this.* In the silence, she heard Barton's deep intake of breath and she imagined what the superintendent was thinking. *Marva's not cut out to lead. Marva was never cut out to lead.* And maybe she wasn't. Her hands were shaking slightly. She felt as if hundreds of taut rubber bands were wrapped around her chest. So many things would have to be done today beyond the normal routine, and she was already overwhelmed. Teachers would have to be informed. Children would find out. They would cry. They'd be frightened. They'd want their parents. The parents would panic. What should she do first?

Barton's voice startled her to attention. "Listen to me, Marva. As of right now, you're in charge over there. You're the acting principal. Do you understand?"

"Yes," said Thomas. "Of course."

"I know you weren't happy last year when I chose Hector over you, but forget about that. It's water under the bridge. For now, you have the top spot, and six hundred children will be looking to *you* for answers, for stability, for reassurance."

"I know." Marva stared at the blue, green, and pink pixels of her mesmerizing screen saver.

"This is a shock for us all, but you need to let the teachers, the students, and the parents know that the school is going to be all right. A terrible tragedy has occurred, but they are not leaderless."

"How?" The word escaped her lips before she could censor it.

"You have to get in front of this crisis, Marva. You have to let your troops know that you're not afraid. You need to take charge. You can do that, can't you?"

Every muscle and sinew in Marva's body wanted to cry out *no*, but she forced herself to say, "I think so."

"You *think* so?"

"I know so. I can do it," Thomas said with a little more energy as Janisa opened her office door and stuck a phone message slip on her desk with the message, *Call your mother back ASAP.*

"Look," Barton said in a gentler voice, "we're going to do this together." It struck Marva that now the administrator sounded like an air traffic controller talking a novice private pilot through an emergency Airbus jetliner landing. "Don't panic. I'm going to get you the support you need right away. As soon as we hang up, I'll call Tweed. We'll get the communications liaison involved. There'll be lots of press on this. Thanks to Hector's little Proud Families campaign, everyone who rides the buses and subways has 777 on the brain. But forget about that. You just worry about the teachers and the children. I'll worry about the press."

"How should we break it to the children?"

"We have procedures for everything, Marva." Barton sounded so nurturing now that Marva guessed her goose was cooked as far as school administration in District 124. Barton was never nice without a motive. She was demanding, egotistical, and mercilessly honest. Marva still remembered how her interview for the PS 777 principal slot had ended. Barton had stood dismissively after twenty minutes and announced, "You're not tough enough, Marva. You're not even close to tough enough to lead that school." Now, she imagined, Barton was only being kind to her out of self-preservation. "I'll have grief counselors over there within the hour."

"Okay," said Thomas numbly.

"And I'll send Ellie Friedman over, too. She can help you set up assemblies and break the news. You're going to be swamped." Marva knew what that meant. Friedman would play principal until a suitable replacement could be found.

As soon as Marva hung up, she buried her head in her hands. She had wanted the top spot so badly—she had wanted it every day she'd walked past Hector's door into her own little closet of an office—but now that she possessed the title, now that she had this chance to show her strength under fire, she realized she didn't have any strength. She didn't have what it took to "get in front of" anything, let alone a crisis like this. She was no leader. She would never be a leader. She stared at the message *Call your mother again ASAP* on the pink message slip. She had been raised to live in the shadow of people stronger than herself. Even her mother, with advanced Parkinson's disease, was stronger than she was.

Marva took a deep breath. She felt completely alone. But then she remembered Sofia Reyes. Kind, confident Sofia Reyes, who she had never gone out of her way to support. Sofia would know exactly how to take charge of this situation. Sofia wouldn't judge her. Sofia could guide her through. Sofia could help her keep face. She picked up her phone and called Sofia instead of calling her mother.

CHAPTER 7

Codella stared at the dead principal's desk close to the wall facing the door. The desktop was neat. The message light on his phone was blinking. The Dell computer on the right side was at least five years old. She powered it on, but a login screen requesting a user ID and password blocked her progress just as Safety Officer Rivera stepped through the door. Rivera was short and overweight but sturdy in a way that made Codella wonder if she might have pitched for a high school softball team years ago.

"I'm Detective Codella and this is Detective Ragavan. We're here because your school's principal was murdered last night."

"Mr. Sanchez? Oh my God." The officer sat down. "Who did it?"

"Did you know him well?"

"Not really. Where did it happen? Who found him?"

"There was an incident here yesterday. A student was attacked. I'd like to hear about that."

"You think it's related?"

"I think you'll be most helpful to us if you just answer our questions," said Codella.

Rivera got the message. "It happened about one o'clock. I was sitting at my desk. All of a sudden, I hear a scream from the boy's room, so I get up and go check it out, and he's sitting on the floor in one of the stalls."

"John Chambers?"

The officer nodded. "He was all wet from toilet water. He didn't look hurt, but he was crying and rambling. I got him on his feet and walked him out of the bathroom. I walked him straight to the nurse—Brenda Sparks. He was—how do you call it when you're breathing too fast?"

"Hyperventilating."

"So Brenda, she got a brown paper lunch bag and told him to breathe into it. But then his nose started bleeding—it gushed all over the bag and his T-shirt—so she got an ice pack and made him lie down, but he didn't want to stay still. He was kicking and screaming and saying, 'My skin, my skin,' over and over. 'My skin. My skin is burning.' I went upstairs for Miss Thomas, and on the way back, we ran into Miss Bernstein. She was looking for him. We all went to the nurse's office, and John was still screaming about his skin, and Miss Thomas was telling Brenda she better call an ambulance, but Miss Bernstein, she took over. She grabbed John's arm and said, 'Let's wash those hands.' Brenda tried to stop her because his nose was still gushing, but Miss Bernstein did it anyway, and then he calmed right down."

"Miss Bernstein is his teacher?"

"That's right. Jenny Bernstein."

"Then what happened?"

"Miss Thomas went back to the office to call John's mother, and while she was gone, John told us who attacked him. A fifth grader, Miguel Espina. You don't think he did it, do you?"

"What happened next?"

"I went to look for Miguel. First I went to his classroom, but he wasn't there, and Mr. Bosco had no idea where he was. In fact, Mr. Bosco was sleeping at his desk when I came in. I had to wake him up."

Like every media consumer in New York City, Codella had read and watched her share of exposés about incompetent New York public school teachers, but she found this a little hard to fathom. "He was sleeping? In front of a class full of kids?"

"That's right. He swears he wasn't, but I saw it plain as day. Why should I lie? I had to shake his shoulder twice before he opened his eyes. I can tell when somebody's sleeping, and if you ask me, you can't blame Mr. Sanchez for suspending him."

"Mr. Sanchez suspended this teacher yesterday?"

Rivera nodded.

"Where did you find Miguel?"

"I didn't. Milosz did—Mr. Jancek, the head custodian. He and Mr. Rerecic searched downstairs while I looked upstairs. They found him hiding in the school auditorium."

"Mr. Rerecic is a custodian, too?"

"Maintenance worker."

Codella typed these names into her iPhone, guessing at the spellings. She typed in Brenda Sparks's name, too. "Then what?"

"I took Miguel to the office."

"Mr. Sanchez had arrived?"

"Not yet. But John was already there with Miss Thomas, and he told us the whole story. Then I took Miguel into the hall and wrote up what happened while we waited for Mr. Sanchez and the parents to get there. I was still with Miguel when John's mother arrived. John rushed out to her, and he was talking a mile a minute and blinking and pulling at his hair, and she told Ms. Thomas she had to get him home right away to take his medication."

"When did Sanchez get there?"

"A few minutes later. Maybe one forty-five. And Miguel's mother got there pretty soon after that."

Codella noted these times in her iPhone. "What happened next?"

"First Mr. Sanchez talked to Ms. Thomas in his office. Then he talked to Miguel's mother. Then he talked to Miguel alone for a *long* time."

"Did you see anyone else?"

"Lots of people were in and out. It was crazy."

"When did Miguel and his mother leave?"

"Just after three."

"And Sanchez?"

"He walked past me around three thirty and left the building."

Codella nodded. "I appreciate your help, Officer. I wonder if you could show Detective Ragavan around the school. He's going to be stationed here to help with our investigation. He needs to get familiar with the layout."

When Rivera and Ragavan were gone, Codella peered out the door and caught Janisa's eye. The young woman was wearing a short tight skirt and three-inch heels. Her long, thick hair was ponytailed and resting on her right shoulder. She met Codella's eyes. "I couldn't help but overhear things. It's terrible. Really terrible," she said.

"Were you here yesterday afternoon?"

"Until two o'clock. My filling fell out last Thursday, and I went to get it fixed. They say the city is safer than ever, but when something like this happens, you wonder, is it really?"

Codella had no intention to debate crime statistics. "What was happening here just before you left?"

Janisa clicked her gum. "Mrs. Chambers had left. Mr. Sanchez got back from the meeting, and he and Ms. Thomas went into his office and shut the door. They were in there when I left."

"Do you know what they were they talking about?"

"Not really." Her eyes darted to the cork bulletin board above the bench.

Codella followed her eyes to the posted school announcements. "What is it?"

Janisa pointed. "That sign-up sheet for iAchieve. Ms. Thomas posted it yesterday morning, and when Mr. Sanchez got here and saw it, he ripped it off, and that's when he called her into his office."

"Did he strike you as angry?"

She nodded.

"About the sign-up sheet?"

"It seemed that way."

"What made it seem that way?"

"He was waving it as they were going into his office. He was yelling at her."

"What did he say?"

"I couldn't make out the words. He shut the door pretty fast."

"Can you think of any reason he'd get upset about her posting a sign-up sheet?"

"He doesn't like people posting things on that board without his permission. I always get the postings approved by him before they go up."

Codella stared at the sign-up sheet again. The top margin had a two-inch tear where Sanchez must have ripped it off a pushpin. "Who reposted it?" she asked.

"Ms. Thomas. She stuck it back up after Mr. Sanchez left for the day."

"What exactly is iAchieve?"

"I'm not sure. Some computer program, I think."

"Was anyone else in the office when you left at two?"

"Miguel Espina's mother was sitting on the bench over there waiting to meet with Mr. Sanchez."

"Anyone else?"

"Mr. Jancek. He was working on Mr. Sanchez's radiator before Mr. Sanchez got back from his meeting, and Mr. Sanchez asked him to step out so he could speak with Ms. Thomas alone, so he was standing here with me for a little while before I left."

Codella thanked the young woman. "I wonder, could you get Mr. Jancek for me?"

CHAPTER 8

"Tom Broner, please. It's Dr. Barton."

"One moment, please."

Margery Barton stared at her nails as she listened to the soothing instrumental hold music. She replayed her words to Marva Thomas. *You need to take charge. You can do that, can't you?* She remembered Marva's pitiful answer. *I think so.* What kind of answer was that?

There was no way she could rely on the assistant principal to make good decisions today. Ellie Friedman would have to pull her strings. Marva Thomas had to look good so Margery would look good.

"He's on another call right now. Can you hang on, Dr. Barton?"

"Yes, I'll hold." She cradled the receiver against her shoulder, opened her desk drawer, pulled out lipstick, and slid the creamy balm expertly from one edge of her lower lip to the other without a mirror. Then she pressed her upper and lower lips together to spread the lipstick evenly. The soothing music was getting on her nerves now, so she put the phone on speaker so it wasn't right in her ear. She had to play this crisis by the book, she told herself. You didn't get to the top of the Department of Education food chain if you couldn't handle a crisis. She had her own reputation to consider. She was fifty-one. It was time to get to Tweed. She wasn't going to turn into one more postmenopausal administrator whose career flamed out in the district hinterlands. She wanted to sit at the big boys' table with Bernie Lipsie and the other policymakers, and this crisis, she realized, could help her get there. It was like Hurricane Sandy pummeling the Jersey Shore eight days before a presidential election.

"Margery," Broner finally said. "To what do I owe the pleasure?"

"I've got a murdered principal," she said.

"What? Shit! What happened?"

Margery relayed the details as she knew them. "I don't trust the AP to handle the press on this, Tom. We need to get in front of the story. Is there someone we can send over there? The news vans are going to start arriving soon, I imagine."

"Jane Stewart," he said. "I'll send Jane. She's a pro. She'll control the message."

"Good."

"Thanks for the speedy heads up."

Next Margery called the chancellor's office. "Dr. Lipsie," she said to the operator who put her through to Lipsie's personal assistant. "It's Margery Barton," she said, "and I have some urgent news for the chancellor."

Barton had never called Bernie Lipsie directly, and when his assistant said, "I'm putting you through, Dr. Barton," she felt like a West Wing advisor about to speak directly with the president.

"What's up, Margery?" Lipsie's deep voice startled her. "Did I hear the *urgent* word? I don't like that word."

The adrenaline that exploded in her chest was as intoxicating as the rush she had felt the first time she'd knocked on Chip Dressler's hotel room door knowing exactly what awaited her on the other side. She pressed her inner thighs together. She wanted to say, *Me neither, Bernie*, but she had never called the chancellor by his first name, and doing so under these circumstances might strike him as presumptuous or inappropriate.

On the other hand, she didn't want to call him *Dr.* Lipsie, either—especially right after he'd called her Margery. That would make her seem so deferential. True, her status was subordinate to his, but acting subservient could make you seem unsuited for a role of greater authority. If you wanted to be a peer, you acted like a peer. She had those *PhD* letters after her name, too, she reminded herself, and though she wasn't, as Bernie was, on a first-name basis with the mayor and his appointees, she certainly had plenty of experience rubbing elbows with influential people. Just last night, she had shared a table at Cipriani with the head trustee of Memorial Sloan Kettering, and she had kept him laughing all night.

Barton avoided names altogether as she related the sketchy facts. "It's a developing situation. I've called Tom, and I'll be in regular contact with the AP over there. I'm sending in a crisis team to advise her and help with the parents and children. I'm keeping my fingers crossed that this unfortunate event has nothing to do with a school employee, but I thought you should be prepared in case you get calls."

"You're always thinking, Margery. I appreciate that. We'll both keep our fingers crossed." In the silence that followed, she wondered if she was supposed to read anything into his words. Lipsie was newly divorced, according to Gayle Fenton, who knew him well, and at the last few superintendent breakfasts, Margery had noticed him looking over at her, even when she wasn't speaking. Last Thursday he had chosen a seat right next to hers, even though there had been several other seats he could have taken. He wasn't the kind of man you would describe as handsome—he was almost entirely bald and his black eyeglass frames made him look like a nerdy college professor—but neither was he unattractive. He wore expensive suits, his cologne smelled enticing, and he was tall and trim. He was no Chip Dressler, but he might, she thought, be a pleasantly surprising sexual partner.

"While I've got you," Lipsie said, "I hear you have your spring iAchieve pilot results."

"Yes, and the numbers look really impressive."

"Good for you, Margery. Good for you. You've done a remarkable job changing the mind-set over there."

"I've still got a few pockets of resistance, but the numbers tell it all. I have a meeting next week to share the results with my technology leadership team. Then we'll take the results to the schools. We need to make our case at the teacher level and get their buy-in."

"Tell Amanda to put your meeting on my calendar. I'll try to make it."

"That would be great," she said, and in the three-second silence that followed, she felt something shift through the satellite connection, like molecules speeding up and changing state, and she decided to take a chance. "Thanks, Bernie. And I'll keep you posted on this situation."

"I'll be waiting, Margery."

CHAPTER 9

Milosz Jancek had short, coarse hair that stood up like the bristles of a brush. It was the kind of haircut Codella associated with army drill sergeants in the movies. He had a long face and a slightly crooked nose, and his sunken eyes made him seem permanently pensive.

"I'm Detective Codella from the NYPD," she said. "Please have a seat, Mr. Jancek."

He nodded and sat with an expectant lift of his eyebrows.

"Your school principal has been murdered." She lobbed the news like a stone into a bush to see what would fly out.

His forehead rippled like the earth over a fault line during an earthquake. "Mr. Sanchez? Dead?" He had a slight accent she couldn't place. He shook his head. "How? How can that be?"

"You're the head janitor, is that correct?"

"Head custodian."

"Some events occurred here yesterday. I don't know if they have any bearing at all on Mr. Sanchez's death, but I'd like the whole picture."

"You mean the boy."

Codella decided his accent was Eastern European. She had lived in New York nineteen years—since she was eighteen—and that was long enough to know the majority of building superintendents and janitors were from Baltic republics with constantly changing names and borders. Every ethnic group in the city dominated certain professions. Indians ran newsstands and worked in eyebrow-threading outlets. Koreans gave manicures. Pakistanis drove taxis. Greeks ran diners. There were plenty of exceptions, but ethnic typecasting had a kernel of truth at its core. "Tell me what you remember."

"I was in Mr. Sanchez's office. Janisa called me in because it was very cold in here. It's still cold. You feel it? I was trying to fix the radiator, and Officer Delia rushed in and asked me to help her find a student, so I called one of my janitors, Mr. Rerecic, to help me, and we found him in the auditorium, hiding between the rows."

"What did you do when you found him?"

"We took him out to the hallway, and I watched him while Mr. Rerecic went for Officer Delia. She came for the boy and then I came back to the radiator."

"What did you see in the office when you came back here?"

He winced apologetically. "Not much. I was kneeling over there with my back to the door." He pointed to the radiator behind Sanchez's desk, just below the window.

"I see. When did Mr. Sanchez come in?"

"I'm not sure. I didn't check my watch."

"Did he speak to you at all?"

"Just to say he needed his office for a while. He asked me to come back later."

"What did he need his office for?"

"Some private meetings, I suppose."

"What meetings?"

"I'm not sure."

Codella waited for him to mention the principal's meeting with Marva Thomas, but he didn't, so she asked, "Did you see Ms. Thomas?"

"Yes, she was in the office too."

"Did Mr. Sanchez speak with her?"

"They went in his office."

"And then?"

He shrugged. "I left to tear down the lunchroom. Our gym doubles as a lunchroom. Mr. Rerecic and I had to fold up the tables before the afternoon PE classes."

"According to Janisa, you stood with her for a while in the outer office."

"Yes, but not for long. Just a minute or two."

"Did you hear anything Mr. Sanchez and Ms. Thomas said to each other?"

Jancek shook his head.

Codella ran her fingers through her hair. "How long have you worked here, Mr. Jancek?"

"This will be my thirteenth year."

"I imagine you see and hear many things around the school. Are you aware of anyone who might have wanted to harm Mr. Sanchez?"

Jancek shook his head. "I can't see that. People complain, sure, but kill?" He shook his head again. "Mr. Sanchez was hardworking. He was a good man. He's an immigrant like me. I was an engineer in my country," he said proudly. "In Croatia. Then the war started. I came here for a better life. So did Mr. Sanchez. And he's just trying to help all these kids who came here for a better life. Why would anybody kill him?"

Why did anybody kill another person? Codella thought. "When he asked you to leave his office, was that the last time you saw him?"

"Yes."

Codella stared at the custodian like an insect under a magnifying glass. Was he nice, or was he too nice? That was always the question you had to ask yourself. In her job, trust had no place. You couldn't take anyone at face value. "Where were you on Monday evening, Mr. Jancek?"

"When I left work, I went straight home. I work. I go home. That's about it for me." He shrugged. "I watched the Knicks."

"Do you live alone?"

He nodded.

"The Knicks had a good third quarter."

"But a terrible fourth. They have no defense," he said.

"What about Carmelo's dunk?" She was testing him.

"They should have called the foul on him, but I'm a Knicks fan, so I'm glad they didn't."

She nodded. "Is there anything else you can tell me?"

He shook his head. "I wish I could. Nobody's perfect, but he was a good principal. He was good for this place."

She took out a card and handed it to him. "If you hear or think of anything that might help us, please call me."

It was 10:48 AM when Jancek left and Codella returned to Thomas's office. The assistant principal looked up from her computer and Codella said, "You didn't mention that Mr. Sanchez called you into his office yesterday."

"He calls me into his office every day."

"Does he tear down sign-up sheets every day, too?"

Marva Thomas didn't answer.

"Tell me about iAchieve."

"It's a technology program the district piloted in four schools last year," she said.

"Why did he pull the sign-up sheet down?"

"He doesn't like notices to be posted without his permission."

"Then why did you post it in the first place?"

"It came in a pouch from the district office—straight from Margery Barton."

Codella stared at Thomas's thin fingers poised above her keyboard. "You also didn't tell me Sanchez suspended a teacher yesterday."

Thomas shrugged. "You didn't ask, and it didn't seem particularly pertinent."

"I would rather be the judge of what is pertinent, Ms. Thomas. Tell me about this Bosco."

"There's not much to tell. He's been at the school for seventeen years. He swears he wasn't sleeping."

"And you believe him?"

"It's his word against Delia's. I certainly don't intend to ask a classroom full of ten-year-olds to testify one way or the other."

"What did you think of Sanchez's decision to suspend him?"

Thomas shrugged again. "Eugene has his faults, I admit, but I would have handled it differently."

"Did you often disagree with Mr. Sanchez's decisions?"

Thomas looked her straight in the eye. "I wouldn't say that."

"What time did Sanchez leave the school yesterday?"

"Around three thirty."

"Is that when he usually calls it quits?"

"He wasn't calling it quits."

Her incomplete answer sat between them like a challenge. *Ask the right question and you* might *get what you're after.*

"Then what was he doing?"

"Visiting a student's home."

"What student?"

"Vondra Williams."

Codella hid her irritation. "Who is Vondra Williams?"

"One of our third graders. She lives in the Jackie Robinson Village."

"And he went there by himself?"

"I assume so."

"Why?"

"Vondra's missed a lot of school this year. We called Child Protective Services, but they hadn't gone to her home yet, and Hector, well, he always likes to take matters into his own hands."

"So he makes home visits?"

"Once or twice a week lately. He thinks he can improve our truancy rates."

"And is he?"

Thomas shrugged noncommittally. Codella was more than a little annoyed that the assistant principal hadn't mentioned the home visit sooner. She was even more annoyed with herself for not having asked a question to elicit the detail sooner. Was her mind not fully engaged? Was she rusty? Was she showing signs of that posttreatment condition cancer survivors referred to as "chemo fog"? She certainly had the other typical aftereffects—the persistent dry mouth and neuropathy. "Is there anything else you haven't told me, Ms. Thomas? Now would be the time."

Thomas shook her head.

"Do you have that list of teachers and parents I asked for?" She didn't hide her irritation.

Thomas held it out.

"E-mail it to me as well." Codella placed her card on the woman's desk. "Right away, please. And I need a recent photo of Sanchez. Do you happen to have one?"

Thomas called out to Janisa. When the assistant appeared, she said, "Janisa, please print a copy of Mr. Sanchez's photo from the website."

Janisa walked out, and Codella turned back to Thomas. "Who's his next of kin?"

"He isn't married. I don't know of any relatives in the city. His mother lives in Puerto Rico. I can check if we have a number on file."

"Do it, and while you're at it, please e-mail me Margery Barton's contact information. And Ms. Thomas?" She waited until the assistant principal made eye contact. "There's to be no one in his office until we review its contents."

"But our student files are in there."

"I understand, and we'll be as expeditious as possible. In the meantime, no one in that office and no one on that computer."

"I'll lock the door," she said a little too casually.

"And Detective Ragavan will seal it with tape."

CHAPTER 10

Barton was still thinking about Bernie Lipsie when she picked up her Samsung. *Call me now,* she touch-typed with two thumbs. As she waited for her cell phone to ring, she imagined Chip in one of his crisp Brooks Brothers shirts sitting in a McFlieger-Walsh conference room feeling the vibration of his Blackberry in his front pants pocket. She replayed Monday afternoon in her mind—Chip sitting on the edge of the king size bed at the Mandarin, looking down at her as she kneeled next to the bed and took him deep in her throat. She had taken him in so far that she had gagged a little, and the sound had gotten him so excited that he had lifted her off her knees, spread her legs, and pounded her into the mattress so hard that she had cried out. It would have been rape, except that she had enjoyed it as much as he had. What would sex be like with Bernie Lipsie? Would he want the same things Chip wanted? Would he have the nerve to demand them?

A text message came back. *In a meeting. Call you in an hour.*

Barton texted again. *Leave the meeting. Call me NOW.*

What is it?

She couldn't risk transmitting more information. She was no fool. How many careers had been ruined by indiscreet texts, e-mails, and tweets? She waited. Three minutes later her cell rang. "What's up?" The voice sounded concerned.

"Are you alone?"

"Yes. What is it?"

"You're not going to believe it."

"Tell me," he said.

"Hector Sanchez is dead."

He didn't say a word, but she could hear the silent smile spread across his face on the other end of the line, and she smiled too. "I'll call you back as soon as I can," he said.

CHAPTER 11

Codella's breath fogged the mid-November air as she stood on the school steps and speed-dialed Vic Portino.

"You're back. I didn't know you were back, Detective," he said. "How does it feel?"

"No complaints yet, Vic."

"And already they send you back to us. Ironic, huh?"

"I suppose you could say so." She remembered McGowan's call this morning. *It's your old stomping ground, Codella.* He could have sent any Manhattan North detective to that crime scene. Sending her wasn't just ironic. It was a loud and clear message. *Go back where you came from.* "Did you get the list I e-mailed you?"

"Yeah. I got it right here."

"Start with the teachers and staff. Run as many through as you can. Flag anyone with a record, anything that makes you suspicious."

"It's a pretty long list."

"I know. Just do what you can while we get a team assembled. We need something to go on."

She ended the call, turned up her collar, and walked toward her car. But she did have one thing to go on. Apparently, Sanchez had left the school yesterday to visit a student in one of the most dangerous housing projects in West Harlem. She had to trace his steps, and she wasn't going to do it alone.

When she pulled up to Sanchez's building, she saw him. He was standing on the front steps next to a uniformed officer guarding the taped-off entrance to the building. She stared at his curly blond hair and his pouty lips around a cigarette, and her emotions fluctuated like the weather at the confluence of opposing fronts.

She got out and slammed her door and watched him notice her. He flicked his cigarette to the ground. For several seconds, neither one of them moved. Then he slowly approached her. He stopped three feet away, and his watery blue eyes swept over her body from head to toe. Surface capillaries spread out like spider webs across the sclera of his eyes.

He'd had a late night, she thought, and too much to drink—but didn't he always have too much to drink? And then she remembered the last time they'd stood alone together, outside the St. James bar, when he had pulled her against him and held her head between two hands and looked into her eyes as if he'd wanted to absorb her whole being into his. He had whispered her name over and over again. He'd said, "You feel it, too. Don't you?" He never said what *it* was, but she knew. And then he had clumsily kissed her. His lips had tasted like vodka and beer nuts. She had tried to push him away.

"What the fuck are you doing? You're drunk, Brian. Go have some coffee. You have absolutely no idea what I feel," she had said.

She'd had almost a year now to think about his words and to scrape past her denial and admit that he *had* known what she was feeling. She had wanted to wrap her arms around him that night as much as he'd wanted her to. In the intervening months, she had tried to explain away her desire. Yes, she had felt something that night, but only because—unbeknownst to her—the lymphoma had invaded her body and started to make her unwell, and everyone feels vulnerable and needy when they're unwell. In the end, however, she had admitted to herself that her feelings for Brian had taken root long before the lymphoma. He had only needed a few too many drinks to be honest about his feelings; she had needed cancer to be honest about hers.

She studied him now. He smiled warily. They were like two animals circling each other, she thought. She wanted to say, *I missed you.* Then she wanted to ask, *Why didn't you come and see me?* And finally she let her anger take over and she wanted to say, *Fuck you. Why are you here?*

He should have been with her ten months ago when her test results had come back and she had had to meet the oncologist—Dr. Abrams—for the first time. The day before that appointment, her neighbor Jean had paid her a visit. Jean's apartment shared a wall with Codella's living room, and their front doors were right next to each other on the third floor. Jean and Codella had become acquainted because they saw each other so often: coming and going, at the garbage bins near the service elevator, or emerging simultaneously to retrieve their *New York Times* early in the morning after they heard the familiar plop when the delivery person flung it toward their doors.

Jean was a freelance journalist and had documented her own breast cancer story in an article for *New York* magazine a few years earlier. Now she wrote a syndicated women's health column. "Who's going with you tomorrow?" she had asked with a forthrightness Codella wasn't used to hearing from others since *she* was usually the one who demanded the information.

"No one." Codella had shrugged.

"No one?"

"It's fine. I don't need anyone."

"Yes, you do," Jean had insisted. "You can't be alone at that appointment. I'll go with you."

Codella had protested, but her protests hadn't been all that strenuous. She had been terrified, she realized now, although she was in denial. Most single people, it occurred to her much later, would have called their mothers to come and be with them at a crisis moment like that. She had thought several times about her mother in the days leading up to the appointment, days when she knew something was terribly wrong with her but didn't yet know just *how* wrong. In those prediagnosis days when she and Brian were not speaking, she had been more tempted than ever to seek her mother's comfort and protection. In the end, however, she had clung to reality and to her personal code of ethics: her mother had *never* been protective, and you didn't call on someone after twenty years of self-imposed silence only because you didn't have anyone else to lean on. Codella had no siblings to help her either—at least none that she knew about, though it was quite conceivable her father had contributed countless children to the population of Providence, Rhode Island, considering his prolific extramarital adventures.

As a police detective, she was trained to ask questions, listen to people, and evaluate their responses. But in the oncologist's office, she had not managed to apply these critical skills of her trade at all.

She had absorbed only intermittent words, as if she were someone in a foreign country trying to understand a language she had
studied only briefly. Aggressive non-Hodgkin's B-cell lymphoma,
she had heard. Hyper-CVAD, she had heard. Mostly, she had been
aware of an intense ringing between her eardrums, as if a roadside
bomb had just detonated at close range.

Jean had asked most of the questions in her clear, calm voice.
"Tell us about hyper-CVAD."

"It's an aggressive chemotherapy treatment administered incre-
mentally over several days."

"So Claire will be staying in the hospital during the chemotherapy?"

"Yes. These are highly toxic dosages, and patients need to be
monitored continually for adverse reactions."

"How long are the treatments?"

"Four to five days," he said.

"And how many treatments is Claire likely to need?"

"The typical protocol is to start with six rounds, alternating
between the A-cycle drugs and the B-cycle drugs. That is going to
be my recommendation here."

"Can she work during the treatments?"

He had smiled slightly. Maybe, she realized now, he had actually been wincing. "Most people aren't up to that."

"When will her treatments begin?"

"I'd like to admit her the day after tomorrow."

"So soon?" These were the first words Codella had uttered
herself.

Abrams had looked at her directly. "You have a fast proliferat-
ing B-cell lymphoma. It could be a form called Burkitt's, which
is very rare in this country. We're still doing additional stains on
the tissue samples to confirm that. Aggressive B-cell lymphomas
move fast, so we need to hit yours very hard and very quickly. The
good news," he smiled in a gentle way that Codella would come
to find reassuring, "is that because these cells are multiplying so
quickly, they are less stable than other cancer cells. They can actually respond very well to the drugs. Our job is to level everything
we can at them and knock them out thoroughly right away. That's
our best chance of curing you."

"So this is curable?" Jean had asked the question Codella was
too afraid to ask.

"A complete cure is our goal," Abrams had said definitively but without a promise. And Codella had held onto that. She had not used her investigative skills to find out more about Burkitt's lymphoma. She knew instinctively that she would not like or be reassured by anything she read. She knew Jean would be scouring the Internet in the privacy of her apartment next door, and she told Jean not to share what she learned. It was better not to know.

She had expected Brian to visit her as soon as he'd learned she was in the hospital. She had imagined him visiting countless times during the first few chemo treatments. In her fantasies, he entered her room silently and curled up beside her on the bed, careful not to get tangled up in her chemo lines. He stroked her head and whispered, "Don't worry. We'll get through this together." But he hadn't come. He hadn't helped her. Jean had been the one at her side, not her friend and partner of seven years, not the man who supposedly loved her, and she wasn't going to forgive him for that. She looked at him now. "You haven't changed a bit."

"You have," he answered, but there was no malice in his tone. "You look—" He hesitated. "Good. Healthy. Maybe a little too thin."

"What are you doing here?"

"Checking in with Muñoz."

"He doesn't need your help. He knows what to do."

Haggerty smiled. "How are you feeling?"

"Better than you probably wish I were." The words, like an impulsive slap, were delivered before she could stop them.

"That's not true," he protested, and his gentle, contrite tone made her feel guilty for her sarcasm. But why should she feel guilty?

"Excuse me." She stepped around him quickly and entered the building, careful not to land in the same sticky spot as earlier this morning. She ignored the tightness in her stomach as she dialed Muñoz. "Where are you?"

"Seventh floor."

"Get down here as soon as you can."

When he appeared in the lobby, she asked, "When did Detective Haggerty get here?"

"About an hour ago."

She stopped short of saying, *You should have called me.* "Follow me." She led him out of the building, down the stairs, to the car.

Haggerty followed them. "Where are you taking Muñoz?"

"I need some backup. It's urgent."

"Let me have your back. Muñoz can keep going here."

She hesitated. Jackie Robinson Village wasn't the kind place you went to without a good backup. Anything could happen in a place like that. She and Brian had been there once to track down a witness who didn't want to be tracked down, and when the elevator doors had opened, five or six gang members had greeted them. Codella had pressed the close button immediately, but their welcoming party was already holding open the doors.

Brian had pulled out his service revolver and aimed it squarely at the closest face. "I'm only going to say this once. Back off right now. I'll give you to five to let go of the door." They didn't let go of the doors until the count of four, and in those seconds, Brian had counted calmly and slowly and his steady aim had not wavered. That was the kind of backup you needed, and she had no idea what Eduardo Muñoz was capable of. She looked at his towering figure. She was going to take a chance. "Get in," she told him.

Muñoz folded his large body into the front passenger seat while Haggerty stared at her. "Claire."

She remembered the last time he'd said her name, in that hoarse, drunk whisper. She stiffened. "Call me if you get something relevant here." *And not before*, she wanted to add.

She opened her car door, climbed into the driver's seat, and started the engine. She resisted the overwhelming impulse to punch the steering wheel. She wasn't going to give him the satisfaction of seeing that he could unnerve her. "We're taking a ride," she told Muñoz calmly as she pulled out.

"Where to?"

"I'll ask the questions for now. What did you find out in there?"

"The building's one of those reclaimed city properties where you get low-interest mortgages, but you can't resell at market value. There are a hundred and twelve units."

"You talk to any neighbors? They know anything?"

"The guy on his floor—the one who called about his barking dog this morning—didn't get home until after ten last night, and the dog was barking like crazy even then."

"So Sanchez was probably already dead. I've been wondering about that dog. Why didn't the murderer just kill it too? Why leave it there to howl and draw attention? Anyone see him come home last night?"

"Not that I spoke to, but his neighbor one flight up—Cameron Swain—knew him pretty well. She had the keys to his apartment. She walks his dog while he's at work. She saw him yesterday a few minutes after five."

Codella turned. "In his apartment?"

Muñoz nodded.

"What was he wearing?"

"The jeans and T-shirt. Not the suit."

"Interesting. What did they talk about?"

"Dog treats."

"Dog treats? That's it?"

"People with dogs have conversations like that," he said.

"You're into dogs?"

"Me? Not really. I could be, I suppose."

"I like dogs, but I don't like to think of a dog cooped up in my one bedroom. Where was this neighbor last night?"

"Out with friends."

"What else?"

"His laptop was still in its case on the vestibule floor." He paused. "I'm sorry I didn't call to tell you Detective Haggerty had arrived. I guess I should have."

"Forget it." She pressed the accelerator harder, and they flew up Amsterdam through green light after green light until the fourteen-story redbrick towers of Jackie Robinson Village loomed in front of them and the bittersweet taste of Haggerty in her mouth faded away.

"That's where we're going?" Muñoz shook his head with a wry grin that she couldn't decipher.

"You've been here before?"

"Yeah, I've been here. I was a narc, remember?"

The public housing project was a sprawling eyesore that dominated three city blocks and provided shelter to chronic welfare recipients, violent felons on parole, the formerly homeless, and the drug and alcohol dependent. Ordinary citizens of Manhattan had the good sense to stay clear. Even the NYPD preferred to circle the perimeter from the safety of their blue-and-white patrol cars.

Codella swerved into the complex. "Sanchez left school yesterday at three thirty. His assistant principal, Marva Thomas, said he was coming here to make a home visit to a student who's missed a lot of school. I need to know who he talked to, what he said, when he left, and where he went from here. We've got to trace his steps from the time he left that school until he was killed. That's why we're here." She pulled into a handicap space. "And you're my bodyguard," she added with a smile.

They walked to tower nine and stepped into an ancient elevator. The lighting was dim. The walls were covered in graffiti. The black buttons were worn from decades of repeated use. The car jerked and the cables above made strange squeaking noises as they slowly ascended. Codella couldn't help but consider how ironic it would be if she'd survived six brutal rounds of chemo and two episodes of C. diff only to plummet to her death as soon as she'd reclaimed her life.

Finally the doors opened and they stepped onto the ninth floor. Overamplified bass from powerful speakers reverberated from somewhere. She stared down the long, narrow corridor toward an imaginary vanishing point. Most of the frosted glass ceiling lamps had long ago been broken, leaving bare bulbs to cast a harsh, uneven light. A half-empty beer bottle, cigarette pack, and lighter lay on the floor just to the left of the elevator.

Muñoz pointed to them. "Looks like a sentry's left his post."

Two feet from the bottle, an inch-long cockroach lay on its back. Its legs were jerking in futile motions. "Come on," she said, "let's do this and get the hell out of here."

Apartment 905 was halfway down the hall. Codella was about to knock when Muñoz caught her arm. "Who we looking for here?"

"Shalon Williams and her daughter Vondra."

"Let me do this." He pushed her back from the door and knocked gently. "You in there?" he said with his face right up to the doorframe. "Hey, baby, you in there?" He knocked again. "Hurry up! Lemme in."

The deadbolt turned. The door opened five inches, and black eyes peered up at Muñoz. A male voice demanded, "Who the fuck are you?"

"Who the fuck are you? I be lookin' for Shalon."

"She be somewhere else right now."

"Open up, bro. I don't wanna advertise myself to the world."

"I got no time for you." Black Eyes tried to close the door.

"Wait!" Muñoz held the door open.

"You a copper?" said Black Eyes.

Muñoz ignored the question. "What's that crazy smell, bro? You cookin' in there?"

"Yeah, fried chicken."

"Don't smell like fried chicken." He pulled back his jacket and showed his identification. "Smell like I gotta get in that apartment."

"You got no warrant, copper."

"I got a nose, bro. My nose is a warrant. I know ingredients when I smell 'em."

Then Black Eyes shrugged. "Whatever." He opened the door and let Muñoz into the darkened room, and then he made a bolt. As he rounded the corner, he slammed into Codella, knocking her against the wall. By the time she got her balance, he'd opened the door to the fire stairs and disappeared. Muñoz raced down the hall after him. When Codella reached the stairwell, Muñoz was two flights below her and Black Eyes was even farther down. She could hear each man grunt with the effort of taking three or four steps at a time. She willed her legs to descend the steps faster and faster until her muscles could no longer keep up with the signals from her brain.

When she reached the ground floor, all she wanted to do was sink onto a step and catch her breath, and she thought, *Jesus, I'm not ready for this yet*, but she forced her leaden legs to carry her out of the stairwell in time to see Black Eyes racing away from the building toward an identical adjacent tower. Her heart was throbbing in her chest, and her quads and hamstrings burned. Muñoz's arms were pumping like a hundred-meter sprinter's, and she watched him close the gap between himself and Black Eyes in long strides.

He grabbed Black Eyes by his collar and pulled him back in one powerful jerk that sent him crashing to the walkway. His head hit concrete, and as he sat up, blood gushed down one side of his face. "Fuck you!" he screamed.

Muñoz kicked him back to the ground and rolled him onto his stomach with his long shoe as Codella finally caught up. Black Eyes was wearing a cheap, too-tight gray sweater that hugged his thin arms and concave, underdeveloped torso. His mouth was covered with open, red sores. His hair was a wild mass of wiry, oily, black curls. He had pinpoint pupils, his skin was pallid, and perspiration seeped from the pores all over his face. "Hands behind your back. Do it *now*." Muñoz pressed his shoe into the small of the man's back as Codella reached for her cuffs and slapped them tightly around his wrists.

They got him up and walked him back to Tower Nine and returned to the apartment. Codella felt around for the light switch. When she flipped it on, the two detectives stood still and stared. The small living room was bare except for a pedestal table piled with containers of acetone, coffee filters, rubber tubing, rock salt, a turkey baster, measuring cups, buckets, tin foil, and a propane tank. Blankets over the windows blocked all traces of daylight. Muñoz pushed Black Eyes onto a chair. "No fried chicken here, bro. We're gonna need to call in Narc. I just know they'll wanna chitchat with you."

Codella continued to the far end of the living room and opened the door to one of the two back rooms. "Better call CPS while you're at it," she told him.

A little girl was sitting on the bed, and she didn't move when Codella stepped over and turned on a lamp. "What's your name?"

The girl didn't answer.

"Are you Vondra?"

She nodded.

"Where's your mother?"

Vondra shrugged.

"When did you last see her?"

"Yesterday," she whispered.

"When yesterday? Do you remember?"

"Bedtime. She wasn't here when I woke up." Tears glistened in the corners of her eyes.

"Was he here?" She pointed out the door toward Black Eyes.

Vondra shook her head.

"When did he come?"

"Today. I thought he was my mom. I let him in. He told me to stay in here and close the door."

The little girl started to cry. "Where's my mommy?"

"I don't know, but we'll look for her. And while we're looking, we'll get you something to eat and drink, okay?" Codella put her arm around the girl. "I have a couple of important questions for you. Were you home here yesterday?"

Vondra nodded.

"Did anybody come here to see you and your mom?"

"Like who?"

"Mr. Sanchez, your principal."

"Mr. Sanchez? Why'd he wanna come here?"

"To check up on you. To find out why you weren't in school."

"Nobody come here," she said resolutely.

"You're absolutely sure?"

Vondra Williams nodded. "Nobody be comin' here 'less they have to," she said with more insight than a nine-year-old should possess.

CHAPTER 12

As Codella started the car, Muñoz stared at the spot where he had tackled Black Eyes. The spot was imprinted in his mind. He could close his eyes and still see the tall oak trees on either side of that sidewalk the way they had looked three months ago in full foliage. He could remember staring up at the leaves and thinking they were a lush but blurry rainforest canopy. He could still see the dense row of pigeons sitting on a low branch. Bird shit from those pigeons had formed a speckled pattern all around him, and as he'd watched those birds jockey for positions, he'd wondered when some of that shit was going to land on him.

The last time Muñoz had been at the Jackie Robinson Village, he'd chased down a crack dealer who'd bolted when they showed up at his door with a warrant. Muñoz was ten feet behind him when the guy had fished a .22 out of his backpack, turned, and taken a shot that sent Muñoz to the concrete. He had lain there on his back with another narc pressing against the bullet hole in his shoulder at the edge of his bulletproof vest and he'd lapsed in and out of consciousness waiting for the EMT. Was it simple irony, he wondered as Codella pulled out of the parking spot, that his very first homicide case had brought him to the scene of his final narcotics case? Was it a sign that your past always followed you into your present?

Working narcotics had never been his end goal, just the only available game plan to get a gold shield. He'd paid for his the hard way, with two years of street work, a shattered shoulder, and a four-hour operation. And to what end? So he could get targeted by the precinct bully? So he could be humiliated in a smelly pub? He pictured Marty Blackstone last evening tossing back shots with his self-satisfied smirk, and he almost felt nostalgic for the past. Wasn't it better to face physical danger doing buy-and-busts on the corner of 179th Street and St. Nicholas than endure psychological torture? He had pondered this question last night all the way from the pub to a gay bar in Chelsea, where he'd anaesthetized his mortification with two strong martinis and used his Grindr app to find a nearby hook-up so he wouldn't have to hear New Dick in his brain anymore.

"What's wrong, Muñoz?" Codella's voice snapped him back to the present.

"Nothing," he said.

She threw him a skeptical glance, but all she said was, "You eat breakfast? I didn't. Let's go."

Ten minutes later, they slid into a vinyl-upholstered window booth at Metro Diner on 100th and Broadway. The restaurant was quiet. The breakfast rush had ended and the lunch crowd was still an hour or so away. She was reading the laminated menu when the waitress came for their order, so Muñoz went first. "Bacon burger, fries, and a large vanilla shake—*extra thick*."

Codella looked up at that, and he could tell she was tempted to make a comment—maybe about men and their craving for meat at all hours of the day or night—but she only smiled and turned to the waitress. "Green tea, and can you do an egg white omelet?"

When they were alone, she said, "That was good work back there. Really good. I wasn't up to that chase. You saved my ass."

"Well, you didn't take me there for my great conversational skills."

She smiled appreciatively as the waitress set down her tea. "So how do you like life in the 171st?"

"It's okay."

"Just okay?"

"Does everyone new get a nickname there?"

"Blackstone?" she guessed.

He nodded.

"So what's yours?"

He shook his head.

"Come on. I had one too. Miss Marple."

"New Dick," he admitted.

"New Dick? That's the best he could do? Not Blue Giant or something? He's losing his touch. He usually does a lot better."

They both smiled. The waitress slid Muñoz's milkshake across the Formica table. He inserted his straw and tested the viscosity. There was nothing he hated more than a thin milkshake, but this one measured up to his standards.

"He'll forget about you sooner or later," Codella assured him.

Muñoz didn't know about that. *How many times*, he thought, *did a bully cop get a fag cop to whip?* But he didn't want to dwell on that now. "So what did you learn at the school?"

"That Sanchez has an equal share of fans and critics. Everyone I talked to had a different impression."

"Any possible suspects?"

"I've got some hunches, but I try to ignore those, and you should, too. Let's follow the evidence. That's why we went to that apartment. Sanchez told his assistant principal that he was going over there to check on a student—but apparently, he lied to her."

"Where next?"

"I'm not sure. But a lot happened at that school yesterday. And I'm going to find out what it means." She blew on her tea and looked out the window as a large, black caregiver pushed a double stroller toward West End Avenue. "I'm going to solve this murder." She took a sip. "I'm going to solve it before that bastard can yank it out from under me." She squinted across the street in the direction of the Wang Chen Table Tennis Club. Her mind was somewhere else, he thought.

Just then the waitress appeared and set their plates in front of them. When she left, he leaned his long torso over the table and spoke in a low voice. "I don't mean to be presumptuous, Detective Codella, but I imagine being a woman who just got back from a medical leave puts a lot of pressure on you."

She unfurled her paper napkin and arranged it on her lap. "What's your point?"

"Just that you probably have a lot to prove right now, at least as much as a gay detective who just got outted on his first night drinking with the other precinct boys." He paused.

"Oh." She cringed. "I'm sorry."

He held her stare. "Then let me stay on this case with you. Let me help you solve this." He wanted to say, *Please*. He almost said, *I need this too.*

Her eyes narrowed appraisingly. A New York City diner had never felt so silent to Muñoz. Finally she lifted her tea mug and held it over the table between them. "You're a good bodyguard. Let's see what else you can do."

He raised his milkshake glass to meet her mug. She smiled. He smiled, too.

CHAPTER 13

Network news vans with satellite uplinks lined the curb in front of the school, and local reporters were spread out, interviewing anyone they could. Codella and Muñoz climbed out of the car and flashes went off in her face. "Detective, give us a comment!"

They hurried past the cops blocking the press from the school. Ragavan met them just inside. "What's been happening?" she asked.

"They brought kids into the auditorium one or two grades at a time. Psychologists talked to them. Now the kids are back in their classrooms. I've mostly been helping keep parents and reporters out of here. It's a zoo."

"How are your computer skills?"

"Good enough."

"Follow me." She led him to Marva Thomas's office. Thomas's thin fingers were dancing across her keyboard, and she didn't look up until Codella rapped loudly. "I'd like you to meet Detective Muñoz, Miss Thomas. He'll be assisting me in this investigation. We plan to speak to some of your staff while Detective Ragavan examines Mr. Sanchez's computer. He needs the login information."

Thomas nodded and pushed back her chair.

"And you still haven't e-mailed me his mother's contact information. The media have this, Ms. Thomas. Do you want his mother hearing about his death on the evening news fifteen hundred miles away? Would you want to hear about your son's death that way?"

"Of course not. I'll get it right away. I've been very busy."

Codella thought, *Right. Busy being clueless.* She wanted to shake the woman and say, *Don't you realize Hector Sanchez was lying to you?*

Don't you know that he wasn't checking on those children he was supposed to care so much about? She wanted to ask, *What the fuck's going on here?* Instead, she simply stated, "However busy we are, we have certain obligations to the dead."

Then she led Muñoz and Ragavan next door to Sanchez's office and took out her frustration by ripping the crime scene tape off his door. "Get on that computer," she told Ragavan. "Read his e-mail. Look at his bookmarks. Search his hard drive. Find out what was going on in his life. Who did he speak to? What did they talk about? Which names keep coming up and why? Write things down for me. I'll be back."

She and Muñoz climbed to the second floor and peered through the windows of closed classroom doors. In room after room, children were sitting at their desks, working on assignments or participating in conversations with teachers who paced between their tables. Were they discussing the dead principal? Were they sharing what they had admired about him? Were they asking hard questions that no teacher was really trained to answer, like "Why do people kill other people?" or "Is anyone else going to die?" How did you possibly make a murder sound nonthreatening to elementary schoolchildren without diminishing the terribleness of the act?

They found Jenny Bernstein sitting alone at her desk. Bernstein had shoulder-length brunette hair with bangs and glasses with dark, fashionable frames. She was chewing the end of a No. 2 pencil like a middle-aged graduate student.

Codella stepped into the room first and introduced herself and Muñoz. "Your students are done for the day?"

"I'm sure they wish they were, but no, they're with their math teacher. I can't imagine they're really concentrating on math, however."

"How did they take the news?"

"A few of them broke down."

"You're John Chambers's teacher, aren't you? I heard about the incident yesterday. Did you speak to Mr. Sanchez after the attack?"

Bernstein shook her head. "I went to see him as soon as school ended, but he had left for the day."

"Do you know where he went?"

"No."

"What can you tell us about him?"

She shrugged. "I didn't know him that well."

"But you must have formed some impression."

Bernstein set her pencil down. "Look, I'm sorry this happened to him. I am. It's awful—more than awful. There aren't really words for it. But I have to be honest with you. He wasn't the person he was made out to be."

"The 'Savior of PS 777'?"

She nodded. "His idea of saving the school was throwing perfectly good teachers under the bus. I'm sorry, but you want me to tell the truth, don't you?"

"Of course. I'll solve this case a lot quicker if people tell me the truth."

"He treated us like a bunch of recalcitrant children. He was always popping into our classrooms unannounced as if he expected to catch us misbehaving. He'd slip into your back row," she pointed to the back of her classroom, "and pull out his Observation Checklist and start assessing all your deficiencies with his four-point rubric. We all lived in dread of being in his crosshairs." She opened a desk drawer and removed several sheets of paper. "Here, look. My October report card."

Codella took the pages. Muñoz glanced at them over her shoulder. Bernstein had been evaluated on various categories, including her creation of a respectful learning environment, her management of classroom procedures and student behavior, her classroom organization, her teaching strategies, her questioning and discussion techniques, and the level of student engagement. She had received a score in each of these categories as well as an overall grade of C+ for the month. Sanchez's handwritten observations filled the pages, and at the bottom of the final page was a note to Bernstein: *You need to work harder, Jenny. You need to demand more of them and yourself.*

"And that's a relatively good score," said Bernstein, "for a legacy teacher."

"Legacy teacher?"

"I was here before Mr. Sanchez was appointed. Other legacies have fared much worse than me. Evelyn Robinson, for instance. She teaches second grade. Two weeks ago, he skewered her at a faculty meeting."

"What did she do?"

"Mr. Sanchez showed up in her room five minutes before recess. Evelyn had just finished small-group reading and the recess bell was about to ring. There wasn't much time to start something new, so she and the kids were playing vocabulary hangman and in walks Mr. Sanchez. Well, he didn't approve of hangman—even though Evelyn was using the game to review words from their reading—and at the faculty meeting the next afternoon, he told everybody how she had wasted precious instructional time and that PS 777 students deserved better than hangman. And then he announced to everyone that Evelyn had the lowest overall October grade—a D minus."

When Codella and Muñoz left Bernstein, they made their way to the opposite end of the corridor where third-grade teacher Christine Donohue was reading on her iPad in her empty classroom. "What can you tell us about Mr. Sanchez? We're trying to get a sense of who he was."

Donohue lowered her cheap reading glasses and let them dangle on the fake gold chain around her neck. The quarter inch of natural silver at her roots contrasted sharply with the rest of her bottled red hair. She set down her iPad, folded her arms, and arranged her face into a smirk that revealed deep creases in her freckled skin. She had a husky voice. "Don't expect me to give you the standard 'Isn't this awful?' and 'He was such a great principal' speech. He was a naïve Johnny-come-lately who thought he knew more than everyone else."

Codella moved closer. "Go on."

"I've been teaching third grade longer than he's had facial hair, and I didn't appreciate him and that Hispanic crony of his coming into my classroom to say I've been doing it all wrong for three decades. That's really all I've got to say about Hector Sanchez."

Another legacy victim, thought Codella. "Who's his crony?"

"Sofia *Rrrrreyes*." Donohue mockingly overaccentuated the rolled *r* in the last name as she rolled her eyes. "Our new literacy coach. Supposedly she's here to make us better teachers. But we're not fooled. She's his cover—well, she was. If anyone complained about his policies, Sofia was there to quote the research about why teachers needed to change. Mind you, she hardly speaks English better than my students. I can only imagine what she's getting paid to tell me *my* business." Her eyes narrowed. "Let me spell things out for you, Detective. Sanchez was on a big ego trip bankrolled, in case you're interested, by a sleazy actress."

"You mean Dana Drew?"

"It's obvious they were having an affair. Why don't you look into that?"

"Drew's a lesbian. She and her partner have a child."

Donohue raised one overly plucked eyebrow. "Do you honestly think what you see on a bus stop poster is reality? The child is Drew's. The girlfriend is just her latest diversion. They've only been together a year. Obviously, she's bored and Sanchez was her new distraction."

"You've put a lot of thought into this."

"No I haven't, because it doesn't take much thought. Don't you know about actors and their loose boundaries? They're all borderline and narcissistic. They'll sleep with anyone. None of their relationships amount to anything. She was using Sanchez, and he was using her."

"How so?"

"She wants everyone to see her as the big public-education advocate. She enrolls her daughter here in September, and the media eat it up just in time for the opening of her new play. How convenient. Everyone's *Oh, isn't Dana Drew so great? She's a regular person like us.* But I assure you her daughter isn't having the typical PS 777 experience. She's dropped off each morning in an Escalade, and Drew has single-handedly funneled enough money in here to hire that coach, put a teacher's aide in every classroom, and start an after-school program. Who's really running this school? Meanwhile, I happen to know she's quietly applied to private schools for next year."

"How do you know that?"

Donohue smirked. "You have your sources. I have mine. And if the daughter goes, you mark my word. The funding will dry up as fast as it started to flow. The great public-education advocate will be on to her next cause, and those 'We're a Proud Family' posters you see all around? They'll be rotting under some new ad campaign."

"Proud Families was Dana Drew's idea?"

"I suppose they cooked it up together—probably in bed. They both wanted the spotlight however they could get it, and we were all expected to be the extras in their drama. I for one wanted no part of it. Nowhere in my contract is it written that I have to smile and say cheese for a big-shot photographer. You're not going to find my mug shot on that wall of pride downstairs, and I wasn't the only one who refused."

"Who else did?"

Donohue squinted. She seemed to read aloud the names off a mental roster as she counted them on her hands. "Anna Masoutis, Norma Feinstein, Gene Bosco, Kristin DeMarco, Roz Porter, Natalie Rapinoe—even Mr. Jancek. After what his family went through, he didn't want to go anywhere near that camera." Then her eyes lighted up. She was clearly a born gossiper. "His niece was raped in a Bosnian camp while a bunch of soldiers took pictures. They made him watch. He has no love of cameras, but that didn't stop Mr. Sanchez from pressuring him. You see, Sanchez punished anyone who didn't participate in his projects. He thought he could railroad you into doing whatever he wanted you to do. He never let up."

Donohue wasn't ready to let up either. "This September he decided the male teachers should all wear dress shirts and ties so the boys would have models of how you dress for success. As if working here makes you a success!" Her laugh was a raspy smoker's rattle that augured future lung cancer or emphysema. "Gene told him if this was Wall Street and he had a Wall Street salary, he'd be happy to dress like the One Percent, but not until. That's Gene, always saying it like it is. We had a good laugh about it over dinner that night. And the very next day, Sanchez started going after him."

"Going after him? What do you mean?"

"He put Gene on his hit list," she said matter-of-factly.

"How do you know?"

"Because he did all the things an administrator does when he's out to get a teacher. Wrote him up for every little infraction he could think of—turning in his lesson plans late, missing a faculty meeting, that kind of thing. He even accused Gene of holding onto a student's arm and shaking it—which is nonsense. Gene's not stupid. He'd never do that. And then—thanks to that fat security guard—Sanchez finally had the ammunition he needed to banish him to temporary reassignment until he can fire him like everyone else he's fired this year. I bet he's had a list of all the teachers he wanted to fire since day one of his tenure. I bet you'll find it if you look at his computer. And I'll bet my name is at the top of that list. Let me know if I'm right." She leaned forward and interlocked her fingers like a church steeple. "Now do you have a *sense* of who he was?"

Codella certainly had a sense of who Christine Donohue was. "When did you last see him?"

"Yesterday morning on the front steps shaking hands like Mr. Candidate for mayor. He was always posing for the camera, whether or not it was there. He was always tweeting his little social media messages of wisdom, too. His Twitter username was MrFixit777. That tells you everything about his big head, doesn't it? You should have seen him stalk around here like a celebrity after that magazine article came out last spring." She rolled her eyes.

Codella thanked Donohue for her time and placed her card on the teacher's desk. "Call me if you think of anything that might help our investigation." But she had a pretty strong suspicion the card would end up in the circular file next to the desk.

CHAPTER 14

Marva Thomas's cell phone rang, and she recognized Carla's number. She braced for her sister to chastise her for not dropping everything this morning to help her mother—Carla was nothing if not judgmental—but this time Carla surprised her. "I heard you on New York One just now, Marva. You were incredible. I never knew you could sound so—" she paused. "Well, so professional. You were so in charge."

"Thanks," Marva answered with no emotion. The compliment only reinforced her feeling of utter inadequacy, since she knew she wasn't responsible for the professionalism Carla has witnessed. She wasn't responsible for anything she had said or done today. As soon as Tweed had authorized the statement to reporters on the school steps, Jane Stewart from the Department of Education communications office had told her exactly what she was going to say and made her rehearse it three times before they had walked outside together. And Ellie Friedman from Margery Barton's office had orchestrated the assemblies with the children and told her exactly what to say about Sanchez's death and how to introduce the grief counselors who spoke to each grade-level group.

"Do they know who did it?" asked Carla.

"Not yet."

"Do they think it's someone at the school?"

Marva heard only self-serving curiosity in Carla's voice. Carla's son Justin attended the Rockwell Academy, an elite private school, and Carla was probably trying to collect whatever tidbits Marva tossed her way so that she could pass them on to the white stay-at-home private-school moms whose acceptance she desperately wanted. Carla's dark complexion, Marva suspected, meant that her membership in their social circle was provisional at best and had to be constantly renewed. But that was the world Carla had chosen. That was her problem. "Look, I can't talk right now, Carla. There's a lot going on here. I'll have to call you later."

"Sure, Marva. Call me when you can."

Marva hung up and closed her eyes. She could hardly breathe. She felt claustrophobic with the door to her tiny office closed, but she needed a break from all the handlers. Ironically, she'd taken more orders from them today than she'd ever had to take from Hector Sanchez. He had usually just ignored her. Today she was like a piece of furniture they kept rearranging. She wanted to speak to someone who would really understand, but who was she supposed to call? Who did she have in the way of friends? Rita Monroe from church? They'd sat together on the bus on a spiritual retreat last month, and they always had nice chats during coffee hour after the St. Michael's service, but Rita wasn't really a friend. She wasn't someone Marva could spill her guts to. The truth was that she had no one. She was alone in this. Not even Sofia Reyes had bothered to return her call.

She heard a knock on her door. She sat up and reached for her keyboard to look busy. "Come in," she said with a blend of authority and annoyance meant to deflect the criticism of whichever handler had come for her now. The door opened, but it was just Milosz holding out a Dunkin' Donuts cup. He set the coffee on her desk in front of her. "I put in sugar and milk, the way you like it."

The aroma expanded her nasal passages, and her eyes started to burn. She had to stop herself from crying over this small act of kindness. If she cried, he would think she was unstable. Maybe she was unstable. In truth, there was no question—she *was*. But she couldn't let on. She took a deep breath. "Two cups in one day? Thank you, Milosz. You shouldn't have."

He smiled. "It's been a hard day for you. And yesterday was even harder."

Marva grasped the warm cardboard cup. Was he referring to her run-in with Sanchez? How much of that conversation had he heard, and if he had heard it, who else had heard it? Janisa? Other teachers? She was mortified to think about that. She still remembered Hector's exact words because they had stung her so painfully.

"Goddammit, Marva." He had not even waited for his office door to be closed. "You're not here to post sign-up sheets. You're not here to make decisions. You're here to keep the heads out of toilets. That's it. And you can't even do that. How the fuck did this happen?"

Marva had never in her life been spoken to so vehemently or vulgarly. Even her supercilious mother and sister never spoke to her like that. "You're the least effective administrator I've ever worked with." He had continued his verbal assault on her self-esteem. And then he had gone for her jugular, disdainfully flicking his index finger against her favorite quote from Ephesians, ripping the tape that held the Post-it note to the side of her computer monitor. "What are you, anyway? One of those simple-minded church ladies? This is a *public* school, for God's sake. You don't belong here. You're out of my school at the end of this year."

Now she forced herself to look up at Milosz despite her deep humiliation. "Thank you," she said. "You're very kind."

He nodded and smiled. He wasn't attractive with that angular face, she thought, but he was nicer to her than anyone else in this place. She watched him close the door on his way out, and then she let herself cry. It was a harder day than anybody realized. But no one ever thought of Marva's feelings—no one except a custodian. She sipped the hot coffee. It was sweetened to perfection.

CHAPTER 15

At 4:15 PM on a weekday, there were few public places on the Upper West Side—or anywhere in Manhattan, for that matter—where you could hold a private conversation on the spur of the moment without the world listening in. Codella had no intention of dragging Vickie Berrard, the teacher of Dana Drew's daughter, to one of the sterile interview rooms at Manhattan North or the 171st Precinct. Those were hardly the sort of places in which the young kindergarten teacher was likely to relax and let down her guard.

There were plenty of Starbucks up and down Broadway, of course, but those were crowded venues with wobbly, crumb-covered pedestal tables that discouraged you from settling in. Codella could think of only one suitable place for a meeting near PS 777, and that was Edgar's Café on Amsterdam between Ninety-First and Ninety-Second Streets. Codella had been frequenting Edgar's since she'd moved to the West Side more than a decade ago. Back then the restaurant had been located on the block of Eighty-Fourth Street west of Broadway called Edgar Allen Poe Street. It was adjacent to the Ohav Shalom Synagogue, and late on a Friday night, young orthodox couples would file in for key lime pie after a Kiddush ceremony. Benny, the smiling old Italian owner, had made his restaurant look like a café in Sorrento, and his friendly Ecuadorian barista made the best lattés.

Benny always made sure Codella had a good table, and if she came at night, he always offered her a piece of key lime pie on the house. When he'd been priced out of his lease on Eighty-Fourth Street, she had followed him to Amsterdam Avenue. Her ancestors were southern Italian, and Benny was from Sicily. They both valued constancy.

Codella and Muñoz silently sipped their drinks and waited for Berrard. When she came through the door, she looked pale and tired. Muñoz pulled out her chair. Codella got the waitress's attention. "How about a coffee or tea?" she asked the teacher. "Maybe a slice of chocolate cake? They have amazing chocolate cake here, and I think most people would agree that this is a day for chocolate." She smiled warmly. Most women, she knew, resorted to desserts in times of stress, even if she didn't. "This must have been a hard day for you."

Berrard peeled out of her quilted Land's End coat. "It's just so sad," she said. "The children and I have been painting pictures for Mr. Sanchez all afternoon. The grief counselor suggested we do something so the children could express their feelings for him."

Codella smiled. "That's a wonderful way to honor him," she said.

"The children loved him so much. He came into our classroom twice a week and read them stories aloud. He always brought the most interesting books to read them. Last week, he read them *Diary of a Worm*, and we used that to start our journaling unit."

Codella nodded politely. "I'm trying to understand who he was, and frankly, everyone I speak to has quite a different perspective."

"I'm not surprised by that."

"No? Why not?"

"Well . . ." She glanced around the restaurant as if she might be under surveillance. "777 is a pretty polarized place. You've got the teachers Hector recruited—like me. And then you have the ones who were here before he came, and a lot of them are—" She paused. "Well, in my opinion, really unprofessional. Lots of them are just clock punchers. They're riding out the years to full retirement benefits. They don't really care about improving students' educational experience."

"What can you tell me about Sofia Reyes?"

"Oh, I *love* Sofia. She's our literacy coach."

"Tell me what that means. She comes to the school and trains you?"

"Twice a week." Berrard nodded. "She runs workshops and leads demonstration lessons to show us new techniques. You can ask her to come in your classroom and watch you teach, and then she'll mentor you privately."

"But I take it some of the teachers feel threatened by her. Why do you think that is?"

"They don't want to admit they could be doing a better job," Berrard answered matter-of-factly. "They're mad because Mr. Sanchez is—I mean was—forcing them to work harder."

"I get the impression he was a pretty harsh evaluator."

"He had to be," she said. "If it were up to most of these teachers, they'd keep doing the same one-size-fits-all teacher-directed lessons they've been doing for two or three decades. They think it's okay to stand up there and read out of the textbook. They don't create opportunities for the children to discover things on their own. They never group the kids for discussions. They don't want to do small-group reading. They don't use their interactive whiteboards. They're the kind of teachers who give our profession a bad name. There's a lot of new research about how kids learn, and they're not paying attention. Sometimes in faculty meetings, Hector passes out a *Reading Research Quarterly* article or copies of a new professional development book he's purchased for everyone, and they just roll their eyes. It's obvious they have no intention to read what he gives them. They checked out long ago. This school has been a dumping ground for lazy, incompetent teachers, and the test scores prove it. So you see, he had to be tough."

"Did he fire anyone?"

Berrard did another visual sweep of the restaurant. Her coffee and chocolate cake arrived. "Well, Christine Donohue would have you believe he was on a witch hunt. In my opinion, she's the legacy teachers' ringleader. She's convinced he trumped up charges against tenured teachers so he could fire them and staff up with cheaper untenured ones like me. She claims he fired two of her buddies."

"Who? Can you give me their names?"

"Imogene Burke and Ron Davis. They both left in mid-September. But I don't think he fired them. I think she's just spreading rumors."

Codella touch-typed the names into her notes app. She noticed that Muñoz had removed a small notepad from his jacket pocket and was also jotting the names. "Which teachers on the staff felt the most threatened by Sanchez?"

Berrard stuck a fork into the dense, dark wedge of cake on her plate. The fork traveled to her mouth and she closed her eyes in obvious pleasure. "I'm sorry. What was your question?"

"Which teachers felt the most threatened by Sanchez?"

"Well, for sure Christine Donohue and her little clique, of course. Anna Masoutis, Roz Porter, Eugene Bosco—they've been here the longest."

"And yet their names were all on the iAchieve sneak preview sign-up sheet down in the office. Why would they sign up to learn about a technology program if they weren't interested in changing their teaching methods?"

"Oh, that's easy!" Berrard laughed. "Mr. Sanchez didn't want iAchieve in our school, and they were doing everything they could to make sure it got adopted. In fact, Christine Donohue even got herself on the adoption committee."

"What's an adoption committee?"

"It's a group of teachers that vote on which program a district will purchase."

"How did she get on the committee?"

"She volunteered, and the superintendent picked her."

"Margery Barton, you mean?"

Berrard nodded.

"So Margery Barton wants iAchieve for the district?"

"She doesn't just want it. She's leading the charge for it."

"And why was Sanchez so opposed to it if he's interested in innovative education?"

"Because he saw it for what it is: just another big expensive program from McFlieger-Walsh. Hector wanted to do something truly innovative. He and Sofia were designing their own apps for intervention. They were working with a little company downtown called Apptitude. I've been testing the beta versions with my students since September. Hector got a small Gates Foundation grant to build the learning apps, and he's hoping to get even more funding to use them in the afterschool intervention program he and Dana Drew are—*were*—about to launch. Hector had so many big plans. This is just terrible for the school."

Codella waited out her commentary. Then she said, "So what I'm hearing is that Hector Sanchez and Margery Barton disagreed about the best way to bring technology into the schools."

Berrard nodded. "And I think that's why Christine has been spreading gossip about him—to make Hector look bad, to influence his credibility."

"You're referring to the rumors that he and Dana Drew were having an affair?"

She nodded.

"Do you think there's any truth to the rumors?" Codella glanced across at Muñoz as she waited for an answer. He had not inserted himself into the interview at all. In fact, he had quietly and deliberately pushed his chair back from the table about a foot so that he was an unobtrusive observer in Vickie Berrard's peripheral vision. Codella had worked with inexperienced detectives who felt compelled to make their mark on an interview whether or not their involvement was useful, and she was impressed by Muñoz's intuition and self-control. He apparently understood and accepted that sometimes fading into the background was the best contribution you could make.

Berrard said, "I think the rumors are ridiculous. Zoe Drew is in my class. I've seen Ms. Drew and Ms. Martin many times."

"Ms. Martin is her partner?"

"That's right. Jane. Jane Martin."

"And you would say that they have a happy relationship?"

"It certainly appears that way to me," said Berrard. "Whenever I see them together, they're smiling, holding hands, glad to see Zoe."

"So you see them together at school quite often?"

"Well, I did at the beginning of the year. They both dropped Zoe off in the morning and picked her up in the afternoon. Lately I see more of Jane, because Dana is at the theater, of course. She gave me house seats to the show during the preview in October. She's wonderful, by the way. I highly recommend it."

Codella's iPhone was vibrating in her pocket. She smiled at the teacher. "You've been very helpful, Miss Berrard. Detective Muñoz and I appreciate your taking this time to see us." She passed her card across the table and pushed out her chair. Muñoz paid the bill, and they left Vickie Berrard to finish her chocolate cake and coffee by herself.

Outside of Edgar's, Codella listened to her voice mail. Hanlon, the NYPD communications liaison, had called her. A press conference was scheduled for 5:00 PM on the steps of the 171st Precinct station, and she needed to be there in fifteen minutes. Ragavan had left a message asking her to phone him, and she did. "Find anything on his computer?"

"Nothing out of the ordinary. I've skimmed his inbox and all his sent and deleted e-mails."

"And? Who does he talk to?"

"Someone named Sofia Reyes. They go back and forth a lot."

"She's his literacy coach. Get her number from Thomas and e-mail it to me. I need to talk to her. Who else?"

"Dana Drew."

"How often?"

"Pretty much every day."

"Judging from the messages, do you think they could be having an affair?"

"Not unless you get turned on talking about funds for student iPads."

Codella checked the time. "When did she last e-mail him?"

"Saturday."

"Read me the note." She waited while he found it.

"It just says *Give me a call.*"

"Did he get any notes from Eugene Bosco?"

"No, but he sent a note to someone named Margery Barton on Monday afternoon. He mentioned Bosco in that note."

"Barton's his district superintendent."

"He told her about Bosco's temporary reassignment."

"What time did he send that note?"

She heard Ragavan flip some pages. "Just before three," he said.

"What else?"

"He talks to a guy named Ivan Schiff."

"Who's he?"

"The e-mail signature says Apptitude. I Googled it. It's in silicon alley. A little start-up. They create all kinds of apps."

"When did they last speak?"

"Last week."

"What's on his hard drive?"

"I'm just starting to look."

"Did Marva Thomas give you his mother's telephone number?"

"Yup. Got it right here."

She turned to Muñoz. "You speak Spanish, right?"

Muñoz nodded.

"Okay, e-mail it to Muñoz right away. He'll call the mother. Then keep going until they kick you out. And make sure you seal that office before you leave." She ended the call and turned to Muñoz. "Come on. We've got a press conference to attend."

CHAPTER 16

Chip Dressler kicked off his shoes, lay on the bed, and called Margery first. "How did it go today?"

"Fine—aside from the fact that the AP over there is a complete idiot. My Caribbean administrative assistant could do a better job. She's why we've got so many problems in these schools. But I've got it under control."

"I'm sure you do." He stared out the window at his skyline view. It was getting dark and the office towers gleamed with soft, golden light. He stared at the black lacquer chest across from the bed. It was tasteful and elegant, he thought. He loved having this room of his own at the Mandarin.

"And here's the good news," Margery added. "Bernie Lipsie may sit in on the pilot results meeting next week."

"How'd you swing that?"

"I have my ways."

"I bet you do," he said.

"What is that supposed to mean?"

"Just that maybe I should be a little jealous?"

"Don't be silly," she said, and he could tell she sounded pleased.

In truth, he didn't care who else she fucked or fondled or flirted with. He and Margery were hardly a long-term proposition. He knew it, and she knew it too. They were together because of iAchieve. The sex was just a byproduct of their intense collaboration. And when the sale was over, well, the collaboration would dissolve.

"Bernie's a real data-driven guy, Chip," Margery was saying now. "If he likes the numbers, then you've got the potential for multiple districts. Bernie will get behind an integrated tech solution with scientifically proven efficacy. The time is right."

"Oh, he'll definitely like these numbers." Chip thought about the impressive bar graphs the research company had prepared. It was amazing the success story you could tell by selectively choosing what data to show or not show. You didn't have to cook the numbers. You just had to artfully arrange them like a delicate composed salad.

"Good," Margery said, "because I want to seal this deal."

He read between the lines. She wanted her promotion. He pressed his lips to the phone. "Have dinner with me," he whispered, calculating that she would turn him down.

"You know we can't be seen together right now."

He sighed convincingly. "I know, I know. It's a good thing you've got more self-control than me."

"Women generally do, Chip."

"I suppose." But he doubted that was actually true in Margery's case.

When they hung up, he dialed Charlene. He had no choice. She had texted him to call her, and it was better to choose the time than have her interrupt inopportunely.

"Chip, sweetie." Her voice came through his earphones like a mother's soft caress. Charlene never betrayed the slightest suspicion that he might be unfaithful. She seemed to him unconditionally trusting, in a way that surprised and even irritated him. Lately he found himself wondering how a wife could possibly fail to notice that her husband was having sex with another woman, unless she was naïve, foolish, and therefore undeserving of his fidelity.

He sat up on the bed and pushed this thought out of his mind. No, she wasn't a fool, he told himself looking again at his panoramic view. She hadn't suspected him because he had given her absolutely no reason to do so. He was not one of those careless, indiscreet husbands. He contained his infidelity within this distant city where his wife had never and would never come. She had no interest in a place like New York, and what he did here, in this anonymous urban bubble, did not even count in the grand scheme of his marriage.

"How did the principal's meeting go?" Charlene asked with genuine interest.

"Great. Really great. We're right on track." Why go into the details? Why mention how Hector Sanchez had openly challenged his research during the meeting? Charlene just wanted everything to be okay. He considered telling her about Hector Sanchez's murder and how he had met Sanchez the very day he had died—Charlene was always interested in a little gossip, and she would be fascinated by his proximity to a murder victim—but he didn't feel like thinking about work anymore, and his omission wouldn't get back to her anyway. A New York City elementary school principal's murder was never going to make the local news in Dallas, Texas. "Everything's fine here," he said. "Tell me about the appointment. How did it go?"

She sighed. "I don't know. Schurr's still not sure. He doesn't deserve his name. He mentioned two other tests he wants."

"More tests?"

"I just want to know, sweetie. Don't you?"

Chip swung his feet off the bed and stood up. He already knew. It was obvious to him. He pictured his three-year-old son who had never spoken a word while the infants and toddlers of their friends and neighbors successfully achieved the happy milestones of babbling and speech. But he didn't say this to Charlene. "Of course I want to know," he said instead.

"I called the insurance company. They won't cover any more tests."

"If we need more tests, then get the tests," he said, because he knew Charlene would not accept the facts before her until she had jumped through every hoop that might offer the slim hope of an alternative truth. "Don't worry about the insurance. We're not going to wait on some Oxford authorization to get our son what he needs."

"You're sure, Chip? It could be expensive." And he could hear the undiluted gratitude in her voice. He could hear how much she loved him for giving her the permission. Why should he feel any guilt about private pleasures in this faraway room when he was giving her everything in life that she wanted? He thought of Margery and what he would ask her to do for him when she came over.

"I'm sure," he said. "Just get the tests."

CHAPTER 17

Haggerty watched Claire emerge from the car and cross the street with Muñoz. Although she was ten or fifteen pounds thinner than before she'd gotten sick, she looked strong and fierce as she neared the gathering of cops, reporters, and bystanders. She had made an incredible recovery, it occurred to him, and he remembered almost too vividly the day he had tried to see her in the hospital.

He had waited a shamefully long time to go to her. By then, she was on her third treatment. He'd brought her flowers, not realizing that flowers were forbidden and would be promptly confiscated by the nurses at the desk. He had naïvely assumed that he and Claire would talk about their falling out, that he would repair the damages, that they might even laugh about it, but as he approached her room, he realized how stupid he had been to think that she would even care about their little fight.

From outside her door, he heard her voice, hoarse and belligerent. "Get me the goddamn morphine. *Now. Please.*"

"It's been ordered," a second voice assured her.

"But it's taking so long. *Please.*"

"It has to get authorized before they'll send it up."

And then Claire was crying. He had moved to where he could see into the room. She was standing next to the bed in a pale-blue hospital gown. Her hands trembled as they gripped the rails for support.

"Let's get you back into bed," the nurse beside her was saying, but Claire only shook her head over and over.

"I can't! The spasm is worse there. I have to stand. Just get me the morphine. Just get me something, goddammit!"

Her eyes had been closed. Her head was shaven. Her facial muscles were pinched by pain. Somehow in the course of six terrible
months, she had metamorphosed into a thin, frail waif. She was
like a tiny old woman. He had stood there listening to her pleas
and curses until the morphine finally arrived, and then he'd backed
away from the door, found the nearest bathroom, and locked himself in. He had pressed his palms against his eyes to keep from
sobbing.

He had waited too long. How could he go to her now? She
wouldn't want him there. She wouldn't want him to see her like
that. She would hate him even more if she knew he'd seen her
like that. He would only make her feel worse than she already did.
And so he had left.

Now he saw her approach Hanlon with the same confidence
she'd had the last time she'd done one of these press conferences.
That was after arresting Wainright Blake for the murder of Elaine
DeFarge and five other women over a twelve-year period. At that
press conference, reporters had fired question after question at her
hoping to get the lurid details. Had Blake raped DeFarge? How
many times? Had he mutilated her body? How long was the lock
of hair he'd cut off her head? Where had they found it? How many
other locks of hair had she found? What did he do with them? Had
she found instruments of torture?

And Codella had finally said, "That's it. We're done here," and
walked away from the microphone. She didn't take any shit. Not
from reporters. Not from him. Not from anyone. That's what he
loved about her. And that's what he hated about her too.

He watched her introduce Muñoz to Hanlon, but Hanlon barely
looked at Muñoz. His smile was all for Claire. Was he attracted to
her, too? Did he think he had any chance with her? Or was he
one of those guys happy just to orbit in the gravitational pull of a
woman like her?

Haggerty moved a little closer. "You look good, Claire," Hanlon was saying. "We were all rooting for you." He pumped her
hand like a guy desperate to pump something else.

"Thanks, Mike. Thanks for all you did for me." Her eyes
scanned the gathering crowd of cops and reporters and landed on
him. He nodded. She nodded back. Then she looked away. She
pulled Muñoz over to Dennis McGowan and introduced him.

"Keep it short and sweet up there," Haggerty heard McGowan tell her. "Let's not have another Claire Codella Show."

"Yes sir," she responded with such uncharacteristic deference that Haggerty knew she was not in his favor. She was treading carefully.

McGowan walked away from them, and Marty Blackstone moved in. He slapped Muñoz on the back. "Hey, we missed you at the morning meeting, Rainbow Dick."

Muñoz seemed too stunned to speak.

"You like it? Rainbow Dick. I thought it suited you. A little nickname upgrade." Blackstone grinned.

Codella turned to Muñoz. "Go talk to Portino. After this press conference, I need you to help him slog through more background checks."

When Muñoz was gone, she stepped closer to Blackstone, so close, Haggerty thought, that she could probably smell whatever he was burping up from lunch. Haggerty was only two feet behind her now.

"You know," he heard her say, "after what I've been through in the last several months, it really gives me comfort to know I can count on certain things."

"Huh?" Blackstone had a perplexed frown.

"For instance, I can count on the sun always coming up over the East River. That's reassuring to me." She tapped her chest. "I can count on that same sun sinking over New Jersey every night, too. And in between," she smiled pleasantly, "I can count on assholes like you to always act like assholes." She patted his arm. "Well done, you asshole." She turned and walked away.

Haggerty moved in beside Blackstone. "She's right, you know. You really are an asshole."

"Maybe so, but she's Muñoz's bag hag. Get it?" He laughed. "*Bag*, as in chemo."

Haggerty waited for Blackstone's laughter to stop. "Listen to me, you dumb motherfucker. I'd beat the shit out of you for saying that if there weren't twenty network news cameras here. But I'm warning you, don't find yourself alone with me."

"You think I'm afraid of you?"

"You should be." Haggerty walked away.

He stood next to Vic Portino and Muñoz as Hanlon got behind the makeshift podium and started the press conference. Hanlon was smooth, he had to admit that. He knew exactly how to fill silence without revealing anything that would jeopardize an investigation. He presented the basic facts—victim's name, occupation, approximate time and place of death, and who was in charge of the investigation, and then he brought up Codella for the Q and A. She was his secret weapon to calm the parents and make the NYPD look good.

The first question came like a rocket-propelled missile. "What's the cause of death?"

"The medical examiner's official report isn't in," Codella answered calmly. "We expect it tomorrow."

"Do you have a suspect?"

"We're only eight hours in."

"So you're saying you don't. What about persons of interest?"

Codella didn't hesitate. "I can't comment on that." Haggerty knew what that meant. She had no one yet.

"What about witnesses?"

"We're speaking to many sources with pertinent information. I'm not at liberty to discuss any of those details right now." She pointed to another hand. It belonged to the nasal voice Haggerty had spoken to several hours ago in front of Sanchez's building.

"Is there any evidence his murder was related to his role as principal, and if so, how can you be certain the students at PS 777 are safe?"

This was the question they had all known would come, and whatever response Codella gave would be replayed on every TV network's and radio station's local news. She'd be quoted in tomorrow's tabloids, he thought, and her answer would spread across the Internet through RSS feeds and tweets and public school bulletin boards. He watched her take a deep breath as she stared at the reporter.

"So far we have absolutely no evidence linking Hector Sanchez's murder to his role as the principal of Public School 777," she said with a tone of utter conviction. That was Claire. She could spin anything—just like him—and get away with it. Strictly speaking, she wasn't lying, of course. The fact that Sanchez's body had been arranged to look like Christ on the cross and that he had been dubbed the "Savior of PS 777" in a national magazine still qualified as a circumstantial association. The killer had left no note decrying the victim's work at the school. So far, there was no forensic evidence to connect the killer to the school, and they still had no witnesses to draw that connection. But he knew she was faking a tone of conviction she didn't really feel, and she was keeping her fingers crossed that someone in the department didn't leak the gruesome details to that nasal voice or some other reporter with a wad of cash.

She continued to look at Nasal Guy. "That said, we're taking every precaution to ensure the safety of the staff and students of PS 777. Until we determine who did perpetrate this crime, we'll keep the security threshold high to ensure that students and staff have a safe learning environment. Their protection will be absolutely paramount during our investigation."

"What precautions are you taking?" the reporter probed.

"I'm not going to discuss security measures explicitly," she said. "They're in place. That's all I'll say."

"Sanchez was an outspoken critic of the teacher's union," said another reporter. "Could that be a factor in this case?"

"People are outspoken critics of many things without getting murdered," she pointed out. "This investigation won't be built on speculation. We'll look for solid evidence. I'll take one more question." She pointed.

"The actress Dana Drew was a big supporter of the school. Are you looking into their relationship?"

"We're looking into *all* of his relationships," she said dismissively.

"That's not an answer."

"Yes it is. And that's it for now. Thank you."

She stepped away from the microphone. Hanlon patted her shoulder. "Nice job."

"Thanks."

McGowan turned and walked toward his waiting car and driver without a word to his detective. Muñoz and Portino entered the station together.

Haggerty watched Claire disappear behind the station, where cop cars were parked and fueled. A minute later, she pulled out of the driveway and turned toward Broadway. Cancer hadn't changed her work ethic, he thought. She would keep going until there was nothing else to do tonight, and then she would go home and drop into bed and get up early and do it all over again. That's what she was like. That's what he was like, too.

He got into his car and drove uptown to Queen Smith's apartment. A day and a half of tracking down the boyfriend had only proven that he could not have killed her baby. He had been in the Harlem Hospital recovering from a crack OD. Queen Smith had lied to him, and now he had to bring her in.

CHAPTER 18

Codella parked in front of the hydrant. Ten feet ahead, a meticulous green awning supported by gleaming brass poles welcomed visitors to 375 Riverside Drive. She peered up at the Beaux-Arts structure. She was as susceptible to apartment envy as any other New Yorker crammed into a small apartment on a low floor, and the lucky river-facing residents of this address, she knew, overlooked the churning Hudson River and the long narrow strip of waterfront green that was Riverside Park. Tonight the New Jersey skyline offered up a spectacular pink sunset that probably added tens of thousands to the value of the uppermost apartments. She climbed out and slammed the car door. Who wouldn't be envious of that?

The doorman announced her arrival via house phone, and she stepped into an immaculate walnut-lined elevator. The smooth ascent made her remember the bumpy ride at the Jackie Robinson Village several hours ago, and she found it hard to imagine a child from that dismal project sharing the same school as one from this elegant building. Granted, public school catchments in Manhattan were as winding as gerrymandered voting districts, but affluent families who found themselves in unappealing zones usually moved or opted out of the public school system.

The elevator opened on fourteen. Codella stepped out onto plush carpet and read the numbers on the nearest doors looking for 14G. Her search ended when a door behind her opened. The woman standing there was at least five foot ten, and in person, she was even more arresting than in her "We're a Proud Family" photograph. Her short hair had been styled—quite expensively,

Codella guessed—to create the artful illusion that it was acciden-
tally tousled. Her gray T-shirt matched her gray eyes, and the tight
fabric advertised broad shoulders and strong upper arms.

Codella displayed her shield. "I'm looking for Dana Drew."

"I'm afraid she's not here right now."

"You're her partner?"

"That's right. Jane Martin. I heard the news about Hector. Is
there something I can help you with?"

"You can help by telling me where to find Miss Drew." She
didn't hide her impatience.

Martin said, "She'll be at the Booth by now. You might be able
to catch her before she goes on. Curtain time is seven o'clock."

Codella looked at her watch. She had an hour and a half.
She thanked the woman, rode the elevator back to the lobby, got in
the car, and sped toward West Forty-Fifth Street.

Once, after the performance of a musical she couldn't remember the name of now, she had waited with friends at the stage door
of a Broadway theater for the actors to emerge and sign playbills.
But she had never actually been backstage at a Broadway theater,
and she had never stopped to consider what a dressing room there
might look like. The one she now entered reminded her of a cluttered, unglamorous prewar study, with racks of clothes rolled
in and a long makeup counter installed where the bookshelves
should be.

"Visitor for you, Miss Drew," said the stagehand who had led
her here. "Detective Codella."

Drew rose from the couch, smiled, and held out her hand.

Codella shook it. "I'm sorry to barge in like this, Miss Drew."

"Nonsense, Detective. Please come in. I have a few minutes
before I dress." Her casual tone suggested that she hadn't heard
about Sanchez. Her eyes were as green as they looked on the large
screen, and they followed the contours of Codella's body like a
human PT scanner.

Codella stared back at the eyes. They were like a riptide that
swept you away from shore.

Drew was still holding her hand. "I didn't know I had any
fans in the NYPD. I'm honored." She pulled Codella farther into
the room, to a spot right in the center where Codella caught a
glimpse of her reflection in the makeup mirror over the actress's

shoulder. She saw her spiky inch-long hair, her leather jacket, and white blouse, and it all made sense.

She thinks I'm a lesbian. And why wouldn't she? I look more like one than she does.

And then she recalled the afternoon her stylist, Jonathan, had come to her apartment between her second and third treatments to shave off what was left of her shoulder-length black hair. It had been falling out for two weeks. She would wake up in the morning and find clumps on her pillow. She would see it in the drain after a shower and then on the tile floor after she blew it dry.

"Let's just get it over with," she had said as they sat in her kitchen, and he had done it quickly, efficiently, and then swept clean her parquet floor so she wouldn't have to look at all the hair she had lost. After that she had worn soft baseball-style caps sold on the American Cancer Society website. No wig for her.

Finally Drew released her hand, returned to the couch, and patted the opposite cushion. Codella remained standing.

"I'm a *huge* fan, Miss Drew, but I wouldn't presume to impose on you this close to curtain time unless I were here on business. I've come because of your acquaintance with Hector Sanchez."

The actress frowned. "Hector? What about him?"

"He's dead, I'm afraid. He was murdered. Last night."

The actress uncrossed her legs, sat forward, and shook her head. "Is this some kind of joke?"

"I assure you, death is something I don't joke about." *At least not anymore*, she thought.

"But how?"

"We've just begun our investigation. How well did you know him?"

For several seconds, the actress just sat there with a look of confusion on her face and shook her head.

"How well did you know him, Miss Drew?" Codella repeated.

"I'm sorry." She forced herself to attention. "My daughter attends his school. I've gotten to know him because of that."

"A photo of you and your family was in his apartment. Did you know that?"

"We ran an ad campaign. Proud Families of PS 777. You've probably seen the billboards."

Codella nodded.

"Hector asked me to sign a print." She shook her head again. "I'm sorry, when did you say he died?"

"Sometime last evening. When did you last see him?"

Drew massaged the bottom of her bare foot. "I beg your pardon?"

"Sanchez, when did you last see him?"

She thought a moment. "Friday."

"Where?"

"At the school."

"Were you alone with him?"

"No. Sofia Reyes was there too. And Jane, my partner."

"Some people say you were having an affair with him."

Drew gave a shrug of resignation. "People say all kinds of things about me."

"Is it true?"

"Of course not."

"Then why do you think they say it?"

"You'll have to ask them," she said stiffening. "Not all celebrities fuck around, you know, despite what the gossip mill says. And if I window-shop at all, it isn't at the men's store, Detective." The green eyes watched her closely.

"You e-mailed Sanchez on Saturday. You asked him to call you. Why?"

"We're working on a project."

"What project?"

"Afterschool Apptitude."

"What is it?"

"An afterschool intervention program. The school day isn't long enough. Most of the kids at PS 777 go home to a television at best. They fall further and further behind. The apps students will use in this program directly support their math and literacy skills. And they don't require large teacher staffing, which is costly and difficult to recruit for after school."

Codella held the actress's stare. "I'm curious. Why does your daughter attend that school? Why not a private school?"

Drew bristled at the question. "Should I assume from all these questions, Detective, that you think I'm somehow involved in this?"

"Not at all." Codella smiled. "I'm just trying to understand things."

"Well, you obviously haven't done your homework on me, or you'd know my mother was principal of that school when I was growing up. I went to that school. I'm very committed to the public schools. I wanted to give it a chance."

"And how's it working out?"

She frowned. "I'm not going to lie. It's challenging. But if everybody who can opt out of public education does, what happens to the people who can't?"

"Most people who can wouldn't care."

"Well, I'm not most people." There was defiance in her voice.

"Can you think of anyone who might have wanted Sanchez dead?"

Drew shook her head. "Not unless bitter, lazy teachers kill their principals. No, I can't." She looked at the clock behind Codella. "I'm sorry, Detective, but it's getting late. I have to . . ." She gestured toward her dressing table as she pulled off her cardigan.

Codella noticed a purplish-yellow bruise on her left bicep. "What happened?" Codella asked.

Drew followed her eyes. "Oh that? I don't know." She moved toward the rack of clothes.

Codella fished a card from her pocket. "Please call me if you think of any information that might help us."

"Of course." Drew took the card and smiled, but her green eyes looked troubled.

CHAPTER 19

Vic Portino's hair was thinning, and he had a little paunch. He always reminded Codella of the Rhode Island Italian men she had grown up around, except that he wore suits and they didn't. Portino's suits were the kind you bought off the rack at discount stores like Men's Warehouse, but as cheap as they were, they still looked better than unflattering polyester sports shirts stretched across too many plates of pasta. "What have you got for me, Vic?"

"Muñoz and I have gotten through most of the faculty and staff with a little help from some of the duty officers."

She peeled off her jacket, pulled up a chair next to Muñoz, and settled into it like an audience member at the Booth Theater just before curtain time. She thought about that bruise she'd seen on Dana Drew's arm. Was it really nothing? She remembered how Drew had taken one look at her and assumed she was a lesbian. She wondered if Portino and Muñoz also thought she looked like a lesbian with her short hair. What about Haggerty? She pushed the thought aside. What did she care? "Tell me about our cast of characters."

"Let's start with Bosco, the suspended fifth-grade teacher." Portino leaned back and rested his notepad on his stomach. "He's got two DWIs. One six years ago, another one last year. His blood alcohol was point one five."

"Okay, so he's a drunk, but that won't help us pin a murder on him."

"What if he's an angry drunk?"

"How angry?"

"He's got a suspended license right now for a road rage incident."

"Go on."

"An elderly woman tried to go through the E-ZPass lane at the JFK Bridge. Only she didn't have an E-ZPass, so of course she stopped traffic. Bosco was the car behind her. He couldn't back up, and it took the bridge and tunnel cop about five minutes to issue the woman a ticket and raise the gate, and by then Bosco had gotten so pissed that he climbed out of his car and started ranting and hammering on the old woman's hood. Gave the cop some attitude, too. According to the arrest report, they almost took him in for a psych evaluation. He ended up pleading no contest and got a reduced sentence by attending anger management classes."

"No wonder Sanchez wanted him out. Anything else?"

"His credit cards are maxed, and he's filed a lawsuit against his landlord. Claims he slipped on an unshoveled walkway after a snowstorm two winters ago and injured a disk. That's it so far."

"I guess we'll have to meet him. What about Marva Thomas?"

Portino flipped to another page of notes. "Unmarried. Lives in Washington Heights. Has a car loan. Pretty decent credit rating. No arrests. Clean."

"Christine Donohue?"

"Nothing to speak of. Married 1978 in Sudbury, Massachusetts. Divorced in 2004. Been with the DOE since 1983."

"And the others?"

"The typical stuff. A few foreclosures. Some ugly divorces. Personal injury claims. Someone by the name of Natalie Rapinoe has about ten speeding tickets. Lots of unpaid parking tickets, too. Emily Truesdale has a restraining order on her ex-husband. Roz Porter has a misdemeanor arrest from the Occupy Wall Street demonstrations in 2011. She refused to leave Zuccotti Park when the police tried to clear everyone out for sanitation reasons." Portino summarized the records of the other teachers.

"What about the staff? Those janitors, the nurse, cafeteria workers."

Muñoz cleared his throat and took over. "Milosz Jancek is the head custodian, as you know. He's been with the DOE since 2001. He's from Croatia. Rerecic, the maintenance guy, is from Albania. He got his citizenship in 2004. Neither one has a record. It's like the United Nations over there. Over half the parents are foreign nationals. We posted lots of queries with immigration. We're waiting for results."

"What else?"

"Janisa Lopez, the school secretary, defaulted on a student loan, so her wages are being garnished."

"What about cafeteria workers?"

"Pretty clean," he said. "A couple domestic violence issues. Nothing out of the ordinary."

"Did we run any checks on his neighbors?"

Muñoz looked at his notes. "We started. We need help."

"I'm working on that. I've got a call into McGowan. We need a task force on this. What have you found so far?"

"Only one name with a criminal record, for marijuana possession. Nobody else looks bad on paper."

"Which isn't the same as not *being* bad." Codella swigged water. "What about his laptop?"

"It's still in the evidence room. There wasn't time," said Vic.

"Make the time," she said firmly. "I want all the data up front. What about his phone?"

"He's a Verizon mobile subscriber. We'll have his records tomorrow."

She got up and paced. "So we don't have much. Just a dead body that looks like Jesus on a cross." She leaned forward. "But there's no mistaking the message in that body, is there? *The savior is dead.* Who would want to send out that message?"

"Someone really angry," suggested Muñoz. "Someone who wanted to rub his reputation in his face."

"Maybe. Or someone who wanted to use his reputation to cover a less obvious motive."

Portino patted his stomach. "Was there any helpful trace at the scene?"

"The inside and outside doorknobs were wiped clean. Banks says most of the prints in the apartment belonged to Sanchez or that neighbor, the one who walked his dog."

"Cameron Swain," said Muñoz, remembering her yellow-green eyes.

"Did Haggerty file the canvass results?"

Portino held up a printout. "It's not very helpful. No one saw anybody come or go. Nobody let someone in. Nobody heard anything."

"So all we really have right now is a bunch of cranky educators like Bosco, Donohue, and Thomas."

"And the angry blogging mother," said Muñoz. "Helen Chambers."

"Right." Codella pulled out her iPhone and opened her notes. "The kindergarten teacher Vicki Berrard mentioned two teachers Sanchez may have fired in September. Ronald Davis and Imogene Burke. And Sanchez was working on apps with a guy named Ivan Schiff at some little Silicon Alley tech start-up—Apptitude. Run reports on them, Vic."

Portino made a note.

"And what about cameras around his building?"

"There's one on his corner," said Portino. "I'll have the data tomorrow. But the camera's on a maintenance list," he warned, "so I don't know what we'll get."

"Let's hope we get something." She looked at her iPhone clock. It was 10:23. Then she looked at Muñoz. "You and I will see Bosco first thing in the morning. Ragavan will go back to the school. Portino, keep going here. Haggerty can help you. Now go home. Tomorrow's gonna be a long day."

But she didn't intend to go home, not yet. Ragavan had e-mailed her Sofia Reyes's address, and now she got in her car and sped across Central Park to the literacy consultant's brownstone apartment on East Ninety-Third Street. She rang the bell three times, but the woman wasn't home.

It was almost eleven when she got to her own apartment. She hung up her jacket, stripped off her jeans and sweater, and climbed into the running shorts and NYPD T-shirt she slept in. Then she made green tea with honey, took her mug and takeout vegan burger into the living room, switched on the news, muted the volume, and got on her laptop. Muñoz had e-mailed her the article about Sanchez from the *New York Times Magazine*, and she took a bite of the burger and started reading where she'd left off that morning.

Few administrators threw their hat in the ring last December when district administrator Margery Barton fired then acting principal Dr. Peter Kelly for incompetence. "School leaders don't get to let kids down on my watch and get away with it," Barton said at the time, and she scored points with school board and central Department of Education officials for her candor and toughness. District parents weren't as impressed. Many felt Barton should have acted a year sooner than she did. "PS 777 had been on the Schools in Need of Improvement list for a year with no actionable plan from the principal or district officials," said one parent of a PS 777 student.

Barton plucked Sanchez out of the Queens International Academy, a middle school serving the needs of recent immigrants and refugees. He was shocked at the conditions in PS 777. Here was a school that, in his words, had "gotten the scraps far too long." The staff consisted of tenured teachers clocking their time until retirement, new teachers no one had bothered to train, and an aging, undermaintained infrastructure.

By anyone's standards, what he's done in just five months at the school is nothing short of miraculous. He took the reins in mid-January. By the end of March, he had not only given the school a physical makeover but also raised fifty thousand dollars from corporate donors to purchase a new school-wide bookroom, written and received a small Gates Foundation grant, hired a part-time literacy consultant, and partnered with actress and public school advocate Dana Drew to create a technology-driven intervention program that will launch next fall with the help of tutors from nearby private high schools looking to fulfill community service requirements. And all the while, he was calling parents—as many as twenty a day—until he'd spoken with every one of them. "If you want the school to work, then you have to get involved," he told them. And slowly but surely, attendance at the new weekly Parents as Partners workshops started to increase.

She finished half of the vegan burger, trying to convince herself that she liked it. Then she switched off the TV and got ready for bed. Nothing was going to keep her awake tonight, she told herself, not after her first seventeen-hour day in almost a year. But the instant her head hit the pillow, she imagined that same pole next to her bed, that same bag of Doxorubicin dangling from the pole. One bag of that drug, she remembered, had turned her into a trembling, frail shadow of a person.

She sat up and pulled back the sheet. When would she stop having these memories? When would she get a solid night of sleep in her bed? If being hooked up to chemo bags in a hospital bed had been prison, then these memories were like a permanent form of probation—the constant reminder that when she least expected it, her body could deploy another death squad of invisible cells.

But at least she had the luxury of worrying about the next death squad. The second roommate she'd had during her treatment, a woman named Patty, had not been so fortunate. Patty was also being treated for Burkitt's lymphoma, but hers had spread to her bone marrow before it was diagnosed. She had been in the hospital for almost two months straight. On the third day of Codella's treatment, she and Patty had taken a pitifully slow and short walk down the corridor together—the two Burkitt's victims—rolling their chemo poles along the polished linoleum floor and comparing their worst treatment experiences. Mouth sores that wouldn't heal, painful bone marrow biopsies and lumbar punctures, blocked chemo ports, deadened taste buds, middle-of-the-night sleep interruptions to get fresh bags of chemo, and the ultimate indignity of wearing adult diapers during C. diff infections.

The day after that walk, Codella had finished her second treatment and gone home with Patty's telephone number in her iPhone directory. She never saw or spoke to Patty again. But three months later, just before her last treatment, when she already knew she was cancer free and would soon be able to focus on getting strong again, Patty's son had called her.

"My mother had your number on a piece of paper by her bed," he had explained. "I thought you might want to know that she died two days ago."

Codella climbed out of bed and returned to the living room. Ironically, she knew, the only way she'd take her mind off her unpleasant past and her uncertain future was to think about someone else's tragedy. She pulled up a photo of Sanchez on her iPhone. She zoomed in on his dark brows and his full lips. She focused on his Adam's apple, which was made more prominent by the unnatural angle of his broken neck. She dragged the image upward to center on his hairless torso, his upward facing palms. She let her mind travel back to his apartment. She remembered his unmade bed, his suit pants neatly hung on a hanger dangling off a doorknob, his suit jacket on the back of a chair, jeans and T-shirt tossed across spin bike handlebars.

Where had he really been after school yesterday? Why had he lied to his AP about going to see Vondra Williams? When had he gotten home? Apparently he'd had time to change from his suit into casual clothes before 5:00, when his neighbor had brought him dog treats. That left about an hour and a half unaccounted for. What had he done in that span of time? When had he undressed? Who had come to kill him, and why? Did it have anything to do with a boy's head getting pushed into a toilet? A controversial program called iAchieve? The polarizing war between young and old teachers? She pondered these questions until she finally dozed off on the living room couch.

CHAPTER 20

Muñoz got off the A train at Thirty-Fourth Street and checked Grindr on his phone as he walked up the steps. For two years, he had arranged virtually every sexual encounter on Grindr. He could justify the random nature of his sex life with the rationalization that work prevented anything more. How could he commit to a relationship when he was working the streets at all hours, buddying up to dealers and junkies, making middle-of-the-night busts and searches? He had rarely seen the same man twice, and he had avoided guys who seemed to need something more than sex, and yet now he found himself wanting more. He sent a message to the software engineer he had hooked up with last night, and then he zipped his jacket and headed west facing the cold river wind.

There was still no message back when he got to where the High Line started south of the Javits Center. Muñoz walked home via this long, uplifted park as often as he could. He especially loved to walk the High Line after dark, when he could have it mostly to himself. Winding between West Side buildings above street level, the path—built on the disused tracks of an elevated railroad spur—provided a voyeuristic view into windows of anonymous city dwellers. Whenever he peered into one of those windows and happened to see people living their private lives, he felt as if he knew them and that they were connected in some strange way through the city they shared.

He checked his phone as he descended from the High Line at Twenty-Third Street, but the software engineer had still not replied. Muñoz was a little surprised by the extent of his disappointment. After most sexual encounters, he left the scene immediately and rarely thought about them again, but the software engineer had been different. He had not wanted Muñoz to leave right away.

"Stay," he had said as he'd gotten out of bed. He had left the room and returned five minutes later with bowls of ice cream. His guileless enthusiasm as he'd crawled back under the comforter and handed over one of the bowls had charmed Muñoz and made him open up. He'd found himself recounting the episode with Blackstone, and he had felt better when the man—Kevin was his name—had said, "What a fucking asshole. They should make a separate state for people like that. Put them all in one place where they can feel superior together and pass their bigot laws without bothering the rest of us."

Muñoz looked at his phone yet again. The message was still unanswered. Would he ever see the guy again?

He was standing in his kitchen sipping a bottle of cold water when the answer finally came. *Are you still there? Did I miss my chance?*

It was after eleven now, and Muñoz remembered Codella's last words. *Get some rest. Tomorrow's gonna be a long day.* He imagined Kevin waiting for his text right now.

I'm on a case, he wrote, *but if you can wait a few days, I'll bring the ice cream next time.*

Chocolate, came the immediate reply. *I'll be waiting.*

WEDNESDAY

CHAPTER 21

Muñoz hopped in the car and held up the *Post*. The three-inch headline screamed, "PS Dead," and below it was a photo of Codella climbing the steps to PS 777. "You made the front page."

She glanced at the tabloid and rolled her eyes. "Who thinks up those headlines anyway?" She pulled away from the curb. "I always wondered. Do they have a special headline SWAT team that sits in a room all day trying to be offensively clever?"

"What do you think they get paid for that?"

"More than we do, I bet. You know about the Wainright Blake case, don't you?"

"Sure. The one who killed and raped nurses."

"That's right. When we went in his apartment, there was this little box under his bed with locks of hair from all six of his victims. The next day, the *Post* headline was 'Dead Locks.' They must have been pretty amused with themselves."

"Good thing they don't know how Sanchez died." Muñoz tossed the paper into the backseat. "I wonder what they'd say. 'Father, Son, and Holy Sanchez'?"

"'Holy Hector'?"

"'Lamb of PS 777.'"

"'Divine Sanchez.'"

"'Sanchez of God.'"

"Hang it up," she said. "We'd never get on that SWAT team."

"Where are we headed?"

"Gambarin called me early this morning. He's got preliminary autopsy results. We'll visit him first and then go see Bosco."

When they peered through the medical examiner's door ten minutes later, he was incising the chest of an emaciated-looking corpse whose jaw hung open in a hollow position that reminded Codella of Edvard Munch's *The Scream*. She watched him expertly lift and pull back a flap of the old man's skin to expose the corpse's sunken rib cage and lungs. Cherry-red blotches of lividity colored the victim's stomach where he had lain face down after death while his blood had thickened and settled. He looked like a cancer victim, but she knew a different killer had ended his life. Gambarin only autopsied homicides.

She did not enter his autopsy room, and she held Muñoz back as well. Gambarin didn't appreciate uninvited infringement on his territory. Instead, they waited in the doorway inhaling the strong odor of formalin and decomposed flesh until the medical examiner acknowledged their presence. Only when he lowered his instrument, lifted his goggles, and came toward them did she speak.

"I got your message, Rudolph. Thanks. This is Detective Muñoz. What can you tell us about our principal?"

"He's an interesting case." Gambarin emitted no emotion.

She waited.

"His killer didn't leave so much as a finger impression on the neck. It was a very clean kill."

"What do you make of that?"

He shrugged. "Either he got lucky or he was a trained professional."

"As in military?"

"Possibly."

"You say *he*. So you're convinced it was a man?"

"I can't be positive, but it takes enormous strength to snap a neck. Your victim isn't going to stand still while you do it. This victim was six foot two. I don't know many women who would have the strength to subdue a man that large and get the right angle to snap a head so cleanly."

"So we're looking for a tall man?" said Muñoz.

"Not necessarily as tall as the victim. Certainly not as tall as you. Average to tall, I'd say. Five foot nine or more. But I couldn't get on the stand and say any of this with absolute certainty."

"But you'd say the killer was physically very strong?" asked Codella.

"I'd say that."

"That describes an awful lot of men in New York City," observed Muñoz.

"How exactly did Sanchez die?" Codella took out her iPhone to take notes.

"Technically, heart failure."

She looked up. "Heart failure?"

"Stemming from the spinal cord fracture. His third cervical cord was snapped clean."

"Would that have resulted in immediate death?" she asked.

"Probably not. But as soon as the cord was snapped, he would have been incapacitated. He either fell right to the ground or was lowered there by the killer. In a C3 fracture, all the motor functions below the fracture site are compromised. Shoulders, arms, chest, diaphragm, legs. He would have been struggling to breathe, but he could have still been conscious for a while. Interestingly, the killer was prepared for this. He stuffed a cloth or rag of some kind in the victim's mouth."

"A rag?"

"White cotton."

"It wasn't there when we got to the scene."

"I know. He'd removed it and apparently took it with him since CSU found nothing. But there were fibers in the mouth."

"Any trace that might indicate who stuffed it there?"

"Nothing I could see, but I sent the fibers to the lab for analysis. This killer must have been wearing gloves, and assuming he brought the cloth with him, he must have carried it in a sealed bag or envelope. The fibers weren't tainted with hair or other particles."

"So Sanchez was immobilized but possibly conscious when the killer staged his crucifixion." Codella tapped open one of the photos she'd snapped at the crime scene.

"That's my guess. It could have taken several moments before he stopped breathing completely, lost consciousness, and died from heart failure. It's likely he watched—in total paralysis, of course—as the killer positioned him into that pose."

Codella considered. "So based on the autopsy results, would you say this was a planned, premeditated murder?"

"I would. Because of the lack of fingerprints and the cloth he used and then took away. I'd testify to that."

"Are we looking for a serial killer?" asked Muñoz. "Some psycho with a Jesus obsession who was out trolling and followed Sanchez home?"

"I'm not the detective." Gambarin looked over his shoulder at the waiting corpse.

"I don't think so," said Codella.

"Why not?" asked Muñoz.

She magnified the same photo she'd studied on her iPhone last night and stared at Sanchez's splayed arms on the living room rug. She held it up for all of them to view. "This doesn't look to me like the work of a deranged serial killer. I could be wrong, of course, but I'd expect a serial killer living out a Jesus obsession to take the staging much further. I'm thinking he would have brought nails, for instance, and hammered the hands to the floorboards, or put a crown of thorns on his head, or carved a biblical passage into his chest or written it on the wall in his blood. This staging seems, I don't know, tame. Too tame." She turned to Gambarin. "You've described a quick, surgical killing that a trained professional would do—an execution. This staging feels more like a sane person's deliberate message. A giant fuck you. The *New York Times* had dubbed Sanchez the 'Savior of PS 777.' I think whoever did this was telling the world, *Here's what happens to saviors.*"

Muñoz was paying careful attention. "So you think the murder does have something to do with the school."

"I didn't say so at the press conference last night, but yeah. I think someone connected to PS 777 killed him, or someone who wanted us to *think* his murderer was someone at that school. And right now the killer—whoever it is—is waiting to read about his mock crucifixion, only that's not going to happen. We can't let that detail find its way into the paper. That detail is going to be *our* weapon, not his last laugh." She tapped her iPhone screen to close the photo.

Gambarin nodded. "What else can I tell you?"

"Is it conceivable that the killer left the victim before he died?" she asked.

Gambarin considered. "Possible," he said, "but unlikely. Although the victim was paralyzed, he might have been able to cry out for several moments. I doubt the killer would have removed the gag if there were any remaining danger of him calling for help. If Sanchez was still alive when the killer left, he was most likely unconscious. I would speculate that the killer was in that apartment for at least fifteen to thirty minutes seeing his job to the end."

Muñoz frowned. "Nothing appears to have been taken from the apartment. His laptop was there. His wallet was still on his bedroom bureau with money and credit cards in it. Only his phone is missing."

"Was the perpetrator left or right handed?" asked Codella.

"The head was snapped violently to the right. My guess is the killer came behind him and grabbed his head around the front with the right hand and the back of the head with his left, like this." He moved behind Muñoz to demonstrate. "He would have pushed hard against the victim's left temple with the palm of his right hand."

"So right handed," concluded Codella.

"Almost certainly."

"What was the time of death?"

"The rigor was completely fixed. Between five and seven, I estimate, but I can be more specific if you find out when he last ate."

"There was no indication he ate anything at his apartment before he died." She turned to Muñoz. "Call Ragavan. Tell him to find out if Sanchez ate lunch at the school."

Gambarin nodded. "He was moved into the crucifixion pose soon after the attack and remained in that position. The blood settled into the lower back and legs."

Codella looked at Muñoz again. "He left the school at three thirty. If he went straight home, he would have been there in five to ten minutes, but if he went straight home, why did he tell Marva Thomas he was going to visit Vondra Williams?"

"Maybe he visited a different student. Maybe he went somewhere he didn't want her to know about. People duck out of work early all the time."

"Yeah, but they don't end up dead on their living room floors."

He acknowledged her point with a rueful expression.

"We have to look at the street cam footage as soon as we get it. We might get lucky and spot him coming home." She turned back to Gambarin. "Anything else?"

"Not until we get lab results. I'll call you if I have more."

She nodded. "We'll let you get back to your work."

They emerged from the First Avenue building into the brisk winds off the East River and walked in silence toward the car as Codella fitted the new details into the scene forming in her brain. Muñoz took longer strides, and she had to quicken her own pace to keep up with him. They got in the car and she said, "Let's go meet the suspended teacher with anger issues."

CHAPTER 22

John McGreevy slid the *Post* across his polished, paper-free desk. CEOs of publishing companies didn't have to deal with the manuscripts, page proofs, catalog layouts, schedules, and tracking sheets that cluttered the desks of the low-paid editors who actually put out the multimillion-dollar programs McFlieger-Walsh published. "Did you see this?" he asked.

Dressler read the blaring, all-caps headline. "No, but I saw the news."

"This guy was in Barton's district," McGreevy observed. "Did you know him?"

"I knew of him. He was at the meeting on Monday."

"Where did he stand on *iAchieve?*"

"He wasn't a fan," Dressler acknowledged without elaboration. Why mention the heated technology debate Sanchez had incited at the meeting? It hardly mattered anymore, now that he was dead. Besides, Margery had all the adoption votes she needed lined up.

"Is this event going to affect Barton's purchasing timeline?"

Dressler wanted to say, *How am I supposed to know?* He felt like shouting, *I can't possibly do any more than I've already done.* Instead he said, "I hope not. Margery has a meeting with her Technology Leadership Team next week. Bernie Lipsie may come to that meeting. He's interested. He's heard we have good results."

McGreevy massaged his jaw. How did the man manage to have such a pronounced five o'clock shadow at ten o'clock in the morning? "Will the numbers stand up to intense scrutiny?"

Dressler considered how to answer that question. As long as the district people studied what was presented to them, they would surely like what they saw, but if they hired an analyst to lift the veil of elegantly colored bar graphs and study the raw data below, well, that was another story. Of course, how likely was it that the New York Department of Education would hire its own analysts to audit results already certified by an independent, university-based research firm? "I think we're good," he said.

McGreevy stared at him for several seconds, obviously trying to discern the specks of doubt beneath his words. "This is critical, Chip," he said, as if Dressler didn't already know this. "This sale could put us back in the game with iAchieve."

"I realize what's at stake."

"Two hundred million," said McGreevy. "We've got two hundred million sunk into this, and so far all we've gotten out of that investment is bad publicity."

Dressler nodded. He knew the story end to end. He was sitting here because of that bad publicity. His predecessor had used a significant portion of the iAchieve national sales and marketing budget to send urban school district administrators who controlled lots of federal funding on an all-expenses-paid "educational seminar" to Oahu, where they'd spent exactly one hour a day listening to academic scholars discuss "Literacy 2.0" and the Common Core State Standards until it was time to tan themselves, climb into helicopters, take surfing lessons on the beach at the Turtle Bay Resort, or sit at the beachside bar with McFlieger-Walsh marketing VPs. Dressler knew McGreevy was hoping the sale to New York City would end McFlieger-Walsh's prolonged PR nightmare and jump-start sales across the country. After all, where the biggest district in the country led, others were sure to follow.

"Have you spoken to Dr. Barton since this happened?" McGreevy sipped his coffee.

"No," Dressler lied. "I thought I should stay below the radar for a while. Let her deal with her crisis. I'm sure she's got her hands full."

McGreevy nodded. "That makes sense."

"But I'll keep you posted if I hear anything." Dressler stood. There was nothing more to say. He returned to the small office he used when he was in town and called Margery on his cell phone. "How are you doing?"

"I'm fine." She sounded calm and in control, and he wondered why he had even worried. Margery always knew how to
handle her district. She was more confident than most of the
men he knew. That was one of her qualities that turned him on
the most.

CHAPTER 23

They found Eugene Bosco in a windowless storage closet on the first floor of Middle School 52. He was sitting at a long table tapping on a laptop keyboard as they entered the claustrophobic enclosure. "Mr. Bosco?"

"Who's asking?"

"I'm Detective Codella, and this is Detective Muñoz."

Bosco shut the laptop. A crinkled copy of the *New York Times* lay beside it along with an open can of Coke and a half-consumed packet of Double Stuf Oreos. Stacked against the wall behind him were bulk-wrapped rolls of toilet paper and industrial-sized crates of hand soap. "Took you long enough to get here."

Apparently a professional demeanor was not required of suspended teachers given "temporary reassignments." Coke had dribbled down the front of his wrinkled shirt, and he had not shaved for at least two days. His combed-back hair looked greasy, and his glasses were dirty.

Codella ignored his sarcasm. "We want to ask you some questions."

"I bet you do." He scratched his jaw, flicking his fingers upward against his whiskers to produce an unpleasant sandpaper sound. Codella's father had done that, too.

Muñoz pulled out two chairs on the opposite side of the table, and Bosco picked up his Oreos packet as they sat. His puffy fingers pinched one of the remaining cookies, and he slid it into his mouth whole like a miniature DVD. Then he sat back in the chair with his palms massaging his large stomach.

"You saw Hector Sanchez the day he was murdered. You spoke to him that afternoon. What time was that?"

"You mean when he blew up and suspended me?" He sniffed mucous into his throat while chewing the Oreo. "Honestly? I can't remember."

"Try harder." She leaned into the table and met his eyes.

He shrugged. "Maybe two thirty." A speck of cookie flew out of his mouth and landed next to a deep gouge in the table.

"And who was there?"

"Just Sanchez and his minion."

"His minion?"

"Sofia Reyes. You haven't heard about her yet? She and Sanchez are the dynamic duo. Changing the world of PS 777 education as we know it."

"*Minion* is a pretty unflattering description."

"I just say it like I see it." He wiped his mouth and brushed his hands together. "Which is why I'm in this closet like a roll of toilet paper."

"You sound pretty angry, Mr. Bosco."

His eyes narrowed. "You're fucking right I'm angry. He accuses me of sleeping on the job, which is bullshit. He takes me out of my classroom. And this is my temporary reassignment. You know what my big job was yesterday? Counting the rolls of toilet paper over there." He gestured toward the wall. "The taxpayers of New York City are now paying me eighty-nine thousand dollars a year to count two-ply toilet paper. You're a taxpayer, Detective. Should I thank you?"

She ignored the question. "Were you angry enough at Sanchez to kill him?"

Bosco pushed out his chair and stood. "Why do teachers always get the blame? We're not the problem, you know. The *problem*," he pointed his left index finger between her eyes like a gun barrel, "is rich people who won't pay their fair share to support public education. If we weren't spending all our tax dollars protecting oil in the Middle East, maybe we could have realistic class sizes and special programs for troublemakers like Miguel Espina. Then I could do my job. Instead, they make me babysit delinquents, and it's all my fault when they do something wrong." His teeth were clenched. His fist was so tight it was white.

"You're not answering my question, Mr. Bosco. Did you kill Hector Sanchez?"

He leaned across the table and smashed his fist onto the wood surface right in front of her. "I wanted to. Oh, did I want to."

Codella glanced at Muñoz. The look said, *Get ready.*

Muñoz stood. He towered over the suspended teacher. He said, "Please take your seat, Mr. Bosco."

"Fuck you!"

"If you don't take your seat and relax, you may end up inside a cell."

"Like I said, I'm already in one."

"I assure you this closet is luxurious compared to where we'll take you."

Nice, thought Codella.

Perspiration dripped down Bosco's forehead, and he breathed like someone with a boot pressed into his chest. He collapsed into the chair and looked on the verge of crying. "I don't deserve this. That bastard had no right to take me out of my classroom. He only did it because I had the guts to stand up to him. I'm the only one who wasn't afraid to tell him to his face he was full of shit."

Codella felt an unwanted wave of sympathy for the man. She knew what it felt like to be confined, in her case to an aluminum pole and bed and constant fevers and infections. But he had done things to deserve his fate. "According to the reports I've heard, you were sleeping right in front of your class," she reminded him.

"Says who? That lazy security guard who can barely see past her layers of blubber? She's a fucking liar."

"If you weren't sleeping, how did Miguel Espina get up and walk out of the room without you noticing?"

Bosco shook his head. "You're as bad as he is. You all want to blame the teachers. Now you want to pin a murder on me, too. Well, go ahead. See if I care."

"Where did you go when you left the school on Monday afternoon?" she asked.

"Home. Where else would I go?"

"What time?"

"I left at four o'clock. Ask Chris Donohue if you don't believe me. She helped me clean out my desk."

"When did you get home?"

"Five fifteen. I live in Bay Ridge. It's a long ride."

"Can you prove it?"

"I live alone."

"Anybody see you on the way?"

"Yeah. About five thousand other New Yorkers riding the MTA."

"That answer's not going to prove your innocence."

"What's the point of proving anything?" He laughed. "Is it gonna get me out of the storage room gulag?"

"As Detective Muñoz just pointed out, there are far worse gulags than this."

"I didn't touch the guy. You want me to take a lie detector?"

"We'll find out the truth, Mr. Bosco. Sooner or later. We always do." She stood.

Five minutes later, they were back in the car. "Man, was he on edge," said Muñoz.

She turned the ignition. "Yeah. He definitely has a short fuse and a persecution complex."

"You think he could have done it?"

She shook her head. "Do you?"

"He's pretty small. Doesn't fit Gambarin's profile, but then he did bang all over that old lady's car at the Triborough."

"Exactly. He's the kind of guy who does things in the heat of the moment. He acts on impulse. But I don't see him snapping the neck of a six-foot-two man like a trained professional. Besides, he's left handed."

She pulled away from the curb while Muñoz pondered how she'd figured that out. "Let's leave him on the back burner for now," she said. "You and Portino check out the street footage. I'm going to check in with McGowan and then go meet the superintendent."

CHAPTER 24

Codella was managing him better than he was managing her, McGowan thought when he looked up and saw her in his doorway. She had called him first thing this morning and now she was here to update him. She was playing by the book, giving him no possible reason to find fault with her.

He would have preferred if she *hadn't* called or come in. Then he'd have an excuse to take the case away from her. He could even start a paper trail to document her insubordination. A good paper trail might justify her demotion or reassignment to a low-profile precinct in an outer borough where he would never have to see her again. But she was too savvy. For all he knew, she had her own paper trail. And if it ever came to he said, she said in front of a review board, she could play the cancer card and score more points than him. He kicked himself for handing her this case on a silver platter. Now she was going to make them all look bad compared to her.

She passed him a report, and he skimmed the pages while she sat across the desk from him and waited patiently. "You have no suspects."

"There are people of interest, but no," she acknowledged, "I wouldn't call any of them viable suspects. Not yet."

"This is too big for you."

"It's too big for the team I have," she corrected him.

"Let's split it up between you and Fisk. Two teams. You run one, he'll take the other."

She shook her head. "I need manpower, not a parallel team. It would be counterproductive to bifurcate the flow of information in this case. There's not much forensic evidence to go on. We're not going to solve this with fingerprints and fibers. And everybody's got a different story to tell. This case needs someone to hear *all* the stories and listen to the silence, too."

He laughed. "What are you? A goddamn horse whisperer? You're going to solve this by listening to the silence?"

"In a manner of speaking." She smiled. "I'm going to listen to what people *don't* tell me."

He looked at his watch. Liverpool was kicking off in an FA Cup game in ten minutes, and he wanted to hear the pregame analysis. She had picked a lousy time to play the duteous detective. "So what kind of help do you want?"

"I've got two computers to download. One of them's still sitting in evidence. I have phone records to analyze. I need background checks on thirty-six parents who were in the building the day he died. And there are twenty-two teachers and eleven staff members to follow up on. I've got as many precinct detectives and officers assigned to the case as Reilly can spare, and I'll take anything else I can get. I'd like to shift command up here and start holding briefings here."

She was putting him in an untenable position. He didn't want her to succeed, but if she didn't succeed, he would look very bad. He had thrown her the case, and she was doing her job. What choice did he have? But no one would want to work under her. When she had arrested Wainright Blake, she had made them all look ineffective by connecting the dots five other detectives—including Fisk and himself—had missed. "Send over the names you need analyzed. I'll get your team together. You can hold your first briefing in . . ." He looked at his watch. The game would end at noon. "Let's say two hours."

CHAPTER 25

The District 124 headquarters was an architecturally uninspired brick-over-cinderblock building on West 134th Street. It was surrounded on all sides by equally drab warehouses waiting, Codella suspected, to be snapped up by Columbia University as part of its perpetual land grab across West Harlem. A receptionist shielded behind Plexiglas looked up as she entered. To the receptionist's right was a locked door that led, Codella supposed, to the Department of Education's inner sanctum.

The receptionist's shiny, black hair was braided intricately at the scalp and decorated with small beads. In her uniform days, Codella had once been assigned to a precinct in Brooklyn, and she knew that some West Indian women spent whole afternoons at hair salons on Flatbush Avenue in order to achieve braids like that. She smiled at the woman and held out her shield. "I'm here to see Margery Barton. Is she in?"

The woman slid up the Plexiglas. "She in a meeting right now."

"Do you know how long she'll be?"

The woman's eyebrows rose and fell expressively.

Codella nodded patiently. "I'll wait. I'm here about Hector Sanchez. Did you happen to know him?"

"Oh, yes. It terrible what happen to him. I see him just yesterday. He come for Mr. Dressler's presentation."

"Mr. Dressler?"

"From McFlieger-Walsh School Publishing."

"What was the presentation about?"

"iAchieve. A new program for the district."

"Do you happen to remember when the meeting ended, Ms.—"
She read the woman's nameplate. "Babb?"

"Around one thirty," Babb said. "But Mr. Sanchez rush out of
here before that."

"Oh?"

"Marva Thomas from his school call up and ask me to pass
him a note in the meeting. There was trouble at the school, so he
leave early."

"I see. Did Dr. Barton know about the trouble?"

Babb nodded. "After the meeting, she get a call from the
mother, Helen Chambers. Dr. Barton give me holy hell for putting
that woman through. She tell me every day I lose my job if I don't
keep the parents away. But what am I supposed to do?"

Codella made a sympathetic face. "And Dr. Barton took
the call?"

She nodded again. "Reluctantly."

"And then?"

"When they hang up, she tell me to get Mr. Sanchez on the
phone."

"Do you remember what time that was?"

Babb recalled that she had rung the school around two forty-
five, and Marva Thomas had come on and said Mr. Sanchez would
have to call her back. "He was with a parent. Her Majesty get mad
at me for that, too." She rolled her eyes.

Codella smiled. "So *Her Majesty* didn't actually speak to
Mr. Sanchez?"

"No."

"Did he call her back?"

"About half an hour later."

"So they spoke around, what? Ten past three?"

She shook her head. "By then, Dr. Barton leave for the day."

Codella reached into her pocket for dry-mouth gum. She
offered some to Babb, but the receptionist declined. "Do you happen to know where Dr. Barton went when she left the office?"

Babb shrugged. "You don't ask Her Majesty questions like that."

"No, I suppose you don't." She smiled. "I appreciate your time,
Ms. Babb."

Codella sat and made notes in her iPhone. Five minutes later,
three professionally dressed women and a man emerged from the

inner sanctum and darted toward the door like a small, purposeful school of fish. As soon as they were gone, Karen Babb disappeared behind the door to the inner sanctum. When she reemerged, she said, "You can come with me, Detective. Dr. Barton see you now."

Codella followed her down a narrow hallway lined with small, windowless offices and larger meeting rooms. All of them had white walls, fluorescent ceiling lights, and identical chrome and laminate furniture. Babb stopped at a door near the back of the building and motioned Codella into a much grander office with carpeting, wood furnishings, and framed children's artwork on the walls. Behind her desk was a large window, but the only view was a filthy brick wall.

The woman who held out her hand exuded confidence like a perfume that assaults rather than teases the senses. She belonged in a Midtown boardroom, thought Codella, not a gritty Uptown Department of Education back office. She had carefully coiffed brunette hair, and her green dress and matching jacket showcased her large breasts as much as they de-emphasized her thickening waist. Her gold necklace didn't look like costume jewelry. She was hardly young, but the hemline of her dress was far enough above the knees to display impressively shapely legs, and her three-inch, bone-colored heels seemed to warn, "Don't discount me."

The handshake was firm. "Margery Barton," she said in a deep, bizarrely sexy voice. "Please, sit. We're all just so upset about this tragedy. How is the investigation going?"

Barton returned to the other side of her desk, sat down authoritatively, and with a sweeping hand gesture, invited Codella to sit as well.

"Hector Sanchez reported to you, Dr. Barton?"

"That's right."

"What can you tell me about him?"

Barton pressed her elbows into the desk and leaned in. "Well, let's see . . . He was a typical new principal. A little green. A little earnest. A little overbearing. But highly motivated, intelligent, passionate. I'm sure you saw the article about him. He took over last February after I discovered that his predecessor had tampered with student assessment data."

"So he was a desperation hire?"

Barton sat back. "I wouldn't go that far. Although to be perfectly honest, not too many experienced principals want to captain a floundering ship. And he was hungry for it."

"And how did he do, in your opinion?"

Codella could see the hairline wrinkles below Barton's concealer when she squinted. "Honestly? He came on like a bull in a china shop. He alienated a lot of teachers last spring—but then so do many other new principals. They always come on strong out of the gate." She smiled. "They think they can change the world in a heartbeat just because they've impressed the parents or the media. It takes them a while to settle down and accept the fact that everything in this gargantuan system requires compromise."

"So it's fair to say there was tension between him and his staff."

"Teachers are very independent, Detective. They don't like to be told what to do. If they think they're being pushed around, they call their union. They check the fine print in their contract. Their contract spells out the rules of the game, not their principal."

"Did you ever regret hiring him?"

She shook her head. "I'm not one of those administrators who second-guess their decisions. What's the point? You work with the hand you're dealt. That's what I told him, too."

"I take it he didn't ascribe to your philosophy," Codella said.

"He complained a lot the first few months. He was pretty unforgiving of the legacy staff."

"I understand he fired a few of them. Ronald Davis and Imogene Burke."

Barton frowned. "Principals don't have the authority to fire teachers on their own. Where did you hear that?"

"From a teacher. Christine Donohue."

Barton smiled. "Chris? Well, I'd caution you about getting your intelligence from her or any other teacher on that staff. Hector would have liked to fire *lots* of teachers over there, including Chris, but the two you've mentioned left of their own volition. Imogene Burke retired—it was overdue—and Mr. Davis resigned. He had no more patience for another round of school improvement, which is sad because we have a real shortage of qualified math specialists. You're awfully interested in the staff. Does that mean you think someone at the school is responsible for his murder?"

Codella ignored the question. "Can you think of anyone at his school who had a particularly adversarial relationship with him? Marva Thomas, for instance?"

Barton laughed. "Marva a murderer?"

"Eugene Bosco?"

"Well, he certainly had a motive after Monday, but you can't honestly think he did this. Look, every principal has his supporters and detractors."

"And what camp did you fall into?"

"I always support my team. If they're successful, I'm successful. I'm sure you know how it works." She smiled again. Her teeth were so white they looked like shiny porcelain bathroom tiles.

"When did you last speak to him?"

"At the principals' meeting Monday morning. I said hello to him just before it started."

"What was the meeting about?"

Barton grasped her necklace with the thumb and forefinger of both hands and met Codella's eyes as she slid her fingers up and down the gold links. "There were several agenda items, Detective. None of which you'd find too interesting, I'm afraid." She wetted her lips and her eyes lingered on Codella's. The administrator's default mode seemed to be gender-blind seductiveness.

"Try me." Codella held Barton's eyes and played along.

"Let's see. Test prep plans. Alignment of instruction to the Common Core Standards. School lock-down procedures."

Codella replayed Karen Babb's words in her head. *He come for Mr. Dressler's presentation.* She watched Barton carefully as she asked, "Who is Mr. Dressler?"

Barton's fingers stopped caressing the necklace. Her hands moved to her temples. She opened her mouth. "I completely forgot. We had a presentation at the meeting. Chip Dressler from McFlieger-Walsh School Publishing was here."

"Chip Dressler?"

"Their senior vice president of sales."

"What was his presentation about?"

"A new program we've been piloting and plan to implement next fall—iAchieve."

Codella nodded casually. "Did you speak to Sanchez after the meeting?"

"No. He left in the middle."

"But you called him later, I believe."

Barton looked up in surprise. "Yes, but he was with a parent and couldn't speak to me."

"Why did you call him?"

"I had to." Barton pressed her right fingers into the surface of her desk. Her perfectly polished fingernails reflected the overhead light. Those nails were strangely hard and feminine at the same time, like her whole persona. Codella glanced discreetly at her own short, unglossed nails as Barton explained, "I'd just found out about the incident at his school. Helen Chambers had called me. She was very upset. Hector had decided to give an in-school suspension to the boy who attacked her son. She wanted me to do something about it. She made some not-so-veiled threats about calling the central office and the press. I tried to talk her off that ledge. I told her I'd find out what had happened. We hung up, and I called Hector to get his side of the story."

"What time did Chambers call you?"

"It must have been two forty-five."

"And after you hung up, you phoned Sanchez immediately?"

"That's right. Around three."

"But you didn't speak to him."

"No. I spoke to Marva Thomas. She told me Hector was with a parent."

"And then?"

Barton shrugged. "Then I went back to work."

Thanks to Karen Babb, Codella knew the answer to her next question. "Did he call you back?"

The superintendent shook her head.

"Did you call him again?"

She shook her head again, but offered no words.

He call about half an hour later, Karen Babb had said, *but by then Dr. Barton leave for the day.* Codella leaned forward in her chair. "Why didn't you call him again? That seems a little strange. I mean, this woman threatens to speak with your superiors and you didn't follow through?"

Barton smiled dismissively. "There's never just one brush fire at a time." She eyed the stacks of papers and folders on her desk. "When you get federal funding—and my schools *depend* on it—all you do is gather data and provide documentation. It's exhausting, and you can't be late without jeopardizing Title I jobs and subsidized lunches. I had a deadline to meet yesterday, and I met it." Now her gaze hardened defiantly. "But he was on my mind all that night."

Codella nodded sympathetically. "When did you leave the office?"

Barton looked at her watch as if the answer were there. "It must have been five. I had to meet my husband down at Cipriani at six. For a fundraiser."

Codella stood, smiled pleasantly, and handed Barton her card. "You've been very helpful, Dr. Barton. Thank you. I've taken up enough of your time. Rest assured we'll be doing everything we can to resolve this case as quickly as possible. We've got a lot of manpower devoted to it." She moved to the door and turned back. "Oh, but one more question first. This iAchieve program. How did Mr. Sanchez feel about it?"

"We all share the same concerns, Detective, about how to exploit the power of technology effectively in our classrooms," Barton answered carefully.

Codella left. Outside, a strong smell of diesel fuel was in the air. It emanated from a green oil delivery truck that was pumping heating fuel into a belowground tank across the street. She stood on the sidewalk for a moment. Barton had lied about leaving the office on Monday afternoon, and Codella would have to find out why.

She got in her car and replayed the standard reassurance she'd given the administrator. *Rest assured, we'll be doing everything we can to resolve this case. We've got a lot of manpower devoted to it.* But they didn't have nearly enough. She needed more than the roomful of researchers McGowan might put at her disposal. She needed feet on the ground, but if she used McGowan's favorite feet, she would end up losing the reins. McGowan would make sure of that. And she couldn't let that happen, even if it meant putting personal issues aside.

She picked up her iPhone and dialed the number she knew by heart. When he came on, she spoke in a dispassionate voice. "You busy?"

"Paperwork," he said. "On Queen Smith. We got her. Turns out she's the one who couldn't stand the baby screaming while she was doing a wake-up blast."

"Jesus."

"How does a mother do that to her baby? I'd like to rattle her brains." He paused.

"Hopefully the legal system will. You did your job, anyway."

"What about your principal?" he asked. "Any progress?"

"We've got too many people to sift through, and I don't want to give this to . . ." She paused.

"I get it. How can I help?"

Where to begin, she wondered. There was Helen Chambers. Sofia Reyes. Yolanda Espina. Chip Dressler. The list went on and on. At this point, they just had to eliminate as many names as they could. She said, "Two teachers left 777 in September. It's not clear if Sanchez fired them or if they left of their own volition. Could be a wild goose chase, but we need to check them off the list. Could you pay them a visit?" She cringed, recognizing the trace of desperation in her voice. She waited.

"Just tell me where to go," he said evenly.

"Portino and Muñoz can give you the details."

Then she hung up and took a deep breath and waited several seconds for the adrenaline to dissolve in her chest. *There*, she thought. *That wasn't so hard.*

A minute later, she checked her voice mail. The waiting message was two hours old. "It's Dana Drew," said the voice in her ear. "I need to talk to you."

CHAPTER 26

Muñoz cued up the street cam footage on a computer at the far end of the squad room. This was not footage from the sophisticated NYPD Real-Time Crime cameras located in high-security areas of the city that could pivot, scan, and zoom to read the text message on a cell phone in someone's palm. The static angle of this camera gave it a finite field of vision. It recorded in grainy images only the vehicles and pedestrians that happened to move in and out of a fixed surveillance area at the corner of Frederick Douglass Boulevard and West 112th Street.

He clicked *Play* where the time stamp indicated 3:20 PM, the time Sanchez had left the school. Then he sat back and watched. Pedestrians moved in and out of view. North and southbound cars passed in waves based on the traffic flow around the 110th Street rotary just to the south. But the images were blurred and more pixilated than usual. "Hey, look at this," he called out to Portino.

Portino waddled over. "Yeah, it's on a maintenance list."

"What should I do?"

"Watch it anyway," said Portino. "You gotta rule it out. I'm gonna get coffee. You want some?"

"Sure. Yeah. Black. Two sugars." He turned his attention back to the screen. When the time stamp read 3:25, a figure in a dark, bulky jacket with a hood entered the camera's field of vision from the southwest side of Frederick Douglass Boulevard. The blurry figure crossed 112th Street to the northwest corner and entered the laundromat there.

Muñoz watched the figure disappear through the door and almost immediately reappear as an even blurrier shadow through the laundromat's side window overlooking 112th Street. He continued to watch as the time stamp counted the seconds and minutes. He paused only when Portino's phone line rang. "Muñoz," he said.

Codella asked, "What's going on?"

"I'm watching the street footage. The quality's terrible, but there might be something there. I don't know yet."

"Keep at it. I need Portino."

"He's on a coffee run."

Codella gave Muñoz a quick summary of her interview with Barton. "I just get a funny feeling. Something's off. I can't put my finger on it. She lied about leaving her office Monday afternoon, and on Monday morning, a guy named Chip Dressler from McFlieger-Walsh School Publishing gave her principals a presentation that she didn't volunteer to tell me about. A program called iAchieve. Ask Vic to do some digging. And have him find out if there was a fundraiser at Cipriani on Monday night. Barton was supposedly there."

"Got it. I'll tell him."

"And call me if something shows up on that camera."

He hung up, clicked *Play*, and continued to watch pedestrians and cars stream in and out of view. Portino returned with his coffee ten minutes later, and Muñoz gave him Codella's message, eyes on the screen the whole time. A woman walking five or six dogs—he couldn't be sure because of the focus issue—turned onto 112th Street, and he noted the time. An adult with a small child turned onto the street from the south side of Frederick Douglass, and he noted that too.

As the video minutes elapsed, the sky darkened. Streetlights went on. Twilight turned to night in the short span of thirty sped-up minutes. The blurry shadow in the laundromat window did not move. He still had not seen anyone who could be Hector Sanchez. Was that because the principal had not come home yet? Was it because Sanchez had taken a cab or walked home from the other end of his block, out of this camera's range?

The man who entered the camera's purview at 5:27 PM wore a light-colored parka and a red baseball cap with the visor low. He walked briskly past the laundromat. Muñoz clicked *Pause* as the figure turned west onto 112th Street. He noted the time on his legal pad. Was it just a man who lived on the block? Was it someone on his way to Morningside Park? Muñoz felt an inner jolt of energy he knew didn't come from caffeine. The grainy images no longer felt like footprints from the past. They seemed to unfold in real time, and Muñoz felt a sense of urgency, as if he could still stop a crime in progress.

At 5:35, the man who moved into view on the west side of Frederick Douglass wore a dark coat that blended with the night. He turned onto 112th Street. Muñoz rewound and paused as the figure's face looked briefly toward the camera. He pressed his eyes closer to the screen. The face was almost indistinguishable from the surrounding darkness. "Detective Portino, take a look at this guy. What do you think?"

Portino lumbered over.

"Is he black?" asked Muñoz.

"Maybe. Or dark-skinned Hispanic. Zoom in a little."

Muñoz enlarged the image and they debated. "I'd say dark skinned, but I sure couldn't swear to it," concluded Portino.

Muñoz made another meticulous notation on his pad. His eyes were tired. He stretched his arms. He stood and went to the men's room. He circled past Reilly's office and saw him on the phone. He wondered if he should call Codella now or wait and watch the scene play out. He went back to his desk and continued watching.

At three minutes past six, the figure in the light-colored parka and red baseball cap reappeared from the direction of Sanchez's building. "Hey!" called out Muñoz. "This could be our guy." He paused the video.

Portino stepped over. The face stared in the direction of the camera, but with the lens out of focus and his visor pulled low, his features remained a mystery. Muñoz and Portino stared at the frozen blob of the man midstride as he approached the side window of the laundromat.

Then Muñoz again played the video. The man continued to walk. He came to the laundromat window and turned to look in. Muñoz paused it. "He's looking at the guy inside. I think they're looking at each other. That guy has been there since three twenty. What the fuck has he been doing in there?"

"I don't know, but I'll tell you this. No jury's gonna convict anyone based on these crap images."

"Still, one of these guys could be the killer."

Muñoz watched two more sped-up hours before the figure in the laundromat emerged, crossed 112th Street, and headed south on Frederick Douglass Boulevard. Then he pushed his chair out, stood, stretched, and rubbed his bloodshot eyes.

CHAPTER 27

Dana Drew's faded T-shirt advertised the 2008 Broadway revival of *Hair*. Her feet were bare, her hair was tousled, and she was wearing no makeup. Codella had stood next to her share of actors at the Zabar's bread counter and the Citarella checkout line, and most of them were so ordinary off camera that you'd look right past them if you weren't paying attention, but Drew managed to appear conspicuously beautiful without any effort.

The actress invited her into a spacious entrance hall where signed Broadway playbills decorated the walls. Codella looked beyond this entryway toward sun-flooded windows that confirmed the spectacular Hudson River view she'd imagined when she'd stood at the door yesterday and looked over Jane Martin's shoulder.

Drew followed her eyes. "Would you like to sit, Detective?"

"I'm fine right here. You wanted to tell me something."

The actress ran her fingers through her streaked blond hair. "It's a little complicated." She bit the side of her thumb.

Codella recalibrated her tone. "All right, then let's go have that seat."

They moved to a three-sided sectional overlooking the river. Codella waited.

Drew finally broke the silence. "You know that Proud Families billboard of my family?"

"The one I saw in Sanchez's apartment? The one I see every day at the bus stop on my corner?"

"It's a big lie," said Drew. "My partner Jane and I separated several months ago."

"Then why did I see her here when I came yesterday?"

"She visits Zoe. She calls the babysitter, and the babysitter lets her know if it's a good time—when I'm not around."

Codella remained silent, wondering where this was going.

"Look, I'm not going to sugarcoat my motive, Detective. The play was about to open. I didn't want to deal with a public breakup. The paparazzi would have been all over that."

"And your partner agreed to the cover-up?"

"I'd prefer to call it an attempt at privacy. But yes. She hoped we'd get back together. At the time, I thought we might too."

"But now you don't?"

"No."

"And you're telling me this because it has something to do with Sanchez?"

Drew nodded. "As I mentioned last night, I had a meeting with Hector and Sofia on Friday to talk about the after-school program. Jane showed up for the meeting. I wasn't expecting her to come. She got there before me. They were all chatting when I walked in. Hector came over and gave me a hug and a kiss. I didn't think anything about it, but when the meeting ended and Jane and I were walking away from the school, she grabbed my arm and pulled me toward her and accused me of ending our relationship because of him."

"What did she say to you?"

"She accused me of being in love with him."

"Are you?"

"I thought I answered that question last night."

"What did you say when she accused you?"

"That she was being ridiculous, of course. But she didn't let go of my arm." Drew massaged her bicep now. "She squeezed it so hard my eyes were watering. I told her she was hurting me and then she gripped it harder. She said, 'Good, because you're hurting me.'" Drew pushed up her T-shirt sleeve and displayed the purplish-yellow imprints Codella had noticed in her dressing room last night.

Codella recalled Jane Martin's gray eyes, her broad shoulders, and her strong upper arms. "You could have filed a domestic violence report."

"Just imagine what the press would do with that."

Codella leaned closer. She felt like the hospital chaplain who used to sit by her bed and chat with her during her treatments. "Why do you want me to know all this?"

"I don't know." Drew's eyes filled up. "I don't *want* to know why. I just want you to have all the facts so you can figure out if they mean anything." She wiped her eyes.

The tears seemed genuine, but could you ever entirely trust the emotions of an actress? "You think she could be involved in this," Codella stated rather than asked.

"I don't want to think so."

"But you do."

"She looked so angry."

"Had she ever looked like that before?"

Drew lowered her eyes and shrugged. "When I asked her to move out, she punched the wall next to my head so hard she broke a finger. She couldn't work for six weeks. She's a sculptor."

"Are the two of you married?"

"No, but when we met two years ago, I thought she would be the one. She loved Zoe. Zoe loved her. I thought we'd be a family. But after she moved in, I began to see warning signs."

"What signs?"

"Anger. Jealousy. We'd go out and people would pay more attention to me than to her, and she wasn't able to deal with that, to trust my feelings. We'd leave and fight for the next few days until I calmed her down. Finally I couldn't take it anymore. I asked her to move out. I didn't want it to be over—when it was good, it was very good—but I didn't want to apologize for who I am. I told her we should take things more slowly. I paid for her apartment. I paid for her studio in Red Hook. I went to all her shows. I hoped she'd work out her resentments, but she wasn't working them out, and two weeks ago I told her I needed to move on and that to do that I couldn't keep supporting her."

"If you'd ended things two weeks ago, then why did she come to the meeting on Friday?"

Drew shrugged. "She wasn't giving up, I suppose. In her defense, she did call that night to apologize for what she'd done."

Codella wasn't impressed. "Abusive partners usually feel apologetic, until the next time they're angry."

Drew hugged herself tightly.

"Have you seen her since?"

"No."

"Your show doesn't run on Mondays. Where were you that evening?"

"I attended a benefit at Town Hall."

"Someone can verify that for you?"

"Zoe came with me. My driver picked us up at six o'clock, and we returned at ten. We were with two friends the whole time. I can give you their numbers."

"Did you tell your partner where you were going?"

"No."

Codella stared into the green eyes. *Don't you know about actors and their loose boundaries?* Christine Donohue had said. *They're all borderline and narcissistic.* She leaned forward on the couch. "Some people aren't opposed to manipulating a police investigation," she said, "to get revenge on a former lover." She watched Drew's face.

The actress just said, "I'm not one of those people."

"No? Well, answer this question: Have you applied to private schools for your daughter next year?"

Drew frowned. "That's an odd question to ask me right now."

"Just answer it," Codella snapped. *Just prove you're capable of telling the truth.*

"All right, yes!" Drew snapped back. "I'm thinking about selling out like every other privileged person. I'm not exactly proud of myself. How did you find out?"

Codella ignored the question. "Write down your ex-partner's address, and don't tell anyone else what you've told me."

Drew got a pen and paper, jotted the information, and held it out without looking up. She was angry, or maybe just embarrassed to have been exposed. Well, that was *her* problem, Codella told herself. She should never have lied last night.

Codella yanked the slip of paper out of Drew's fingers and stood, making it clear she didn't appreciate the actress's obfuscation. In the next instant, however, her protective instincts clouded her objectivity and she sat back down. She stared into the green eyes. "If she touches you again, you call me immediately."

CHAPTER 28

"Mrs. Burke? Imogene Burke?"

The former PS 777 teacher opened her door three inches. She had straight blue-gray hair that hadn't been coiffed recently. She was holding a cordless phone in one hand. Her watery eyes gleamed. "Are you here to fix my sink?"

"No." Haggerty held up his shield.

"What's that?"

"I'm a police detective, Mrs. Burke."

She opened the door wider, grabbed his wrist, pulled it toward her, and examined the shield closely. "Is this real?" She banged on it. "It doesn't look real."

He pulled out his NYPD identification card. She studied that carefully, too.

"We okay now?" he asked.

"I suppose."

"I don't have a lot of time, Mrs. Burke. May I come in? I'm here about Hector Sanchez."

"Who?"

"Sanchez. Hector Sanchez. Your principal."

She looked irritated. "He's not my principal."

"Your *former* principal then. Before you retired."

"Who said I retired?" Burke sneered contemptuously, as if he were crazy.

"You're Imogene Burke, right?"

"Of course I am."

"The Imogene Burke from PS 777?"

"That's right."

"Can I come in?"

She stepped back and allowed him to enter a dim, narrow entry hall where boxes and shoes lined half the floor and fading family photos competed for wall space. The air surrounding her smelled like cheap perfume or potpourri masking acrid body odor. The smell got on his nerves and made him feel a generalized disgust. She reminded him of his old aunts, stern and pedantically Catholic.

Her living room was like a three-dimensional model of lower Manhattan. Everywhere he looked were skyscrapers of old *National Geographics*, *New Yorkers*, and *Smithsonians* with ragged yellow edges. Some of them tilted precariously to one side like construction catastrophes waiting to happen. A narrow pathway snaked through the towers and led to a black-and-white couch where a rancid stench broke through the potpourri. Haggerty knew that smell. Once he'd answered a call at the apartment of a mentally ill woman whose whole apartment—to the horror of her neighbors—had been usurped by mice. The building exterminators had shot poison into the walls and under the floorboards, and the whole apartment had become a killing field of smelly corpses. Burke had a rotting mouse somewhere in this room.

"Look, Mrs. Burke, I just have a few questions and then I'm out of here. When did you last see Sanchez?"

"I told you. I don't know any Sanchez." She waved the cordless phone in her hand.

"Don't play games with me, Mrs. Burke. We're talking about murder here."

"Murder? I didn't murder anyone!" she said. "What do you mean, murder?"

"Where were you on Monday afternoon and evening?"

"I came right home from school. I took the B to Rock Center and the F to Forest Hills. It's what I always do."

"We both know that's not true, Mrs. Burke! You haven't been there since September. So where were you?"

But only vacant, slightly panicked eyes answered his demand.

"Jesus Christ!" He shook his head, suddenly comprehending the obvious. The only crime he would uncover here was the vandalism time, bad genes, or too many saturated fats had done to the old woman's brain cells. He would certainly find no answers and make no breakthroughs to advance the Sanchez case, and his frustration got the best of him because he had come here determined to take something useful back, something Claire would want to hear, information that would change the course of the case and melt the frost between then. *Dammit!* He kicked his heel against the nearest magazine towers. It swayed and then slowly but decisively toppled toward the narrow pathway and crashed into Imogene Burke's leg, cutting her off on the other side of the collapse.

"Aaaahh!" she screamed at the top of her lungs. "Get out of here! Get out now or I'll call the police!"

CHAPTER 29

It might only be November, but the inside of the car was like a bone-chilling meat locker. Codella dropped the slip of paper from Drew on the passenger seat. It was one more unconnected detail in a still sketchy patchwork of facts and suppositions. She zipped her jacket, started the engine, and turned up the heater. She'd get to Jane Martin later. Right now, she needed to hear Sofia Reyes's perspective on things. Sofia Reyes's name was coming up on everyone's lips. Who was she and what would she have to say about Sanchez and iAchieve and the teachers of PS 777?

Codella sped across the park and pulled up to the literacy coordinator's address on East Ninety-Third Street for the second time in less than twenty-four hours. In the light of day, the brownstone looked well maintained, though its façade paled in contrast to the elegance of those on either side of it. Rental buildings seldom looked as good as owner-occupied townhouses. She climbed the steps to the parlor level and pressed the button for 2B. There was no answer, and she pressed three more times before she called Reyes's cell phone. After five rings, the woman's polite, bilingual greeting came on, and Codella left an urgent message. Then she headed back to the West Side, to Helen Chambers's address. There was always the possibility that Chambers was an angry mother with a crazy, get-even husband or brother or boyfriend capable of snapping someone's neck. Chambers had to be eliminated as a suspect.

The woman who answered the door was wearing rubber gloves. She had a dough-white complexion that contrasted sharply with her dark-brown hair and eyes. The hair was fine and straight, and she wore it in a pageboy with limp, slightly uneven bangs that

looked self-inflicted. She had the puffy blotched skin of someone who had recently been crying. Codella displayed her shield.
"Mrs. Chambers?"

"Yes?"

"I'm investigating the death of Hector Sanchez. May I come in?"

"It's not exactly a good time."

"I'll keep it short."

Chambers opened the door reluctantly, and Codella stepped
into a cramped vestibule cluttered with shoes, umbrellas, and
a wrought iron coat rack. She followed the woman into a small
kitchen that had not been renovated in at least twenty years judging from the chipped cabinets; the dull, scuffed linoleum; and the
outdated appliances. The first thing that caught her eye was the stiff
beige-and-white corpse of a teddy bear hamster lying on its back
with curled up feet next to the Mr. Coffee. Beside the corpse sat
a cardboard container with air holes. Scratching sounds emanated
from within the box. As Codella watched, Helen Chambers spread
fresh cedar chips into the bottom of a just-cleaned hamster cage,
opened the cardboard box, and lifted a live hamster into the cage.

No graduate degree from John Jay College of Criminal Justice
was required to piece this mystery together. One hamster had died
inconveniently, and it was now being replaced with a body double.
Did the fact that Chambers was covering up an untimely hamster
death mean she was also capable of covering up a murder? Codella
watched her close the cage door and insert an orange carrot-shaped
chew toy through the wire bars. She watched Chambers turn to the
stiff little corpse, which had already lost the soft plumpness of living
flesh. The exposed stomach looked lumpy and matted. "'Farewell
to thee!'" Chambers petted the little head. "But not farewell / To
all my fondest thoughts of thee.'" She looked at Codella and laughed
nervously. "Anne Brontë. I read it at my great aunt's funeral last
month. I still have it memorized. John would have wanted me to
say something like that."

Codella nodded politely.

Then Chambers switched from contemplative to efficient, wrapping a section of the *New York Times* around the dead pet as if she
were wrapping up salmon steaks at the Citarella seafood counter.

"You left the school yesterday before Mr. Sanchez got there, is
that correct, Mrs. Chambers?"

"John was very upset after what had happened. He needed some medication." She set the packaged corpse on top of a stainless push-pedal garbage bin.

"What time did you leave?"

"One thirty or so."

"Did you go back to the school later on to see Mr. Sanchez?"

"No, but I called him."

"When was that?"

"A little after two, I think."

"Tell me about that call."

"There's nothing to tell. He didn't take it. He was with Miguel Espina's mother. Marva Thomas came on instead. I asked her how Miguel would be punished, and she told me he was getting an in-school suspension. I wasn't pleased to hear that, and I told her Mr. Sanchez should at least have had the decency to get on the phone and tell me that to my face."

"And?"

"She assured me she would have him call me right back. I waited thirty minutes, but he didn't call, and then I was just so enraged that I called the district office."

"What time was that?"

Chambers shrugged. "Two forty-five or so. It took me fifteen minutes to track down the superintendent's number."

"Margery Barton?"

"That's right, and then I had to threaten to call the chancellor before the receptionist put me through."

Codella noted the times in her iPhone. "Tell me about your conversation with the superintendent."

"There's nothing to tell about that either." Chambers sniffed. "The *B* word applies. She's dismissive and patronizing. She promised to look into the suspension, but I could tell it was all lip service and she wasn't going to do anything."

"Is that why you posted your comment on the school message board?"

Chambers looked surprised. "How do you know that?"

"Sanchez was reading it the night he died."

Chambers blanched. "I shouldn't have done it. It's just that sometimes you feel like you're screaming in the dark and you want someone to hear you. You know? It just wasn't right for John to get his face pushed into a toilet bowl one day and have to face his tormentor at school the very next day. I still feel enraged when I think about what happened."

"How many parents of PS 777 go to that website?"

"Plenty," she said. "I started checking it in September. One of the parents posted the site on the office bulletin board."

Chambers didn't strike Codella as the type of woman who sought vengeance through violence, but she had been surprised before. "Where were you on Monday night, Mrs. Chambers?" she asked.

Chambers poked her finger through the wires of the hamster cage and watched the little body double nibble her fingers as she spoke. "I was here, with John and my husband. We were angry, Detective, but we're not murderers."

Codella nodded. "Thank you for your time."

CHAPTER 30

Haggerty sped toward the Park Slope section of Brooklyn so fast he got pulled over on Eastern Parkway right across from the Brooklyn Museum. The officer sauntered over from his squad car and asked the predictable question. "Do you know why I stopped you?"

"Sixty-five in a forty-five zone." Haggerty smiled and held out his shield for scrutiny. "Sorry, Officer. This is police business." Then he raised his window and left the cop standing in the road.

When he looped around Grand Army Plaza onto Prospect Park West, it was ten past twelve. He parked on the corner of Third Street and got out.

Tall oak trees canopied the wide block. Most of the branches were bare, and dried-up brown leaves littered the street in front of the limestone row houses. He climbed the stoop of Ronald Davis's address and read the names next to the buzzers. There were eight units in the once majestic single-family Victorian home. Davis was on the third floor. Haggerty rang him and waited for a voice, but the only answer was a long buzz unlocking the heavy parlor door. Haggerty pushed his way in, climbed the stairs, and knocked.

The man at the door had dirty blond hair. His button-down shirt was neatly pressed, and his jeans looked clean and new. "Who are you?" he asked.

Haggerty showed his shield. "I'm here about Hector Sanchez."

Davis nodded. "You wanna come in?" He scratched the side of his head. "I read about him this morning. I never knew a murder victim before."

The limestone's living room had the original wood and tiling around the fireplace mantel. Someone had cared enough about the

Victorian touches to restore the wainscoting and sand the hard-wood floors to a gleaming polish. "Nice place," Haggerty said. "A rental?"

Davis nodded. "Sublet. Off Craigslist. Can you believe it?"

Haggerty pointed to the acoustic guitar on the couch. "You play?"

He nodded again.

"What kind is it?"

"Martin Dread. A vintage one made from extinct Brazilian rosewood. You play too?"

Haggerty shook his head. "I took up the trumpet for two weeks in fifth grade. Old man couldn't stand the racket. How well did you know Sanchez?"

"I only worked for him five months."

"What did you think of him?"

"Not much."

"Why'd he fire you?"

Davis laughed. "Who said he fired me?"

"If he didn't fire you, then why'd you leave in September?"

"Because I didn't feel like working for a prick who gives teach-ers weekly report cards. How would you like to get an e-mail every Monday with your current grade and performance goals?"

"That would depend on my grades, I guess."

"Well, I got C minuses. My buddy Chris got Cs. We used to laugh about it. Maybe other people were motivated by his little stunts, but he motivated me right out the door. Life's too short to work for assholes. You know why he gave me the C minuses?"

"Why?"

"Because I wouldn't stay after school an extra hour and a half three times a week—without extra pay, mind you—to prep kids for the state math tests. Would you work an extra shift for no pay?" He didn't wait for an answer. "That's *my* time. I run a business after school. I tutor private school kids at Berkeley Carroll and Packer and Poly Prep. Their parents pay me two hundred bucks an hour to teach their kids algebra, geometry, and calculus, and they're grate-ful. Why should I give that up?"

Haggerty did the calculations. If Davis had ten clients a week during the school year, he could make more than a grade-three detective just from tutoring. "I'm shitty at math," he said. "Where were you on Monday night?"

Davis laughed. "Why? You think I killed him? I guess you're desperate for leads, huh?"

Haggerty ignored the question. "Where were you?"

"Tutoring Caroline Fenkel on Henry Street in Brooklyn Heights," he said. "She's a junior at Packer."

"How long were you there?"

"From six thirty to seven thirty, and then I met with Matthew Benjamin at the Starbucks on Montague. He's a sophomore at the same school. I left him at eight forty-five."

"I'll need their numbers."

"It's not good for business if people think I'm part of a murder investigation."

"Not my problem. Just give me the numbers."

Five minutes later, Haggerty called the Fenkel and Benjamin numbers from his car and the alibi checked out, which meant he had just wasted two and a half hours trolling for nonexistent clues in the outer boroughs. He had nothing to take back to Claire.

He started the car and headed for the Battery Tunnel.

CHAPTER 31

Eight officers sat around the table in briefing room 3-B at Manhattan North. Two were plainclothes homicide detectives from the North squad. Dan Fisk was a barrel-chested man of fifty or so—McGowan's personal eyes and ears in the squad—and the few times Codella had spoken to him, he had been brusque, even cold. Frank Nichols was a beefy black man with short hair and a thin moustache. She had met him but never worked with him. The other six officers were uniformed personnel who'd been drafted to assist. All but one of them were men.

McGowan had instructed her not to begin the briefing until he arrived, and as the minutes passed, Codella's mouth was getting drier and drier. She pushed a piece of Biotene between her molars and clenched with the force of a car crusher. She had never led a task force at Manhattan North. In the two months she had been in the homicide squad before getting sick, she had been assigned to Joe Cleary's team, and they had split their efforts between unsolved cases from previous years and one or two new homicides that were quickly solved. This would be her debut performance then, and McGowan would be evaluating everything she said. She was just like one of those PS 777 teachers, it occurred to her, who had dreaded the judgment of their impossible-to-please principal.

When McGowan finally entered the room a little after 1:00 PM, she wasted no time. "You've all been selected to work on the Hector Sanchez murder investigation. First, let me give you a quick summary. Sanchez was the elementary school principal at PS 777. He was murdered yesterday evening in his apartment on West 112th Street. We don't believe this was a burglary gone awry. There is no sign of forced entry, and nothing of value appears to have been taken from his apartment. His body was undressed and staged to look like Christ on the cross, and this may be related to the fact that he was described as the 'Savior of PS 777' in a magazine article last summer."

"How'd he die?" Fisk called out.

Codella ignored his premature interruption. She didn't intend to let him interview her in front of *her* task force. She kept her eyes on the uniformed officers, some of whom had probably never sat through a homicide briefing before, as she said, "We believe the victim opened the door to his killer. It's therefore very possible he knew his killer. It could have been a neighbor. It could have been a teacher or parent or staff member at PS 777."

"We got that," said McGowan. "How'd he die?"

He and Fisk were tag teaming her, she realized. They were trying to throw her off her game, make her doubt her approach. She breathed deeply and took her time as she launched a photo from her iPhone onto the large flat-screen mounted on the wall behind her. "We believe the murderer came through the door, stepped behind Sanchez, and snapped his neck in one violent movement. The victim's third vertebra was severed, and that would have paralyzed him from the neck down. He died within a half hour from heart failure. We can assume the killer is strong, that he's tall enough to restrain a six-foot-two-inch victim. And he's more than likely right handed. I say *he* deliberately. Chances are the perpetrator is male."

In her peripheral vision, McGowan reminded her of a patient sniper waiting for his clean shot. He stepped forward and fired. "Fisk, tell us what we need here."

Fisk pushed out his chair to stand. Codella raised her hand in a stop motion. "*I'll* answer that," she said. "This is my briefing. I'll tell you what we need."

Silence followed. Fisk looked at McGowan. McGowan glared at Codella. Codella concentrated on the other faces around the table. She picked up a file folder. "This contains the names, addresses, and telephone numbers of the twenty-two teachers and eleven noninstructional personnel at PS 777. It also contains the contact information of every parent in the school the day Sanchez died. Everyone in this file needs to be contacted. We need to know where they were on Monday evening from 3:30 PM until the following morning. We need alibis verified. We have to identify names that require further investigation." She looked at Fisk. "And I need you to coordinate this effort."

She slid the file across the table. "That's it. We'll have another briefing tomorrow morning. Let's get to work."

Her hands were shaking as she shut off the flat-screen monitor, put on her jacket, and moved toward the exit. She held her breath as she passed McGowan in the doorway.

Half an hour later, she found Marva Thomas sipping coffee and eating a sandwich at her desk. She skipped the usual greetings. "I spoke to Margery Barton this morning, and she told me she phoned the school on Monday at three PM to speak to Sanchez. You came on the line instead and told her he was busy."

Thomas dabbed her mouth with a napkin and finished swallowing. "That's right."

"Who was he with?"

Thomas folded the tinfoil around the uneaten half of her sandwich. "Christine Donohue." She reached for her coffee.

"Why didn't you tell me this yesterday? When I asked you who was in this office on Monday afternoon, you never mentioned Christine Donohue."

"I guess I forgot. I'm sorry."

Codella planted her palms on her side of Thomas's desk. She leaned within two feet of the assistant principal's face. "This is a murder investigation, Ms. Thomas, or did you forget that, too? Your job is to give me every piece of information you can."

Thomas only nodded.

Codella's eyes flashed to the biblical passage on Thomas's computer. "Why was Christine Donohue in his office?"

"I assume they were discussing Mr. Bosco."

"Why would they do that?"

"Because someone had to stand up for him, and Christine Donohue wasn't afraid to do it."

Codella stepped back from the desk. "I understand Sanchez had a meeting here on Friday after school."

"Not here. They couldn't meet here. The floors were being polished."

"Where then?"

"The cafeteria."

"What was the meeting about?"

"I don't know. I wasn't part of it."

"Who was there?"

"Sofia Reyes. Dana Drew. Jane Martin."

"No one else?"

"As far as I know. I left before they finished. It was five. I had to get home. My mother has Parkinson's, Detective. She lives with me. She shuts down if she doesn't have her medication at certain intervals."

"When was the last time you spoke to Sofia Reyes?"

"Monday morning. She called to say she couldn't be in on Tuesday and would reschedule her appointments for Thursday. She may be out of town. She would definitely call if she'd heard the news."

"Did you speak to Sanchez over the weekend?"

"No."

"Did he have any other meetings on Monday that I should know about?"

Thomas shook her head.

"Where were you on Monday after school?"

"I went straight home. I made some dinner. My mother and I watched television."

When Codella left Thomas's office, she found Ragavan in the school cafeteria, and they walked back to the principal's office together. "Have you found anything? Heard anything?"

"He kept meticulous records on everybody in the school. Every teacher has a folder. He has detailed evaluations from his classroom visits. He has a report card with all their names and weekly grades. You gotta see this."

She stepped behind the desk and looked over his shoulder at the Excel document filled with comments and grades. Anna Masoutis had poorly modeled how to use key details in the text to find a main idea; Shirley Weaver had asked too many literal comprehension questions; and Roz Porter had conducted a lesson without scaffolding the beginning English learners in her class.

"Jesus, I'd hate to work for him," said Codella. "What about the voice mail messages? Did you listen to them?"

"He hadn't picked them up since last Friday. There are two from Sofia Reyes and one from the Apptitude guy. That's it."

"Call the Apptitude guy. Find out what he was doing. I've gone to Sofia Reyes's apartment twice already, and I left her a message to call me. We really need to speak to her."

CHAPTER 32

Chip Dressler's cell phone vibrated. He pulled it out of his pant pocket and recognized Margery's number on the display, so he stepped out of the conference room on the twenty-fourth floor of McFlieger-Walsh where he was reviewing promotional collateral with the iAchieve marketing team. He walked quickly to his little office and closed the door. "What's up?"

"I've been trying to reach you for an hour."

"I've been in back-to-back meetings."

"Don't you check your cell?"

"I'm sorry." He was careful not to let her hear his irritation. "What's the matter?"

"The police came to see me this morning."

"That was bound to happen."

"Yes, but the detective asked me where I was all Monday afternoon."

"What did you tell him?"

"*Her.* I told her I was in my office until five."

He wanted to say, *What the hell did you do that for?* Instead he said, "What was your thinking?"

"I *wasn't* thinking," she snapped. "Obviously! It was stupid. Go ahead and say it."

He said nothing. Saying nothing was better than risking another diplomatic response that she would see right through.

"What if she finds out I lied?"

He wasn't used to hearing anxiety in Margery's voice. "She probably won't," he said. "I hardly think the police will be focusing in on you as a prime suspect. No offense." He laughed. "But as imposing as you are, you're no one's idea of a psychotic killer."

She didn't respond to the humor. "But if they find out I didn't tell them the truth, they might start probing, and other things might come out."

"Other things?"

"You know."

"They can't find out about *that* unless you or I tell them, and we're not going to," he said. "That would be a disaster for both of us, Margery."

"I know."

"Listen to me. You're about to unveil incredible research results. You're going to get a lot of publicity for what you're doing in the district. Lipsie's going to take note. You're going to get a big promotion out of this. We just have to sit tight and let this inconvenient little distraction go away. And it *will* go away. They had to visit you. It was pro forma, I'm sure."

He heard her sigh. "All right," she said.

"The last thing you should do is act guilty about something you had no part in. And what you do in your private life is nobody's business but your own—and mine."

"You're right," she said.

"Of course I'm right. Now are you going to be okay?"

She took a deep breath. "Could we meet for a drink later on?"

Chip looked at his watch. He hadn't planned on seeing Margery again before his flight out tomorrow, but he couldn't leave her questioning his commitment to her, not when the purchase orders for iAchieve still needed her careful review and signature. "I've got the PS 777 iAchieve demo at three forty-five. They didn't cancel it. But I can duck out of here in about half an hour. Meet me at the hotel at two. We'll talk there."

"Make sure no one follows you," she said.

"Listen to yourself." He laughed. "You make it sound like we're double agents or something. Ease up on the paranoia." But in truth, now she was making him nervous, too.

CHAPTER 33

Haggerty returned to the precinct at 1:45. Blackstone was sitting on the edge of his desk reading the *Post* and sipping a Coke. It was probably his third or fourth of the day, thought Haggerty as he stared at Blackstone's soda belly. He waved at Portino. Portino had the McFlieger-Walsh website up on his screen, and he was on the phone with someone about a fundraiser on Monday night. Muñoz was bent over his keyboard logging a video segment from the surveillance footage paused on his computer screen. Haggerty walked over to him. "You find anything on there?"

"Plenty, but it's a blurry mess. Have a look." Muñoz played back images of the three figures that might be related to Sanchez's murder.

"Has Codella seen this yet?"

"Not yet. She said she'd be back in an hour."

"Can I give you a piece of advice? Take a quick trip up to the laundromat before she gets here. See if they have a security cam inside. If there's a camera in there, it might give us a better look at that face in the window. Codella will ask for that. You could anticipate her."

Muñoz nodded. "I'll go right away." He stood and grabbed his jacket off his chair. "Thanks."

"Sure thing." Haggerty slapped his back and smiled.

As soon as Muñoz was gone, Blackstone sauntered over. "Nice of you to help out Rainbow Dick." He slurped the last drops of soda in his can and tossed the can into a garbage bin next to Muñoz's desk.

Haggerty walked away.

Blackstone chuckled. "Looks to me like Codella's got herself two bag hags," he called out.

Then Haggerty turned back, moved as close as he could without touching Blackstone, and said, "I think it's real interesting how focused you are on Muñoz. I think maybe you're into him, Blackstone. I think maybe you've got some *urges* you don't know how to handle. You know what they say about guys who protest a little too much."

Blackstone's face reddened.

"Maybe in the spirit of department camaraderie," Haggerty continued, "we should bring this up at tomorrow's roll call. Maybe the other guys can help you deal with your unresolved issues."

Blackstone pressed both palms into Haggerty's shoulders and shoved him backward. Haggerty's thigh hit the desk behind him and the feet of the desk skidded across the floor with a loud screech. Portino pushed out his chair and stood up as Haggerty shoved Blackstone back. Then Blackstone grabbed Haggerty's shirt and yanked on it hard. "Fuck you!"

Haggerty laughed. "You see? You've got issues." He tore Blackstone's hand away from his collar. Then Blackstone threw a punch but it only swiped air. Portino came over and pulled Blackstone away as Haggerty turned and walked out of the squad room. "Go back to your corner," Portino told Blackstone. "It's over."

Haggerty went to the evidence room and signed out Hector Sanchez's laptop. Bag hag or not, he was going to help Claire.

CHAPTER 34

Jane Martin was wearing a steel-blue cable-knit sweater and skin-tight jeans when she opened the door to her fourth-floor apartment. "You found me. That means Dana must have let you in on our *big lie.*"

"There's no room for lies in a murder investigation, Ms. Martin. She hardly had a choice."

"So how can I help you?"

"I have a few questions." Codella stared at Martin's heavily veined, slightly discolored hands. *She's a sculptor,* Drew had said.

"Ask away," said Martin with apparent bonhomie.

"You had a meeting with Sanchez on Friday."

"It wasn't my meeting, but yes, I was there."

"Why?" asked Codella, with an exaggerated expression of confusion. "Why did you show up for that meeting after Ms. Drew had broken things off?"

Martin gave an amused little smile that covered whatever she was really feeling. "Dana doesn't want it to be over," she said. "Dana's just confused right now."

"Confused?"

"About how she feels. Haven't you ever been confused?"

Codella ignored the attempt to deflect her scrutiny. "How long did the meeting last?"

"Forty minutes or so."

"How did Sanchez seem?"

She shrugged. "Same as always."

"Which is how?"

"Businesslike."

"You knew him well?"

"Dana knew him better."

"Did he mention any problems at the school?"

She snickered. "There are nothing but problems at that school. I've been telling Dana all along to get Zoe out of it."

"Who left the meeting first?"

"Dana and I did. Hector and Sofia stayed behind. They had some other things to discuss, I think."

Codella stared at Martin's inscrutable face. *The girlfriend is just her latest diversion*, Christine Donohue had said. *When we met two years ago, I thought she would be the one*, Dana Drew had told her. Codella knew that her straightforward questions would only get her safe, succinct answers. She had to switch tactics. "When you left the meeting," she asked calmly, "did you and Ms. Drew have your fight right outside the school where you could see people coming and going?"

Martin shifted from one foot to the other and didn't hide her annoyance. "My personal life has nothing to do with your investigation."

Codella pressed harder. "Did anyone leave the building while you were holding on to Miss Drew's arm firmly enough to cause a bruise?"

"What's your game, Detective?"

"I'm not playing any game. I merely asked you a question, and I'd like an answer."

"No. I didn't see anyone leave."

"While you were holding onto your partner's arm firmly enough to cause a bruise?"

The eyes narrowed. The arms crossed over the chest. "Are we done here?"

"Not quite. Where were you on Monday evening between four and seven PM?"

"Well, I certainly wasn't with Hector, if that's what you're suggesting."

"I'm not suggesting anything. I'm asking for a straight answer. I'm sure you understand."

"Of course. And I'll give you one. Since you insist. I was at my studio. I'm a sculptor. But I'm sure Dana told you that, too."

"Where's your studio?"

"In Red Hook. In a converted warehouse."

"Where exactly?"

Martin gave the address and Codella touch-typed it into her iPhone. "You drove there?"

"That's right."

"In your car?"

She nodded.

"Did anyone else see you while you were there?"

"I share a space with two other artists, but neither of them was there." Martin shrugged. "I guess you'll have to take my word."

Codella had no intention of doing that. "Okay," she said. "I appreciate your time."

She returned to the building's lobby and phoned Drew. "What kind of car does your ex-partner drive, and where does she park it?"

"It's a Volvo S60. It's mine, actually. It's in the Rapid Park on Ninety-Seventh Street. Why?"

"Did you take it out on Monday?"

"No. I haven't used it for weeks. A driver takes me to the theater and back."

"After you told Martin it was over, did you tell the garage not to give her access to the car anymore?"

"No. I didn't."

"So she could still be driving it?"

"I'm sure she is."

CHAPTER 35

As soon as Dressler got to his hotel room, he ordered Margery's favorite Veuve Clicquot rosé from room service, but when she arrived ten minutes later, she wanted straight scotch instead, so he unscrewed the top on a bottle from the minibar and poured the amber liquid over ice.

She took a long sip and said, "I should never have hired that man."

"It's too late to worry about that."

"He really picked an inconvenient time to get himself murdered."

"Maybe, maybe not," said Dressler. "It could be a blessing in disguise. You and I both know he was going to poison as many principals as he could against the program. You could see that at the meeting on Monday. If anything, this was a convenient tragedy."

"I suppose." She drained the scotch and set the glass on top of the minibar. "Ironically, just before the meeting, he told me I'd have to implement the program at his school over his dead body."

"He said that?"

"His exact words, Chip. And now he's dead. Doesn't that seem strange? And you and I are bound to get on somebody's radar. The minute they zero in on iAchieve, they're going to start looking at me and you—and *us*. We had a motive."

"You can't arrest people just because they have a motive. They need evidence, and they're not going to find any because there is none."

"People get wrongly charged all the time. Sometimes they're even convicted. If the police start digging around and our relationship comes out, I'm through."

"And so am I," he said. "You know that. But it's *not* going to come out, because we're not going to tell them."

"That could be easier said than done. You didn't get the visit from that detective. She kept asking questions. She grilled me about my afternoon. She wanted exact times."

"And I'm sure you answered everything satisfactorily." He prayed that she had.

"Almost everything. But then she asked if Hector had called me Monday afternoon. I told her no. I didn't know because I ducked out of the office to come here. But after she left my office this morning, I checked Karen's log, and he had called me five minutes after I left." She rubbed her eyes. "Dammit! If I'd just stayed put a little longer."

He came up beside her and rubbed her shoulders. "Relax, Margery, the police aren't looking for you. They're looking for a murderer."

"And where do I say I went if they find out I left the office? I can't tell them the truth."

"You tell me," he challenged. "Think of something. Right now. If anyone can think their way out of a box, it's you."

He watched her open the minibar, remove another miniature of scotch, and pour it over her melting ice cubes. She took a long sip and paced back and forth. Eventually she stopped between the minibar and the bed and turned to face him. The alcohol was starting to take effect, Chip observed. A little of her confidence was returning. "I went looking for a scarf," she said.

"A scarf?"

"A silk scarf to wear to Cipriani. I ducked out of the office, and I didn't want Karen to know where I was going, so I told her I had a meeting."

"Where did you go?"

"Saks. But I didn't like their selection, so then I went to Bergdorf's."

"What floor at Bergdorf's?" He quizzed her like a cop trying to catch her in a lie.

"Third," she said evenly.

"Tell me about the scarves."

"There was a Roberto Cavalli, but it didn't quite match my dress. The Emilio Pucci was a little too garish. I liked the Alexander

McQueen, and a sales clerk tried to talk me into that one, but it wasn't a perfect match for my dress, and for that kind of money . . ." She trailed off. "Finally I was running out of time, so I just got in a cab and went down to the dinner." She shrugged.

Chip clapped. "Now *that's* the Margery I know. Stick to that story. The detail is perfect."

"You think so?"

He got behind her and pressed his thighs against her buttocks. "Yes. Now *relax*." He kneaded her shoulders until she let out a deep sigh.

"You're right." She turned around to kiss him on the mouth. "We'll laugh about this a month from now, won't we?"

"Of course we will." He kissed her back, and she pressed her tongue against his and he felt himself respond. He put his arm against her lower back, guided her toward the bed, and pushed her gently onto the mattress.

"Let me go to the bathroom first."

"I don't want to wait," he said because the last time he had waited in bed for her, she had taken five minutes, and in that time, Charlene had called his cell. Her smiling honey-skinned face had filled his cell phone screen and then he couldn't get her out of his mind as he had unbuttoned Margery's blouse and cupped her large breasts.

"Chip," she whispered, now with obvious desire.

He unbuttoned her cashmere cardigan, unfastened the side zipper on her skirt, and pulled the skirt down over her thighs and legs, along with her panties. And then he lowered himself onto the mattress between her legs and buried his face in her bikini-waxed pubic hair. His tongue found the warm hidden flesh, and she said, "What are you doing?"

"*Relaxing* you." He braced her thighs with his strong hands. He'd never given oral sex to Margery before, and he was sure her aging orthopedic surgeon had never done that for her.

He let his tongue explore the passage to her vagina. Her head was back against the pillow, and her eyes were closed. He wet his index finger and found another passage to explore. Margery voiced a quick protest to that, but her body certainly didn't protest. He inserted the tip of his finger ever so slightly, and she said, "Oh, God, Chip," and that was all he needed to hear. He had found another one of Margery Barton's secret and probably unfulfilled appetites. He slowly slid in deeper and she came so hard that he felt the pulsing all around his finger. "Oh God," she said.

Then he climbed on top of her and entered her and rocked to her pace. When she was about to come a second time, he pounded her hard and deep so they both screamed out, and it seemed to go on and on. Then he fell to the side of her, sweaty and sticky and certain. If Margery were forced to lie, she'd give a convincing performance that would save them both.

CHAPTER 36

The 171st Precinct detectives' squad room still felt more like home to Codella than any room at Manhattan North. As soon as she walked through the door, Haggerty approached. "Can I show you something, Claire?"

He had signed Sanchez's laptop out of evidence, and it was sitting on his desk. Her first reaction was outrage. He was just like McGowan and Fisk, she found herself thinking. They were all looking for a way to yank the case out from under her and deny her the opportunity to prove herself. In the next instant, she could feel him reading these thoughts on her face.

"I went to see those teachers," he said. "One of them—Imogene Burke—has dementia. I can't even imagine her in a classroom. The other one—Ronald Davis—is a first-class jerk, but he has a solid alibi. I came back here and figured I'd pitch in while I had a couple of hours."

She looked around the room. Portino and Muñoz were on their computers. Schugren was watching them from his desk across the room. Blackstone wasn't there, thank God. She wanted to say, *I don't need your help*. But she did need help. She just didn't want *his* help. Instead she said, "Show me what you've got."

He leaned forward and tapped the track pad on Sanchez's computer. An instant later, an image filled the high-resolution Retina display.

"Jesus fucking Christ," she whispered.

"I know."

They stared in silence at the familiar faces filling the laptop screen. The faces were only an inch apart. The eyes were locked.

The lips appeared to have just parted from a kiss. The woman's left fingers were combing through the hair at his neckline. His right fingers were brushing her cheek softly.

"I blew up the faces to make sure there was no mistake," he explained. "Here's the original image." The next photo showed the figures standing on the front steps of Sanchez's 112th Street building, about to go in. It had been taken, Codella noted, from a vantage some hundred or so yards across the street. The woman's right hand rested on his chest, and his left palm, placed well below the small of her back, was pulling her into him.

"Where did you find this?"

"In his trashcan."

"Print me out a copy."

She continued to stare at the screen and felt her stomach tighten. She heard Christine Donohue's gravelly voice in her head for the second time today. *Don't you know about actors and their loose boundaries? They're all borderline and narcissistic. They sleep with anyone.* The words were a harsh reminder that rumors, like stereotypes, often had a perverse way of encapsulating granules of truth. She heard Dana Drew's voice insisting, *If I window-shop at all, it isn't at the men's store, Detective.* Could there now be any question about Drew's veracity—or lack of it?

Haggerty looked at her. "I guess she might not be a full-fledged lesbian after all. I'm thinking we put her in the bisexual category. How about you?" He smiled.

Codella didn't respond. What could she say? That Drew was an actor and actors were supposed to make you believe things that weren't true? The simple, undeniable fact was that she had seen all the obvious signs of Drew's duplicity, and she had allowed herself to misinterpret them. She had allowed herself to be duped by a soft tone, green eyes, tears, and a bruise on a bicep.

She stared at Haggerty for several seconds. Finally, she whispered, "Thanks."

He smiled and handed her the printout.

"I'll be back," she said.

Then she turned, raced down the steps, took a side exit to the parking area behind the precinct house, and got in her car.

When she entered the Riverside Drive address, she flashed her shield, growled at the doorman, "Don't even think about announcing me!" and rode the elevator like a caged panther ready to pounce on its prey. When Drew opened the door, she held up the photograph. "You lied to me."

Drew studied the image. "Who took that?"

"You lied to me."

"Where did you get that?"

"He'd had it several days. I take it he didn't tell you about it."

She didn't answer the question. "Whoever took this could be his killer," she said.

"Or maybe *you're* his killer."

"Don't be ridiculous, Detective."

"You were with him Monday afternoon, weren't you?" Codella accused. "You're the reason he left the school at three thirty. He didn't visit any student. He came home to pay *you* a visit, didn't he?"

Drew glanced over her shoulder. "I'd rather not discuss this now. My housekeeper is here."

"Didn't he?" Codella repeated belligerently.

"Yes," Drew acquiesced. "Yes, all right. But please, lower your voice."

Codella moved a few inches closer. "I'm not the kind of person who gets angry easily. I have a slow fuse, but when it burns down, you don't want to be around me. And right now, I'm reaching the end of my fuse. You played me this afternoon, and I don't like to be played. I'm not happy about it, Miss Drew, and I'm thinking it might be time for you to see the inside of an interview room."

"Are you threatening me?"

Now Codella gave her own self-satisfied smile. "Yes, and it's no empty threat, I assure you. You want to end up on Page Six tomorrow?"

Those words seemed to cut deep. "I'd rather not," she answered quietly.

"Then start talking, and don't leave anything out. When did you get to his apartment?"

"We'd planned to meet at three thirty. I got there first. I let myself in."

"So you had a key to the admiral's club. You were a frequent flyer."

"It's not what you think."

"You got right into his bed?"

Drew's silence was answer enough.

"When did he join you?"

"Three forty or so. He was held up by the incident with that boy."

"*That boy?* I thought you cared about those kids. *That boy* has a name. John Chambers." Codella leaned on the doorframe and looked past Drew's shoulder, remembering the plush couch and the river view she had enjoyed earlier in the day. "Then what happened? He joined you in the bedroom? He took off the suit and hung the jacket on a hanger? He laid the pants over the chair? Is that what he did?"

She nodded.

"And after you did whatever you call what you were doing, you left?"

She nodded again.

"When?"

"Just before five."

"How do you know?"

"I phoned my driver. He was waiting a block away. He swung around for me at the prearranged time."

"Did Sanchez get dressed before you left?"

"He put on some jeans. He walked me to the door." Her eyes now filled with tears.

Codella shook her head dismissively. "You kept those tears out of your eyes for a whole half hour in your dressing room last night while you pretended to flirt with me, so don't play your pity game now. If he'd meant something to you, really meant something, you would have come clean on your own, you would have wanted to find his killer no matter what the personal cost, and the fact that you didn't only begs the question, what else are you hiding?"

"I'm not hiding anything else." Drew pushed strands of blond hair behind her ear. "And I did care about him. I could hardly concentrate during the performance last night. I know what it looks like to you. I know, but I only did what millions of other people do every day. I can't help it if people hold me to some unrealistic higher standard just because I'm a Broadway actress."

"Some people hold you to a lower one just because you're a Broadway actress." She thought of Donohue.

"Well, then at least I didn't disappoint them. Look, I'm human. No, I wasn't *in love* with Hector, but I cared about him. He was gentle and funny, and I was lonely. Of course I lied. You would have, too, if you were in my shoes. You've never been drawn and quartered by the media."

"Maybe not," Codella acknowledged, "but we all get drawn and quartered by someone." She thought of McGowan and what he was likely to say to her at tomorrow's briefing.

"If people knew about Hector and me, they'd assume I only helped the school for one reason, and that isn't true."

"But protecting your reputation meant more to you than finding his killer."

"That's not true either. I just didn't want my motives to be misinterpreted. I care more for those kids than most of the people charged with educating them. Let's be honest, public education in this city is a disaster. No one in the Department of Education goes home and frets about the children of PS 777. You think those children ever cross Bernie Lipsie's mind?" She didn't wait for an answer. "Lipsie's never even seen those kids. You think Margery Barton loses sleep over them? To her they're just raw scores in a stanine. And the teachers? They're like equity actors who've been playing the same swing roles for fifteen years. They're practically robots. They had a good thing going. They didn't have to think at all. But then this powerhouse comes in and says, 'Hey, we're supposed to be *educating* these kids. We're supposed to be preparing them for more than a life on food stamps. We're not just babysitters. We've got standards to uphold.' They hated him for that. They would have done almost anything to get rid of him. They couldn't stand the fact that he was actually making a difference. Remember, to some of these kids, PS 777 is their only lifeline. Hector wanted to save those kids. Haven't you ever wanted to save someone?"

Codella forced herself to ignore that question. She wasn't going to go where that question led. "You say you left around five. Think carefully. Who did you see as you left the building?"

"No one," Drew said.

"What about outside? Was anyone standing on the street? Did you see anyone parked in a car?"

The actress shook her head. "I ducked into my car as fast as I could. I didn't want to be seen."

"I'm going to need a formal statement from you."

"But—"

Codella held up her hand to signal the uselessness of Drew's protests. "If you get to the 171st tomorrow morning at seven AM, you might be able to avoid too many eyes. Text me. I'll meet you there." Then she turned to go. As she got off the elevator, she saw the missed calls from Muñoz, Haggerty, and Manhattan North.

CHAPTER 37

Chip positioned his laminated McFlieger-Walsh nametag on the front of his left lapel and slipped the magnet behind the lapel to hold the nametag in place. He hadn't prepped for this meeting—Margery Barton had usurped his prep time in other ways—but he'd given this same presentation to fifteen other schools in Margery's district, so how much prep time did he really need? "Just smile a lot," Margery had told him in September when he'd started to make the rounds. "They'll be staring at your white teeth. They'll be sizing you up in your Euro cut suit." Her eyes had dropped to his belt buckle and below, and he knew exactly what she had meant. *Was Margery still in his hotel room,* he wondered now, *or had she returned to her office to avoid another suspicious absence?*

He smiled broadly at a tall, dark-haired woman who was tentatively peeking into the room. "Are you looking for the iAchieve demonstration?" he asked. She nodded, and he said, "Come on in. I'm Chip Dressler. And you are . . . ?"

"Anna Masoutis." The woman smiled.

"Anna. Great. Thanks for coming. You'll need this." He handed her a charged iPad and an agenda. *Anna. Anna.* He repeated her name in his head several times as she chose a seat in the third row of tables. No one ever chose the first row. *Anna.* A successful sales representative did not forget names. *Anna the Greek Princess,* he thought, cementing the name in his long-term memory. No. *Anna of the Aegean.* He would make Anna feel like his best friend by the end of the hour. He would make them all feel like his best friends.

He turned his grin on a dour teacher with short, gray-brown hair. Teachers, he had observed throughout his career, were seldom glamorous or fashionable like Anna of the Aegean. Many of them inhabited a world of asexuality, and this one was an extreme case in point. Her glasses were utilitarian. Her sweater and pants were drab. She bordered on obese. He dialed back his charisma as he held out his hand. "I'm Chip Dressler from McFlieger–Walsh."

"Roz Porter," she announced.

"Roz, thanks so much for coming. What grade do you teach?" *Roz. Roz. Roz not Rosalind.*

"Second."

"Well, I'm so glad you came, Roz. Here's your iPad. You'll need this. And our agenda. We'll get started in just a couple of moments." He watched her wedge her wide hips under a table.

When all eleven participants were seated, Dressler moved to the front of the small room. "I want to thank you all for taking this time out of your afternoons to learn about iAchieve. And before we get started, I also want to take a moment to tell you how personally sorry I am, as I know all of you are, for the terrible tragedy here at PS 777." But looking into their eyes, he could see that they felt no more grief or loss than he did. This was not a gathering of Sanchez sympathizers. He saw this as *Roz not Rosalind* rolled her eyes at *Jenny Who Needs Jenny Craig*, and six-foot *Kristin Magic DeMarco* cleared her throat for all to hear. He quickly changed the subject. "Let's get started. Oh, but first, I brought snacks." He watched the faces light up as he placed milk and dark chocolate kisses at each table.

CHAPTER 38

Sofia Reyes's small, calloused feet were bare, and her ankles were bound. Someone had expended considerable effort to prop her into a kneeling position between an overstuffed chair and a matching ottoman. The palms of her hands were taped together, and her wrists were bound in front of her chest. Her wide-open eyes stared straight ahead in eternal surprise or panic, but they saw nothing, the clouded corneas dried out and damaged by lack of circulation. The body's decomposition was advanced, speeded no doubt by the heat from hissing prewar radiators. Her face had been pummeled. The left side of her skull was contused, and blood had matted her dark-brown hair, stained her pajamas, and seeped copiously into the carpet beneath her. She looked like a gruesome plaster of Paris supplicant kneeling in prayer.

Codella stared for several seconds. She noted the white nylon twine around Reyes's wrists and ankles and the slash at her neck. "This is part two of an installation," she announced.

"What?" asked the cop at the door.

"Never mind," she said, realizing that he wouldn't know what she was talking about, and she didn't want him to. Sanchez was Jesus on the cross and Sofia Reyes was Mary Magdalene, the disciple who had stayed with him till the end.

She took out her iPhone and snapped a photograph. She moved carefully around the body and snapped several more. She took a photo of the small half-filled brandy glass and the bottle of Courvoisier resting on an end table next to the chair where Reyes must have sat and sipped brandy before her death. She photographed the brass stand-up lamp that had crashed to the floor a foot in front of Reyes. Her eyes moved to a string of wooden rosary beads dangling conspicuously from the shut window blinds across from the body. Someone had jammed them through two slats with the little wooden cross hanging at the bottom. Where had the beads been before the killer arrived? On the end table? In Sofia's lap? In her hands? Had she been in the middle of a prayer cycle when her killer had knocked on the door? Codella scanned the walls and floors, but there were no other obvious disturbances in the pleasant living room.

"Who found the body?"

"The daughter," said one of the uniforms near the door.

"What do you know about her?"

"She's an OB-GYN at NYU Medical Center. She'd been calling her mother since yesterday but couldn't get her so she came over as soon as she finished a delivery."

"Where is she now?"

"Sergeant Peattie took her downstairs to the super's apartment."

"Did she touch anything?"

He shrugged. "She was kneeling by the body when we got here."

"Where's Evidence Collection? They should be here by now."

"Almost here," said the officer.

"And the ME?"

"On his way."

"Who is it? It has to be Gambarin. I don't want anyone else. Let them know. Right now." She turned to the other officer in the room. "No one else enters this apartment until Crime Scene arrives. I want Banks. Is that clear?"

"Yes, ma'am," he said, but just then a burly, gray-haired detective from the 145th came through the door and said, "Who the fuck are you?"

"Codella." She held out her hand. "Manhattan North. Homicide."

"Colleary. What are you doing here?" He didn't hide his anger.

Codella said, "Can we talk in the hallway, Detective Colleary?"

She moved through the door and stationed herself as far from the first responders as she could. Colleary reluctantly followed. "I'm listening."

"This murder is related to the death of Hector Sanchez, the PS 777 principal who died on Monday night."

"What makes you so sure?"

"The victim was his literacy consultant. They worked together, and their murders have certain similarities, Detective. I'm sure you didn't miss the interesting arrangement in there." She eyed the door.

"No," he acknowledged.

"I'll be coordinating both investigations. When your officers do the vertical, I'd like to send over a detective from the 121st, Detective Muñoz, to give them some background. Are you good with that?"

Codella knew how territorial precinct detectives could be—she'd been one of them, after all—but Colleary didn't protest. "He observes chain of command in my precinct. He gives background, that's all."

"Of course."

The detectives returned to the crime scene and Colleary huddled with his precinct cops. Codella stood and stared at the body. She had rung the woman's brownstone buzzer on two different occasions since yesterday, she thought, and all that time, Reyes had been lying here. Based on outward appearances, she had probably been killed the same night as Sanchez and perhaps by the same person. And if so, then Codella didn't need forensics to know that Sanchez had been killed first. Banks had found no trace blood at his apartment, and there was no way Reyes's murderer had walked out of this place without taking some blood along for the ride. She got the attention of the cop at the door. "Any sign of break-in?"

He shook his head. "The daughter had to use her key when she got here."

Codella turned back to the body. So either Reyes had known her killer like Sanchez, she thought, or the killer had used a convincing pretext to make his victim open the door.

She heard heavy footsteps on the brownstone staircase, and Banks's crime scene team appeared. "Long time no see," Banks said cheerfully.

She smiled ruefully. "Get ready, boys. This is one colorful show."

By the time Gambarin signed in two hours later, Reyes's body had been photographed from more angles than a supermodel during fashion week. Banks's team had collected prints that probably weren't the killer's, bagged a few fibers clinging to Reyes's pajamas, and illuminated a trail of footprints leading from the living room carpet to the parquet vestibule, into the lobby, and all the way down the stairs to the brownstone's entrance. They were still engaged in their search, covered head to toe like CDC scientists studying deadly bacterial strains. Gambarin removed a Tyvek jumpsuit from his case. "What do we know?"

"She was a consultant at Sanchez's school. He'd hired her to help him turn the staff around."

Gambarin squinted, stretched his neck, and peered at the corpse as he pulled on his suit and booties. Then he stepped into the room and bent beside the corpse. "She has a gaping wound to the carotid. A head contusion as well." He gazed upward, and his eyes panned left to right across the spotless ceiling before they landed on the thick puddle of blood around Reyes's knees. The blood had dried into a dark crust like thickened lava after a volcano.

Codella knew what he was thinking. "No arterial spurts."

"Right."

"What does it mean?"

"It means he delivered the head blow before he cut her throat. Her heart was still pumping but it wasn't very strong."

"Maybe he had to subdue her before he could make her look like Mary Magdalene."

"He definitely tied her wrists first. Her hands are clean. If her hands had been free, she'd have raised them to her neck and tried to staunch the bleeding."

Codella stared at the frozen terror on Sofia Reyes's face. The woman had died a much slower and gruesome death than Sanchez. But why? What had she possibly done to incite her killer? What motive could explain her barbarous death, and how was it related to Sanchez's, because certainly it had to be related. Were there other decomposing disciples rotting in yet-to-be-discovered locations?

"I hope you can find me some clues, Rudolph. I really need something to go on."

"We'll see," was all Gambarin said. "Call me in the morning. I'll do the autopsy tonight."

CHAPTER 39

"Where's Haggerty?" she asked as soon as she got to the precinct.

"He's down at the prosecutor's office. They're getting ready for Queen Smith's arraignment."

She pulled up a chair next to Portino. "Can you show me the street cam footage?" She dropped into the chair and closed her eyes while Portino cued it up.

"Don't get your hopes up," he warned.

One by one he showed her the segments Muñoz had carefully documented. When they were finished, he sat back and rested his folded hands on his stomach. "Not much help, huh? Nothing here that a grand jury's gonna use to indict anyone."

"Was there a camera in the laundromat?"

"Muñoz checked it out. Nothing. What are we going to do? We can't show these to the public."

"Maybe. But if we hold onto them, it could look like we're hiding something." She sighed and pointed to the screen. "Which one do you think's the killer?"

"Well, Red Cap got there first. Overcoat never shows up on the camera again. He might just live around there."

"What about Laundromat Guy?"

"I don't know. He's in that window the whole time. He can't be the killer. He could be a lookout, I suppose."

"Maybe," she said. "Maybe not. I want you to call Detective Colleary at the 145th. Ask him to check the street cams near the Reyes brownstone as soon as possible. Maybe we'll get lucky and spot Red Cap or Overcoat there. We've got to find out how these murders are connected."

After Portino made the call, she asked, "Did you look into iAchieve and Chip Dressler?"

He grabbed a file off his desk. "There's a ton of information about iAchieve on the Internet. It's supposed to be this amazing new learning and assessment system. The word they keep using is *adaptive*."

"What does that mean exactly?"

"The program tracks each kid's scores and adapts the instruction based on their performance. One article called it the one-on-one cyberteacher of the future. I like that."

"Sounds a little too good to be true, don't you think?"

"I don't know. McFlieger-Walsh partnered with major technology companies and brain researchers at Johns Hopkins University."

"That must have cost them a pretty penny."

"One source says they invested more than two hundred million in a push to lock up the elementary and high school market for technology-based learning. McFlieger-Walsh is owned by Hemisphere Media Holdings, and now they're under pressure from Hemisphere shareholders to see some upside, but the program's not getting the traction they expected. McFlieger-Walsh is dragging down Hemisphere's stock price. They want to spin it off, but there are no takers yet."

"Why isn't the program getting any traction if it's so scientifically proven?"

"Seems it's a little bleeding edge. A lot of districts still haven't installed the sophisticated learning management systems and hardware needed to run a program that requires whiteboards in every classroom linked to tablets in every student's hands that feed data into a database that can diagnose individual student needs and provide reteaching on the spot at the right level."

"It's a lot more complicated than when I was in school."

"And last year McFlieger-Walsh was cited for unethical sales and marketing practices. Their nonprofit division sent twenty-five big shot school administrators on an all-expense-paid trip to Oahu. Supposedly, it was a 'training' seminar for educational leaders—nothing to do with product sales—but every administrator who participated was a long-standing McFlieger-Walsh customer, and it was obvious the company was softening them up for an iAchieve sale. McFlieger-Walsh's competitors cried foul play, and a big investigation was launched. The company got fined and had to back off on the hard sell. They lost a lot of momentum and credibility."

"Was Margery Barton on that trip?"

"Her name wasn't mentioned in the articles. Does she have a suspiciously good tan?" He smirked.

Codella visualized the unnervingly striking administrator. "Tans don't last that long, Vic. Anyway, I have a feeling she would have spent her time under an umbrella at the tiki bar, not under the hot skin-damaging sun. She's at least fifty, but she looks impressively put together. All I know is, she wants iAchieve in her district—she wants it badly—and Sanchez definitely *didn't* want it in his school."

"Would she take him out for being an obstacle?"

"Anything's possible, I suppose. She could have hired someone to do her dirty work."

"Or McFlieger-Walsh could have done it," said Portino.

"They certainly have a financial incentive to keep that sale alive," Codella agreed. "Selling to New York City would mitigate a lot of bad press. What did you find out about Chip Dressler?"

"He's the senior vice president and national sales manager for McFlieger-Walsh. He lives in Dallas, but he commutes to the New York office about once a month."

"He made a presentation to the principals in Barton's district Monday morning," said Codella. "I also saw a sign-up sheet on the PS 777 bulletin board about an iAchieve sneak preview this afternoon. I wonder if he went through with that. All the teachers that hated Sanchez signed up for the session. Anything to get under his skin, I guess. Tell me about Margery Barton."

"She's a pretty ambitious woman if you consider she went from teacher to district administrator in eleven years. Last September the chancellor—Bernie Lipsie—tapped her to head up a citywide technology task force."

"What about her personal life?"

"Married to a big-time surgeon. He's the head of geriatric orthopedics at the Hospital for Special Surgery. He's also a chief of orthopedics at NYU Medical School. He has a publication list a mile long. He's involved in at least twenty research studies on various hip replacement procedures and hardware."

"So I take it she really did attend a fundraiser at Cipriani on Monday night?"

"From beginning to end." Portino sipped his coffee.

She stood and grabbed her jacket from the back of her chair. There was something else going on here, and she couldn't put her finger on it yet. Lies were flying in all directions, and she wasn't even sure she'd heard them all yet. She pushed her right arm through her jacket sleeve. "Go home, Vic. Get some rest. We'll go over the details tomorrow morning with a clear head. We'll hold a briefing at Manhattan North. I'll send a message out."

Then she left the squad room, walked downstairs, and rushed past the raucous front desk area, where even at this hour, Upper West Siders were waiting to file complaints and report incidents. Outside, a cold, misty rain was falling. She turned up her collar. She had to get a winter coat, she reminded herself again as she crossed the dark street to where her car was parked in a long row of cops' cars.

She got in. It was after nine. She phoned McGowan's cell. He would be home, she imagined, and he wouldn't be happy to see her name pop up. Chances were she'd get an earful for standing up to him at the meeting. But he'd ordered her to keep him informed, and she was going to keep doing it.

When he answered, she said, "Sir, I've just seen the video footage from Sanchez's street the night he died. There are three persons of interest on that footage, but they're all too blurred to yield any clear facial images. The camera was defective."

"Shit."

"It was on a maintenance list."

"Goddammit."

"I think we should release it to the press anyway."

"Are you serious? Can't you imagine the headlines?"

"I can," she acknowledged calmly. "But if it comes out that we're sitting on it, it could be even more embarrassing for us. It could look like we're covering up. It could take the press's attention off the murders and put it on us."

He was quiet. She waited. She listened to him breathe. "What are you suggesting?" he asked.

"A news conference. We acknowledge the camera problem. We show the footage of the three persons of interest. We call for anyone who may have seen them to come forward."

"I'll think about it," was all he said. "I'll decide before tomorrow's briefing."

He hung up. She sat in the cold car in silence for several minutes. She considered going home, but she didn't want to go home. She wondered where Haggerty was right now. She pulled out of the parking space and headed toward the Ninety-Sixth Street transverse that crossed Central Park. Maybe, she thought, she could watch Sofia Reyes's autopsy, but when she got to Gambarin's office, Reyes's body had already been incised; her tissue samples taken; and her organs removed, examined, weighed, and returned to her body. She lay quiescent on a stainless table, and her incisions were being sewn together by Gambarin's autopsy assistant.

The medical examiner looked tired, and he skipped formalities as usual. "I estimate she died between six and nine PM on Monday night. She had a deep, ten-centimeter slash to the left side of her neck suggesting a right-handed killer, consistent with Sanchez's killer. The blade severed the sternocleidomastoid muscle; jugular vein; carotid sheath and artery; and everything down to the spine, trachea, and larynx. Her killer didn't take any chances. The official cause of death is exsanguination. She bled out. No surprise, I'm sure."

"Anything else you can tell me?"

"There was blunt trauma to her skull. The murderer hit her with a bronze statuette that was on the floor. CSU found her blood and hair on the base."

"He delivered the blow to her head before he slit her throat?"

"Yes."

Codella pictured the bronze statuette. "What do you make of the head blow?"

"I don't think he intended to kill her with the blunt force, if that's what you're asking. It was just one blow. She may have put up a fight and incited his anger, so he reached for something in order to subdue her. Her hands were tied so tightly that they were getting no circulation at all before she died. He punched her in the face, too. She had a fractured cheekbone."

"What else?"

"She was gagged, like Sanchez. I found the same kind of white cotton fibers in her mouth. CSU has them for analysis."

Codella thanked him and called CSU. Burke got on the line and confirmed that the fibers in Sanchez's mouth were identical to the fibers in Reyes's mouth. "They're just a cheap cotton, the kind in a household rag," he said. "So common they'd never be enough to convince a jury the cases are connected."

"We need more evidence to link the murders."

"I'm afraid you're not going to get it from forensics," he said. "Sorry."

When Codella got home, she rode the elevator with a woman doing late-night laundry, who said, "Hey, I really like your hair short like that."

Codella smiled. *Get cancer,* she wanted to say. *You can have it, too.* She got off on her floor. She stared at her neighbor Jean's door and wondered if she was home. But it was too late to knock on her door, and she wasn't really in the mood for conversation anyway. She let herself in and pulled off her boots in the vestibule. Then she flipped on the television, but all the basketball games had ended so she settled for a low backdrop of news while she cut up an apple.

She plopped onto her couch and stared at the talking head. Now two people were dead, and somehow the deaths were linked, and she wasn't going to solve either murder until she found that link. Hector Sanchez was turning out to have been a very complicated man. The so-called Savior of PS 777 had been quite the self-promoter, she reflected, running a major advertising campaign on the Upper West Side, starting parent groups, developing apps, and openly challenging Margery Barton's technology plans for the district. Were his efforts really driven by superior educational vision, or had he been motivated by hubris and self-interest? Was it possible, as Christine Donohue had suggested, that all his grand initiatives were nothing more than performance art choreographed to distract the world from what was really going on between himself and Dana Drew?

She took a bite of her apple. Milosz Jancek had called him a "good man," she recalled, someone who wanted to make children's lives better, but how could that be so when he had rushed out of school to go have sex with Drew and built his pretext on the sad circumstances of a child like Vondra Williams, a child who could have used a home visit from a concerned adult? How could you say he was a suitable protector of innocent children when he'd bullied his own assistant principal the same morning John Chambers's head was pushed into a toilet? Wasn't he really just a hypocrite? He had fired Eugene Bosco for closing his eyes in front of his class, but hadn't he done something even more egregious, using children for his own glorification?

Codella turned off the television. And how did Sofia Reyes factor into the equation? Had she been a coconspirator in his self-aggrandizement, or was she an innocent casualty? Codella remembered the flagrant positioning of the literacy consultant's body. In her mind, she could still clearly see the frozen fear in Reyes's cloudy eyes. She could imagine her terrifying last moments of life, during which she must have known she was going to die and couldn't do anything to alter the inevitable. Surely she would have pleaded. She would have screamed. But what chance had she had against her assailant?

If you had to come face to face with a would-be killer, Codella thought, cancer had to be a better adversary than whoever had murdered Sofia Reyes. At least cancer gave you time to assemble an army and launch some sort of counterattack. And even if you lost, you still might have a week, a month, a year to reflect on your life and catalog all the small joys you had ever experienced.

Codella remembered lying in the hospital and thinking about the simple perfection of Pink Lady apples and how she hoped she would get to taste them again when all the hideousness ended, if it ended in her favor. Sofia Reyes hadn't had that privilege. She'd had no army of doctors to lob chemo agents and monoclonal antibodies at her killer. She'd had to die alone, defenseless, with no time for last reflections.

THURSDAY

CHAPTER 40

Detectives Fisk and Nichols sat at the far end of the conference table, a nonverbal signal, Codella thought, that they did not intend to give her their full attention or allegiance. The uniformed officers had claimed the seats on the window side of the long table, and the precinct detectives—Muñoz, Haggerty, Portino, and Ragavan from the 171st and Colleary from the 145th—were sitting across from them. McGowan hovered near the door. Crammed into briefing room 2-B, they were an intimate yet uncomfortably segregated confederacy of crime solvers.

"Let's review the developments," she said from her seat at the head of the table. "Gambarin has confirmed that Sanchez and Reyes were both killed on Monday night within a few hours of each other. Reyes was gagged just like Sanchez, and the fibers found in her mouth match the fibers found in his mouth. That's a link, but it's the only link so far—that and the fact that they both looked like cast members in *The Passion of the Christ*. Beyond that, we have no physical evidence."

She picked up a dry-erase marker and stood in front of the whiteboard mounted on the wall behind the precinct detectives. She wrote *Hector Sanchez* in the middle of the board. Below his name she drew three spokes leading to the words *Red Cap, Overcoat,* and *Laundromat Guy.*

"We've established that these three individuals were in the vicinity of Sanchez's apartment before and during the time when he was murdered." She turned to Muñoz, and he played key sections of the footage on the flat-screen behind her chair and described the sequence of events. When he finished, she turned to McGowan.

McGowan cleared his throat. "We're going public with this footage," he said in his clipped, blue-collar accent.

"But you can't see anything," said Fisk. "Are you sure that's wise?"

"If we don't put it out there and the press gets hold of it, then they skewer us for the fuckup," said McGowan, taking full credit for the insight and the decision. Codella didn't care. By helping him, she had scored a victory and embedded whispers of doubt in his mind about Dan Fisk's judgment. "There's going to be a press conference at ten AM down at One Police Plaza," he continued. "We'll ask the public for help. That means the tip lines are going to be flooded, and most of what we get will be sheer crap, as you know, but you'll have to sift through it, so get ready for a chaotic day."

When he was done, she turned back to her diagram. On the left side of Sanchez's name, she wrote *Dana Drew*. "What everybody knows about her is that she has a child at the school, and she's contributed thousands of dollars to fund Sanchez's pet programs— Proud Families, Parents as Partners, Afterschool Apptitude. What they *don't* know is that she and her partner Jane Martin split up last year. They're living apart and *pretending* to still be a couple so Drew can avoid bad press while she's on Broadway. There are rumors that Drew and Sanchez were having an affair." She found Haggerty's blue eyes. "And now we know that the rumors were true."

She drew a line between the names *Hector Sanchez* and *Dana Drew*. She turned to Muñoz, and he flashed the photo of Sanchez and Drew on the front steps of Sanchez's building.

The image provoked suggestive whispers around the table, and Codella recalled the CSU guys' comments at the Sanchez crime scene. *She was hot in* Time's Up*! She's a lesbian. Yeah, a really hot lesbian.* She met the eyes of the gathered officers. "Enjoy your fantasies, gentlemen—and lady—but please keep them to yourselves. Let's remember that two people are dead. Our newest victim, Sofia Reyes, was a sixty-year-old mother, a career educator, and the killer beat her so brutally that her cheekbones were fractured. He cut her throat so deeply, it's unlikely she would have survived even with immediate medical attention."

She paused, watching the grins melt off the faces out of embarrassment more than sincere compassion. She continued, "If her killer is the same man who killed Sanchez—and the murders are undoubtedly connected—then he acted far more violently in his second crime. Why? Was he desperate? Does he feel violent aggression toward women? Is he sending a message to someone? These are the questions I need you to be thinking about. And let me be very clear about something. Nothing you've heard or seen in this room leaves this room. The press and the general public will not hear or see these details. They will not find out how the victims died, and they will not know that Drew had a sexual relationship with Sanchez. The only way they'll find that out is if *you* disclose confidential information, and if you do and I find out that you've done so, you can kiss your future good-bye."

The room grew quiet. "Yesterday I confronted Drew with the photo Detective Haggerty found. She admitted they'd been meeting secretly for months. Sanchez never went to Vondra Williams's apartment on Monday afternoon when he left the school at three twenty. In fact, he went straight home to meet Dana Drew. She was at his apartment from three thirty to five o'clock. She claims her driver picked her up in front of the building at five and that no one saw her leave."

"And we believe her?" asked Portino.

"She gave a formal statement at seven AM this morning. I'm inclined to think she's telling the truth," Codella said, "although we'll need to speak with her driver for confirmation. Supposedly she attended a performance at Town Hall that night. If that's true, then she didn't have time to kill Sanchez and cross the park to take care of Sofia Reyes too. Not to mention the fact that she's only about five foot two."

"She could have an accomplice," pointed out Haggerty. "She could have paid someone."

"That's true," conceded Codella. "She could certainly afford to. So she's still on our list of potential suspects."

"Who else is a possible suspect?" Frank Nichols asked.

Codella turned to the whiteboard and wrote another name. *Margery Barton*. "The district administrator lied about her whereabouts on Monday afternoon. We know she's determined for her district to adopt the technology program iAchieve from McFlieger-Walsh. We also know Sanchez opposed that adoption vigorously. He and Sofia Reyes were developing their own technology tools with a little company called Apptitude. And at the district principal's meeting on Monday, Sanchez voiced his objections to iAchieve. Margery Barton had a clear motive for wanting Sanchez and Reyes out of the picture."

Next, she wrote the words *McFlieger-Walsh*. "The publisher of iAchieve is part of Hemisphere Media Holdings. They've been trying to spin off McFlieger-Walsh for a year now, but there are no takers. The company has a tarnished reputation to repair—they engaged in unethical sales tactics—and there are millions of dollars on the line for them."

Then she jotted the name *Chip Dressler* below *McFlieger-Walsh*. "Dressler is the senior vice president of sales for McFlieger-Walsh, and he is personally overseeing the New York iAchieve campaign. He gave a presentation on Monday morning to the principals in Margery Barton's district. That's where Sanchez publicly questioned the integrity of the program. I think we have to consider the possibility that Dressler could be involved."

"Working alone, with Barton, or with McFlieger-Walsh." Haggerty completed her thought.

"Right." Beneath Barton's name Codella wrote the name *Jane Martin*. "Martin claims she drove to her studio in Red Hook on Monday night, but she couldn't produce any names to verify that alibi. When I saw Drew on Tuesday night at the theater, she had a deep bruise on her bicep. When I spoke to her yesterday, she admitted that Martin put it there. Martin, it seems, is the classic jealous partner. She accused Drew of breaking off their relationship because she was in love with Sanchez. She got a little angry, held onto her arm a little too tightly."

Haggerty raised his hand and spoke. "Martin's jealousy might be a motive for killing Sanchez, but why would she go all the way across town and kill Reyes, too?"

Codella nodded. "For that matter, why would any of these suspects bother to take out Reyes? Once Sanchez is out of the picture, she ceases to have a role at the school anyway. She was just a paid consultant."

Now Muñoz spoke up. "Maybe the same teachers who hated Sanchez hated her for helping him."

Codella turned to the whiteboard and wrote *PS 777 teachers*. "Detective Muñoz brings up a good point. The other potential suspects in this are the 777 teachers who hated Sanchez. And there were plenty of them. We keep hearing that teachers don't kill, but is that true?"

She capped the dry-erase marker and set it on the ledge below the whiteboard. "All we know is that the fibers in the two victims' mouths matched, and it's next to impossible for their biblical death poses to be coincidental. We need to find the link between them, a link a grand jury will buy. We're going to turn over every stone we can today. We're going to find the link."

She paused for her words to sink in. Then she looked at Fisk. "I need their phone records meticulously analyzed. When did they last speak or text? Were they involved in something that got them into danger?"

She turned to Muñoz. "Go see the security staff at Two Penn Plaza where McFlieger-Walsh is headquartered. Be discreet. And go to Dana Drew's garage, the Rapid Park on Ninety-Seventh Street. If Martin went to Red Hook on Monday night, she used Drew's car. Find out if that car left the garage."

"Should I talk to her driver too?"

"Yes. Make sure Drew's story checks out."

She looked at Ragavan and Nichols. "Go back to the school. Interview teachers, parents, staff. Find out everything you can about Sofia Reyes. We don't know enough about that woman. I want a profile."

Finally she turned to Haggerty, who had cut through Dana Drew's lies with one quick sweep of Sanchez's laptop. "Get back on his computer," she said. "Tell me everything that's happened on that machine in the last few weeks. If something else is there, find it."

She looked at her watch. "I'll be back from One Police Plaza in two hours."

CHAPTER 41

Marva Thomas retreated to her office as soon as the morning surge of students into the building had subsided. She stared at the large Dunkin' Donuts coffee Milosz had left on her desk along with the *New York Post*. When she read the headline, she felt an inappropriate reaction—relief. Sofia Reyes had not callously ignored her calls for help on Tuesday. Dead bodies didn't return calls for help.

She sat and sipped the coffee. Milosz had added half-and-half instead of milk, and although she never allowed herself such an indulgence, she realized how much she enjoyed it. She had just begun to read the front-page story when Delia knocked on her door.

"It's Aaliyah Ajam, Miss Thomas. She just tripped over something in that pile," she pointed toward the front hall, "and her knee landed on a picture frame. She got a big cut. I took her to the nurse. We gotta move that stuff. It's not safe there. Someone's gonna call the fire department pretty soon."

Marva nodded. "I'll be right there." Then she watched the overweight safety officer lumber out. Delia was trying to be helpful, she knew, and she supposed she should be grateful, but all she felt was annoyance. Even Delia was coaching her. Even Delia doubted her judgment.

The entire left wall of the school entrance hall was covered by children's crayon drawings, paintings, cards, and handwritten letters to Sanchez. Piled on the buffed linoleum floor were tributes large and small: stuffed animals, dolls, flowers, books, toys, Yankees caps and jerseys, baseballs, beads, crosses, Bibles, and other mementos. Marva's eyes fell on a letter from a first-grade student, and she quickly turned away. She didn't want to read heartfelt messages about a man she had loathed. He had never included her in any of his grand schemes. He had wanted all possible glory to accrue to him. He was like an angry overseer, and she was just one more slave in his metaphorical cotton field.

But now she was free of him, they all were, and as unchristian as the thought might be, she wasn't sad that he was dead. And removing that oversized memorial mound from the hallways would give her nothing but pleasure. "Call Mr. Jancek and Mr. Rerecic," she instructed Janisa. "Have them meet me at the front doors."

When they arrived, she pointed to the piled-high mementoes. "This is a safety hazard. We need to move these things to a less trafficked area and clean up the broken glass."

"Where would you like us to take them?" asked Mr. Jancek.

Anywhere I don't have to see them, she thought. "A corner in the library," she suggested. "Set it up in there."

He nodded and told Mr. Rerecic to bring a cart. Then he leaned toward Marva. "Is there anything else I can do?"

She stared at his blue eyes and couldn't deny the obvious any longer. Milosz cared for her in *that* way. She had recognized the fact for months, she supposed, and just hadn't acknowledged it. What did it say about her that a custodian felt entitled to be interested in her? What did it say about her that she hadn't—as Hector had instructed—nipped his smiles, pats, and Dunkin' Donuts overtures in the bud as soon as they'd begun?

He continued to smile, and if she was honest, she enjoyed his attention. No, he wasn't conventionally attractive, but he wasn't unattractive either. He was tall and strong, and he had a lively glint in his eyes. Most women's husbands weren't any more attractive than he was. What made any man and woman attractive to each other, she supposed, was the invisible alchemy of their private interactions.

She risked a return smile, and she imagined what might happen—what she might *want* to happen—if they were alone. She imagined him reaching up to stroke her hair and gently touch the side of her face with his calloused fingers in a way no one ever touched her. She imagined him leaning close enough that she could inhale his cologne as he pressed her head against his chest. The fantasy set off an unexpected sensation in the pit of her stomach that traveled lower and caused a pleasant drawing sensation between her legs. She swallowed and glanced over at Delia twenty feet away, but Delia was not even looking at her.

Marva knew she should walk away this instant, but she felt caught in the gravitational pull of the imagined human contact. She had not been made love to by a man in many years, and she had not even fantasized about a real man in almost as many. Her intermittent fantasies, alone in her bed when her mother was sleeping in the bedroom across the hall, involved handsome male actors making love to equally beautiful actresses. These were the fantasies that accompanied her occasional solo acts of sexual gratification, and these stolen interludes had represented the extent of her sex life for so long that the thought of a true, intimate encounter was as excruciating as it was compelling.

Milosz, she realized, might actually want her in just the ways she needed to be wanted. She forced herself to turn away from him. She walked self-consciously across the hall to the office—aware that he was watching her—and paused in front of Hector's empty office. As she stared at his vacant desk, an unwanted insight took her by surprise. She had hated Hector expressly because so many parents and children had loved him. She, too, had wanted someone to love her. And now she was ready to accept a custodian's love, if he decided to offer more than coffee.

CHAPTER 42

When Muñoz left the McFlieger-Walsh headquarters at Two Penn Plaza, he took the subway back uptown and walked to Dana Drew's parking garage. The weekday morning chaos of a Manhattan Rapid Park garage had ended, which meant that all the Upper West Siders who reverse commuted to Westchester or New Jersey or Connecticut had picked up their cars and made for the West Side Highway two hours ago. Only one black Lexus idled in front of the exit, and the driver was pointing to his door and berating a Hispanic attendant.

Muñoz watched the familiar little garage drama play out. The driver insisted the scratch hadn't been there yesterday. The garage attendant acted as if he had no idea what had happened. "Get me the manager," the driver finally insisted.

The attendant stepped past Muñoz and went into a little room the size of a ticket booth, and two minutes later, an older, smiling Hispanic man came over. He had shoe-polish-black hair and a meticulously groomed moustache. He stared up at the taller driver and waited.

The driver pointed. The manager looked. The driver said, "Your guys did this."

The manager bent down to touch the scratch. "We can touch that up for you."

"I don't want it *touched up*. I want it looking like it did before."

"We can do that."

"What? With spray paint?"

It went on for several minutes before the driver got in his car and drove away without filling out any forms, knowing that he was just going to have to live with the inevitable nicks and scratches that came with parking a car in New York City.

The manager turned to Muñoz and shrugged. Muñoz followed him back to his little office and showed his shield. "You've got a car in here that belongs to Dana Drew, the actress."

"A Volvo." He spoke English with a thick Spanish accent.

Muñoz switched to Spanish. *"¿Cuánto tiempo hace desde que salió del garaje?"*

The manager thought about it. *"Dos semanas. Quizás tres."*

"¿Estás cierto?" Muñoz asked, and the manager proceeded to explain how cars that didn't leave the garage every day went into a long-term section on the bottom level and that in order to get a car out of long-term, the tenant had to call and ask for the car at least twelve hours in advance. *"Tenemos un log."* He pointed to a tattered logbook lying on the desk behind him. *"La señorita Drew no ha pedido su carro. Estoy muy cierto."*

"¿Y la señorita Martin?" he asked.

"Ni ella tampoco," he said.

Muñoz left and texted Codella with the news. The car hadn't left the garage. If Martin had gone to Red Hook on Monday night, she hadn't used the Volvo. Now he just had to find Dana Drew's driver and confirm her Monday night alibi.

CHAPTER 43

Codella peeked into the pressroom packed with noisy reporters. A few minutes later, Hanson spelled out the plan. There would be no denials, no defensiveness—just the facts and a reasoned explanation of why the camera had failed at such an inauspicious time.

"The last thing we need is someone writing an exposé on the pros and cons of NYPD surveillance technology," said the commissioner.

"Right," said Hanson, "which is why we'll dispense with the facts and move the focus back to the investigation." He looked at McGowan and Codella. "We've got edited clips of the three persons of interest. Which one of you wants to walk them through?"

Codella looked at McGowan.

McGowan said, "This is Codella's case. She'll do it."

Hanson nodded. "Make it quick. Walk them through the key moments. Ask the public for help."

She nodded. *And take the heat*, she thought, *if there's heat to be taken.*

Hanson checked his watch and drank from his Poland Springs bottle. At 10:00 AM sharp, he approached the podium, and the clicking of cameras commenced. He raised his hands for silence. "Good morning, ladies and gentlemen. We're going to get started right now. I have a brief statement to make. Then we'd like to show you some surveillance footage taken near the scene of Hector Sanchez's murder. Please save your questions until the very end of this press conference."

He scanned the audience nodding here and there to familiar reporters. "On Monday, between the hours of five and seven PM, Hector Sanchez, the principal of PS 777 in Upper Manhattan, was murdered in his West 112th Street apartment. On that same evening, we now know, Sofia Reyes, a literacy consultant at PS 777, was also murdered in her Upper East Side apartment. Both murders remain unsolved."

Hanson took a quick sip of water before he continued. "A street surveillance camera located on the corner of Frederick Douglass Boulevard and 112th Street has yielded images of three persons of interest near Hector Sanchez's apartment between the hours of five and nine PM on Monday. We would like to share these images with you and the public in an effort to identify these individuals. However, we must also acknowledge that the resolution—the clarity—of these images is marred by the fact that the camera lens was out of focus at the time the images were recorded."

Hands shot up, but Hanson shook his head. "First let me say a word about the camera. It is an older fixed-image model installed in the mid-1990s. We don't know why it failed, but there are several possible explanations. Vandalism is one of them. In the course of a year, the NYPD surveillance cameras are damaged by vandalism an average of three hundred times. Inclement weather may also have been a factor. In the past two months, the city has suffered the effects of three hurricanes that caused severe wind and flooding in the city. In Manhattan alone, there are more than five thousand public security cameras exposed to the elements twenty-four-seven, so things like this are going to happen. Even the most durable cameras do break down. The NYPD has a schedule of regular maintenance for these cameras, and this particular camera was only weeks away from regular maintenance. The timing of the failure is unfortunate, particularly to the families of the victims who deserve a speedy road to justice for their lost loved ones. It is also frustrating to the detectives who are working day and night to solve these homicides as quickly as possible. A full investigation into the causes of the failure will be conducted, a thorough review of camera maintenance procedures will take place, and the results will be shared with the media and the public." Hanson paused again. "But right now we need to focus the public's attention on the progress we have made and the help we need to find whoever is responsible for these crimes. As I mentioned earlier, we want to show you the surveillance footage. This footage will be available on our website as well. I'm going to turn the microphone over to Detective Claire Codella from

Manhattan North Homicide, who is going to share these images with you and explain what they show."

Codella walked to the podium and waited for the first clip to play on the flat-screens on either side of the room. "We know from the autopsy results that Hector Sanchez was murdered between the hours of five and seven PM At 5:27 PM, the individual you see here in a red baseball cap turned onto his block. We believe him to be a male Caucasian, approximately five foot eleven. His image was captured again just after six PM when he left the victim's street."

She motioned for the next clip. As it played, she said, "This individual turned onto Sanchez's block at 5:54 PM He appears to be wearing a dark overcoat. We believe him to be a dark-skinned Hispanic or African American man, and it may be that his presence is coincidental, but we would like to identify and speak with him."

As the third clip began, she said, "The camera also recorded a potential witness inside the Wash and Wear Laundromat at the corner of Frederick Douglass and 112th Street. This individual entered the laundromat before three thirty and remained there until almost eight PM We don't have enough visual information to determine the ethnicity, age, or gender of this potential witness, but we are asking this person or anyone who was in the Wash and Wear Laundromat on Monday afternoon and may have seen this person to come forward."

The clip ended, and Hanson joined her at the podium. "Let me add to what Detective Codella has said. We urge the public to come forward with any information about these persons of interest. We also ask that anyone possessing still or video images of this area taken Monday evening share those images with us. I'll take your questions now."

"What about Reyes's apartment? Is there footage there, too?"

"The camera nearest her building has not turned up potential suspects."

"Could the murderer be responsible for the damage to the camera?"

"There is no evidence to suggest that."

"Why didn't you come forward with these images sooner?"

"We've only just completed our analysis." Hanson pointed to another hand.

"Are you saying this is the only evidence you have at the moment?"

Hanson deferred to Codella. "No," she said, "that's not at all what we're saying."

"Then what other evidence do you have?"

"We're not going to share details of the ongoing investigation."

"You said that at the last press conference. Either you have something or you don't."

Codella looked at her watch. *What did she really have?* she thought as the questions continued to land at her feet and test her mind's ability to pass and dribble faster than it had for a year, and she was relieved when she was finally back in her car and speeding up the FDR Drive. Months had passed since she had felt every synapse fire in concert with one purpose only: to collect the fragments of truth and connect them before a trail grew cold and a killer escaped detection permanently.

During her treatment, she had tried to stay sharp by focusing on little mysteries to solve in the hospital. Was her roommate an attorney or a librarian? What was her diagnosis? Could answers be ascertained through deduction using clues the roommate gave during phone calls, in the television programming she preferred, by the visitors she entertained, through hints her doctors dropped during bedside visits? Data were plentiful: test results reported by overly loud interns, a new drug introduced by the night nurse, temperature readings, questions about pain level, sleeping patterns, swelling and inflammation. There was no privacy in a hospital room. You could gather abundant facts and details about your neighbor, but the copious information led to no satisfying conclusions. All you ever discovered was that this roommate had just been diagnosed, that one was nearing the end of treatment, and that the next one was going to need a stem cell transplant. The knowledge only added to her own hopelessness, and in the end, her brain couldn't even focus on the details for long anyway with so many toxic chemicals coursing through her system. Now her brain felt sharp, but was it sharp enough?

CHAPTER 44

Haggerty dialed her cell from memory.

"Codella." Her voice sounded brittle and hard through the wireless connection.

He wanted to say her name. *Claire.* He wanted to say, *Don't worry. You'll solve this.* But she wouldn't want his reassurance, as much as she might need it. Instead, he said, "Guess who the savior was Skyping with at five twenty-three on Monday evening?"

Codella's voice snapped to attention. "He was on Skype?"

"Yeah. With none other than Reyes."

"Jesus! How the hell did you figure that out?"

"It wasn't hard. The Skype icon's on his desktop so I clicked. His computer remembers his passwords. He wasn't a very careful guy. I checked his contacts and his call log."

He waited. He could hear her brain chew the data. "His neighbor was in his apartment a little after five that day," she said. "His computer was still in its case near the door at that point, and he was dressed in his jeans and a T-shirt. It was right after Drew left his apartment, because he'd climbed into the jeans to walk her to the door. He must have grabbed the computer out of the bag the minute the neighbor left and put it on the ottoman where it was on Tuesday morning. That means he must have been wearing his T-shirt and jeans when he Skyped—I can't see him tearing back down to boxers to video chat with a sixty-year-old literacy consultant—which suggests that he was dressed when his murderer arrived."

"So his murderer probably undressed him," agreed Haggerty. "The way I see it, his killer must have knocked on the door while he and Reyes were Skyping. In which case, Sofia Reyes might have seen or heard his murderer."

"And that's our link," she said, and all hardness suddenly drained from her voice. She was with him in the moment, like old times, like nothing bad had ever happened between them.

"Exactly," he said.

"How long was that call?"

"Twelve minutes."

"So he was still alive at five thirty-five. And assuming the killer knocked on his door while he was Skyping, Sanchez might have told Reyes to hang on. He might have gone to the door and let his killer in without the killer knowing he was being watched by another set of eyes. The killer must have waited for him to end that call. And that means Sanchez wasn't reading the parent blog that we saw open on his laptop Monday morning. The killer opened that blog site."

"There's something else," said Haggerty. "That photo of Sanchez and Drew. I know how it got on his computer. It was e-mailed to him last week."

"By whom?"

"That I can't say. Whoever sent it used an account with bogus contact info."

"Was there a message?"

"Yes, and it's a little enigmatic."

"Read it to me."

"It's four lines. Four questions. Like a riddle." He read the message slowly.

"*Savior or secret sinner? Proud principal or proud playmate? Exemplary or unacceptable? iAchieve or Apptitude?*" He paused. "What do you make of it?"

She was silent for a moment. "It's a threat."

"A threat?"

"The words *Savior or sinner* are posing a challenge," she explained. "They're asking him does he want to stay the 'Savior of PS 777' in people's eyes, or does he want his sin—his affair with Drew—to be exposed? *Proud Principal or proud playmate* is a reference to his Proud Families at PS 777 campaign. Right now he gets to be the proud principal, but if the photo is leaked, his whole campaign looks like a joke. He looks like a sleazebag."

"What about *Exemplary or unacceptable?*"

"That's a reference to the scoring scale he's been using to rate his teachers. Exemplary is the top rating on the scale. Apparently, no teachers got that grade, no matter how hard they worked. Most teachers got his lowest ranking—unacceptable. I think whoever wrote this was saying, *Change your grades or we'll change your image.*"

Haggerty stared at the message in his hand. "So the last line is telling him to get behind iAchieve?"

"Exactly. And what's curious to me is that he got this warning a week ago, but he didn't change his behavior at all. He went to that principal's meeting and publically challenged Dressler about iAchieve. He fired Bosco, berated Thomas, and left school early to be the 'secret sinner.' He was either stupid or supremely confident that he could deny the truth behind the photo."

"So what now?" asked Haggerty.

"We keep looking beneath the lies. I need to pay another visit to Barton."

He opened his mouth to say, "I'll come with you," but she had already clicked off, and he was right where he'd been before, on the sideline, trying to get back in her game.

CHAPTER 45

Codella got to the District 124 office just after noon. "Detective, please have a seat." Barton greeted her hospitably enough, but her slightly brittle tone and tight smile suggested she was anything but glad to see her. "I am so saddened by Sofia's death. I remember her from our teaching days. She was always a powerhouse. A lovely person. A dedicated educator. I hope you find whoever's responsible for this and lock them up for life."

"We'll find whoever it is." Codella took the proffered seat. "I have a few more questions for you."

"Of course." Barton sat behind her desk.

"Why did you hire Hector Sanchez? Why him and not someone more tried and true?"

"The honest answer?"

"What other kind would I want?"

"I couldn't get anyone else to step in," Barton acknowledged matter-of-factly.

"Why not?"

"Well, you have to understand, a principal's reputation is based on his or her students' test scores. The scores at PS 777 have been low for some time. Any established principal taking that job is gambling with his career. The only principal who'd jump at that position would be a brand new candidate with no record to ruin."

"Based on my conversations, some teachers loved Sanchez but many more disliked him intensely. How did parents feel about him?"

"They adored him." She smiled. "Wouldn't you love someone who puts your family photos on a bus stop and gives you donuts and free English lessons every week? He should have been a politician, not a school bureaucrat."

"How did he feel about iAchieve?"

Barton frowned. "What do you mean?"

"Did he like the program?"

"Teachers like programs, Detective. Principals just care about whether they're effective or not."

"Did Sanchez think iAchieve would be an effective program?"

"No, but his belief was based on prejudice rather than careful analysis."

"How so?"

"He didn't really study the data. He jumped to a conclusion. As I said yesterday, he was a new principal. He wanted to run his own show. For him, the world began and ended with PS 777, and he didn't want anything imposed on his little world—even something with the potential to be game changing. Hector didn't have an open mind. That was his weakness as a school leader. I had to fight him on that. I have to think about more than just PS 777."

"What exactly did he say about iAchieve at the principals' meeting on Monday?"

"I don't remember exactly, but he posed some questions about the validity of the research behind it—the length of the studies and whether they were conducted by an independent research firm."

"And were they?"

Codella detected no defensiveness in Barton's response. "Of course they were. I wasn't about to accept McFlieger-Walsh's own data. I insisted on a pilot in my own schools before I'd even con- sider the program for New York City schoolchildren." Barton folded her exquisitely manicured hands on top of her desk. "I don't have the habit of accepting what people tell me at face value any more than you probably do, Detective, but neither am I closed minded to the possibilities. Hector just didn't want to acknowledge what iAchieve can do."

"What can it do?"

"In a nutshell? Level the playing field for students of many backgrounds and ability levels."

"Level it how?"

Barton leaned across her desk. "In my district alone, I have twenty-six *thousand* students, Detective. They're from sixty different countries of origin, and fifty-five percent of them are English learners. I have fourteen thousand students who qualify for Title I funding—that's more than *half*—which means that they live below the poverty line. In many cases, they have just one parent who's either on welfare or working two or three jobs, and that parent either has no time or energy or inclination to read books with their child before bed or help with homework or go to a museum. Many of them live in public housing projects and homeless shelters. But somehow I'm supposed to educate all of them. I'm supposed to get them all to pass an annual proficiency test. And now with the Common Core Standards, I have to make the curriculum even more rigorous so they're college and career ready by the time they graduate." She laughed at the absurdity. "And I have to do this with a workforce of underexperienced teachers, dead wood—let's admit it—and maverick principals like Sanchez who think they know what's best for their schools and don't want to look across the whole district at what the data tell us."

"And iAchieve is the solution?"

"I'm not naïve, Detective. I know there's no silver bullet. But it's motivating individualized instruction. It's data driven. It tells teachers exactly what each student needs. It takes the decision making out of teachers' hands—and quite frankly, contrary to what he thought and what you may believe, sometimes that *is* a good thing."

"How does it work?"

"Every student gets a tablet. Every student gets assignments based on his or her needs and abilities. All the instruction is aligned to the standards. The software is completely adaptive, and students can't help but make progress over time because the program constantly provides remediation based on their mistakes. With this program, you don't need an army of Sofia Reyeses trying to train teachers who can't or don't want to change their ways. And it provides a level of differentiation that goes beyond anything even the best-trained teacher can give in a classroom of thirty students with grossly different needs. This is the future, like it or not. Technology finally ensures the abolition of one-size-fits-all instruction."

"But does it work?" asked Codella.

"Yes, it works. We've done a pilot in four schools, and the data look excellent."

"It must be incredibly expensive with such a major investment in hardware as well as software."

Barton smiled knowingly. "You never get something for nothing, do you? But in this case, I have something McFlieger-Walsh wants, too. They need a big district to take on this program. And they'll give me significant discounts to make that happen. They know once a big urban district like New York embraces iAchieve, more big districts will follow. I have bargaining chips, and I intend to use them. It's a win-win."

Codella nodded. Barton certainly made a convincing and passionate case. "How do these programs get selected?"

"There's an adoption committee. Teachers, administrators, parents. They all get a vote."

"Was anyone from PS 777 on that committee?"

"There's someone from every school."

"Was Christine Donohue one of the committee members?"

"Yes, Chris is on the committee."

Codella stared at the administrator's perfect nails, her bright gold earrings, her flawlessly highlighted hair with not a strand of gray. "Was she handpicked to spread the good news about iAchieve—and spread some rumors about Sanchez to neutralize his resistance to the program?"

Barton frowned. "That's a pretty serious accusation." She sat back in her Aeron chair. "If I did what you're suggesting, then I shouldn't be sitting in this office. I shouldn't be making the educational decisions for sixty thousand New York City schoolchildren." Her eyes narrowed. "I want iAchieve for all the right reasons. Yes, turning failing schools into successful ones will help my career, but that's just the incidental reward."

Codella had to admit that if the woman was lying, she was a convincing liar. But then, she already knew the administrator was capable of deception. Everybody in this case seemed pretty skilled in that department.

Barton said, "Every superintendent wants committee members who will support them. Obviously I wasn't going to knowingly choose someone without an open mind. That said, I didn't ask Chris Donohue to be a rabble rouser."

"Maybe you didn't have to ask her," responded Codella. "Maybe you just had to let her know how much you wanted the program."

Annoyance spread across Barton's face as she checked her diamond-studded watch. "Now I'm starting to think you're on a fishing expedition, Detective. I assure you, there are no fish in this sea. My policies and my interest in iAchieve for the district are not responsible for Hector Sanchez's death. With all due respect, you're wasting my time with this line of questioning, and worse, you're wasting taxpayers' time. You should be somewhere else looking for relevant information." She stood. "Now I do have another meeting that's about to begin."

"Sit down, Dr. Barton. We're not done here."

Barton's condescension turned to caution. She returned to her seat apprehensively.

"Why don't you quit wasting *my* time and tell me where you were on Monday afternoon, because you certainly weren't here."

And then Barton laughed so hard that her eyes began to water. "Is that what this suspicion is all about? The fact that I didn't admit to you that I slipped out of my office Monday afternoon to go shopping? Oh, Detective, we could have saved each other so much time if you'd just come to the point."

"You should have come to the point on Monday when I asked."

Then Barton moistened her lower lip with the tip of her tongue on an intake of breath. "I just didn't think it mattered."

"This is a murder investigation, Dr. Barton. Every piece of information matters to me."

Barton erased her smile. "You're right, and I apologize."

"You say you left to go shopping?"

"My husband and I were meeting each other downtown at Cipriani at six for a fundraiser. He called me that morning and told me we were going to be at a table with the chairmen of the boards of Sloan Kettering and Weil Cornell. I didn't feel dressed up enough for that, and there was no time to go back to Brooklyn and change, so I thought I'd get a nice silk scarf to, you know, *enhance* the ensemble." Her smile returned.

"Where did you go?"

"Saks."

"And you can prove this, I assume? You have a receipt?"

Barton shook her head. "I didn't find anything there so I walked up to Bergdorf's."

"So you have that receipt?"

"No," Barton said. "I didn't find anything there either. There was one nice Roberto Cavalli scarf, but it was just not quite the right color."

"I see." Codella had heard hundreds of alibis over the years, and this one, she guessed, had been carefully but naïvely crafted so as to be foolproof. Only it wasn't, of course. Few false alibis were. "Okay," she said, "then tell me the approximate times you arrived at each store and which entrances you used."

And now Barton stared at her quizzically. "Why?"

Codella pulled out her iPhone to take notes. "So we can confirm your alibi."

"Is that really necessary?"

"Yes, I think it is."

"But how can you?"

Codella shrugged. "You don't enter Saks or Bergdorf's without getting your picture taken. We'll call up the security footage and confirm your whereabouts, and then I won't have to bother you anymore." She smiled. "Did you use the Fifth Avenue entrance at Saks?"

Barton continued to stare.

Codella waited several seconds while the administrator's thoughts brewed into a thick black espresso of panic. Finally, she stared the woman straight in the eyes and said, "You didn't go to Saks or Bergdorf's on Monday, did you?"

Barton pressed her lips together and breathed deeply through her nostrils. She raised her chin gamely, but she couldn't control the small-muscle twitches around her mouth. Codella sensed her panic. She watched Barton glance at her arms. Right now, she guessed, Barton was feeling as if an enormous gravitational force had suddenly immobilized her limbs. Codella remembered how paralyzed she had felt when she had been cornered by cancer, as if every blood cell in her veins, arteries, and capillaries were a microscopic black hole containing entire compressed galaxies worth of terror. Barton's eyes were closed, and Codella waited for her to decide her next move. Finally, she opened them again and said in a vulnerable voice, "I'm a married woman, Detective. And I have a career that I love."

"And you have secrets," said Codella evenly, "that don't conform with either of those circumstances."

Barton nodded ever so slightly. "Where I went had nothing to do with Hector's death, nothing to do with my commitment to the children of New York City."

Hadn't Codella heard that same argument from Dana Drew yesterday? "I'll have to judge that for myself," she said.

"May I count on your discretion?"

Codella found herself savoring the condescending administrator's reversal of fortune. "I can only keep secrets," she said, "if they don't involve criminality and they don't interfere with my investigation. You'll have to take your chances, but one more lie and I warn you, I *will* see through it, and when I do, I'll haul you to a police station for an official statement so fast your head will be spinning. I have a crime to solve, and you have already wasted quite enough of my time."

Barton again insisted, "I had nothing to do with Hector's or Sofia's deaths."

"I'll give you one more chance to tell me where you were between three and six PM on Monday."

"I was in a hotel room."

"With whom?"

"Chip Dressler."

"The McFlieger-Walsh executive."

"That's right."

"And you're having a sexual relationship with him."

Barton didn't answer.

"Which is unethical," Codella continued, "because you are a Department of Education official and he represents iAchieve, which constitutes an egregious conflict of interest. Is that correct?"

"That's correct." Barton managed to hold her head erect, although the muscles around her mouth continued to twitch nervously.

"I assume Mr. Dressler will confirm all this?"

"He won't be happy about it, but yes, I assume he won't lie. Please, neither one of us had anything to do with these murders, and this could be very damaging to my marriage and to my plans for the district."

"Conflicts of interest usually come back to bite us," observed Codella.

Barton now looked pale and shell-shocked.

"I'll have to confirm your alibi."

"I know." Her usually resonant voice was a whisper.

"I assume you can give me Mr. Dressler's phone number?"

"Of course."

Codella picked up the phone on Margery's desk. "I'm ready."

"You're calling him now?" She sounded like a sixteen-year-old caught by her parents in a lie.

"Well, I certainly don't intend to give you the opportunity to prep him for my questions. The number, Dr. Barton."

CHAPTER 46

Dressler climbed out of the limo while the driver got his bags from the trunk. He pressed a twenty into the driver's palm and walked straight to curbside check-in where he flashed another twenty to get the immediate attention of a skycap.

When his luggage was tagged, he went inside and got in the TSA precheck security line, where he didn't have to strip off his jacket, belt, and shoes or even remove his laptop from its case before he placed them on the conveyor belt for X-raying. He stepped into the explosive detection scanner the same way he'd stepped into the hot shower yesterday afternoon to wash Margery off his body before the iAchieve demo, and as the imperceptible puff of air surrounded his body, he imagined his New York disguise melt away like stage makeup.

When he emerged on the other side of the mass spectrometer, he envisioned his core identities reemerge: Chip Dressler, devoted father; Chip Dressler, husband of Charlene, the former beauty queen; Chip Dressler, deacon of the United Methodist Church of Greater Dallas. These were his true roles in life, he told himself. These were the roles that meant something to him. The role of sales executive, with all the false charm and compromise it demanded, was only a means to his true purpose in life. Charlene. His son. His future children to come. He grabbed his laptop off the conveyor belt and started toward the gate.

He spotted an empty seat near a charging station and plugged in his phone and computer. Forty more minutes and he would be five miles high in the air, in the dead zone between one life and another. It was there that Chip Dressler completed his transformation, clearing his brain and shifting one foreground for another. He sat back in his vinyl chair and closed his eyes. He jumped when he heard his ring tone. He looked at the number. It was Margery. Why was she calling him now? Why couldn't she leave him be? But he swiped his touch screen and said, "Hey, what's up?"

"Mr. Dressler?" came the unfamiliar voice.

"Who's this?"

"Detective Claire Codella with the NYPD. I suggest you find a place where you can speak freely."

"What's this about?" Dressler snapped, now angry that he had picked up the phone.

"It's about Hector Sanchez."

"What does he have to do with me?"

"That's what I'd like to know."

"I have nothing to do with him."

"You made a presentation that Mr. Sanchez attended the morning of his death."

"So?"

"So I'd like to know where you were that afternoon."

"Are you suggesting I had something to do with his death?"

"I'm just asking a question."

"I went several places. I was out and about."

"*Out and about* is a vague and therefore suspicious answer, Mr. Dressler."

The preboarding announcement blared as Dressler debated what to say next. Finally, the voice on the other end said, "Good. You're considering your next words carefully. That's very wise of you under the circumstances."

Dressler sighed. Picking up the call had been a huge mistake. He should have let it go, and there was only one reason a detective could be phoning from Margery's office. "She told you, didn't she?"

"Where are you right now?"

"About to board a plane at LaGuardia."

"You'll regret it if you do. Right now, I just want answers to my questions. But I'm becoming a pretty impatient detective, and I won't be as forgiving if you make me chase you. I suggest you get yourself to Margery Barton's office as soon as possible. I'll give you half an hour."

She hung up on him. He heard the boarding call for first class, and he stood for several seconds debating his next move. His bag was on that plane. He'd told Charlene he was coming. But there was no choice here. He left the terminal and headed toward the taxi stand.

CHAPTER 47

Margery Barton felt her throat constricting as Codella hung up and turned back to her. She tried without success to swallow. She realized she wasn't breathing, that she hadn't inhaled during Codella's entire phone call with Chip. Her ears felt ultrasensitive, and she almost jumped when the detective turned back to her and said, "Okay, Superintendent, tell me how it went down, and you better hope he gives me the same story when he gets here. Where did the two of you meet?"

"The Mandarin in the Time Warner building."

"What floor?"

"Fifteen."

"Room number?"

"I don't remember. Wait. 1520, I think."

"Did you eat anything?"

"No."

"Drink?"

"Champagne. In the room."

"What kind?"

"Veuve Clicquot rosé."

"Did you receive any phone calls while you were there?"

"My phone was off."

"What about him?"

"No."

"Did he make any calls?"

"No."

"When did you leave his room?"

"Around five twenty."

"Is that the last time you've seen or spoken to him?"

Margery paused. Another lie would only compound her problems. "No," she admitted.

"Go on."

"We met yesterday as well."

"For the same purposes?"

"Yes."

"What time was that?"

"Around two."

"Did you discuss Hector Sanchez at all?"

She paused again. The answer was obviously yes, and she didn't want to confess it because she would have to go into details and then she would look guilty.

Codella leaned across the desk so that the arms of her leather jacket were only inches from Margery's face. "I'm this close," the detective held up her thumb and index finger less than half an inch apart, "to demanding a formal statement from you."

"I panicked," Margery said. "I told Chip I'd lied to you on Monday. I was afraid you'd find out. So we made up the scarf alibi—no, I made it up myself—and there's nothing more to it. I swear. Hector and I didn't always see eye to eye. It's true I wasn't very happy with his performance as a principal, and if I could take back his appointment, I probably would, but I didn't have anything to do with his death. I only lied to keep you from finding out about my . . ." She trailed off.

CHAPTER 48

Chip Dressler got to the district office twenty minutes later. Codella had expected to conduct a standard verification of alibis, Dressler in a separate room from Barton telling his version of the Monday afternoon events so that Codella could judge the veracity of their separate claims. But as soon as Dressler appeared in Barton's doorway, everything became instantly more complicated. Dressler, she observed, was African American, a fact she had not detected from his voice, and he stood before her in a dark cashmere coat that at once made her think of the figure in the blurry street cam footage she had replayed for the room full of reporters at One Police Plaza that morning.

Dressler traded quick glances with Barton, and he didn't look pleased. Codella asked Barton to leave them, which she did without speaking.

"Sit down, Mr. Dressler," Codella instructed as soon as they were alone.

"This is really embarrassing," said Dressler.

"You better hope that's all it is," she said. "Give me the facts. Times. Places. You can skip the gritty details."

The stories aligned, as Codella had suspected they would, and when he confirmed that Barton had left his room around five twenty, she said, "All right, Mr. Dressler. I'm convinced you were in each other's company."

"Is that it?" he asked hopefully. "Can I go now?"

"Not quite yet. You haven't told me what happened after Dr. Barton left your room. I know where she was all evening, but where were you?" She watched him carefully now.

"What do you mean?" he said.

"I mean, where were you? Where did you go?"

"Who said I went anywhere?"

"Don't be coy with me," she snapped. "Did you leave your hotel room or didn't you?"

"Yes."

"To do what?"

He shrugged. "To go eat. Have some dinner. Get some air."

She stared into his clear, green eyes that seemed untroubled by the fact that two bodies were lying in cold storage on the east side of Manhattan. She was getting tired of patiently asking questions that people could dance around. "Cut the shit, Mr. Dressler," she commanded, "and tell me exactly where the fuck you went or I swear to God, everyone in New York City is going to know about your extracurricular activities. I've got a guy on video near Sanchez's apartment, and he looks a hell of a lot like you. Did you go to Sanchez's apartment that night?"

"What?"

"You heard me. Now answer the goddamn question."

Dressler swallowed. "All right. All right. I went to his apartment, but I didn't kill him. I didn't even see him."

"Keep talking."

"He was pretty negative during the meeting that morning. Margery told me not to worry about him, but I did. I've been working on this sale for a year. It's worth six million. Sealing this deal for the company would be a huge coup for me. I didn't want to see it fall apart. I thought I could talk to him."

"Did Barton know you were going there?"

"No."

"Did anyone at McFlieger-Walsh know you were going there?"

"No, it was entirely my own idea."

"Did you tell Sanchez you were coming?"

"No."

"What time did you get to his apartment?"

"Around six."

"Tell me what happened."

"I rang his bell, but there was no answer. It was stupid, I know, going all that way without being sure he was home. But I figured he would be there on a Monday night and that we could have a chat, man to man, educator to educator."

"Did you go inside the building?"

He shook his head.

"Did you see anyone enter or leave?"

"No. I stood there and rang the bell three times, and then I gave up and walked back to my hotel feeling like a jerk."

"What route did you take back?"

"Morningside Drive to Columbus. Then I cut over to Broadway in the Eighties."

Codella watched him closely. "Did you ever take photographs of Sanchez with a woman?"

"Photos?"

"Compromising photos."

"Of course not! Why would I do a thing like that?"

"Did you know such photographs existed?"

"No. I had no idea!"

"Margery Barton never mentioned them to you?"

"I don't know anything about any photographs. Look, I wanted the sale, I admit, but I'd never do anything illegal to get it."

Codella considered all the lies she had been told in the last two days. Why should she believe him? "You're going to sit right here until a detective comes to pick you up. You're going to accompany that detective to a precinct and give him a statement. You don't have a problem with that, do you?"

She speed-dialed Haggerty before he could answer.

CHAPTER 49

Miguel Espina slumped into the chair on the other side of Marva Thomas's desk. "Sit up, Miguel," she said and watched him straighten his posture slightly. Every time she looked at Miguel, she remembered the chaos of Monday. She thought of Hector dragging her into his office and screaming, *You're not here to post sign-up sheets. You're here to keep the heads out of the toilets. How the hell did this happen?* In Hector Sanchez's eyes, Espina was *her* failure, not his, so she supposed there was poetic justice in the fact that she now had to administer his in-school suspension.

"Tell me what you did today," she asked him perfunctorily.

"I painted a banner for the lunch room."

"What does the banner say?"

"'No Bullying Zone.'"

She nodded. "That's a very good message for everyone in this school to remember. What else did you do?"

"My math and my history reading. Oh, and I helped Mrs. Broner reshelve books, and I finished the novel I been reading."

"What novel?"

"*Maniac Magee.*"

"Tell me about it."

Miguel shrugged. "He's this homeless kid."

"What happens to him?" She knew the plot, of course.

"Lots of stuff."

"Specifics, Miguel. And speak in complete sentences."

"He runs away from his aunt and uncle. He meets up with this white girl, Amanda, and she's real nice to him but then he leaves her 'cause the neighbors don't want some black kid in their hood.

So then he bunks in with this old dude who used to play ball. Oh, and Maniac is a pretty cool dude who can run and throw and hit a ball and catch a football, and he always be helping a lot of people and things turn out okay for him in the end."

Marva asked, "Did you identify with anyone in the story?"

Miguel looked at her as if she'd spoken Attic Greek. "Huh?"

"Did anyone in the novel remind you of yourself?"

He thought about it. "Maybe Mars Bar. He acts mean to Amanda."

"What about Maniac? Is Maniac like you?"

Miguel shook his head.

"Are you sure?"

"How'd he be like me?"

"Think about it," she said. "Think about it tonight, and come here tomorrow and tell me three ways you're like Maniac Magee. That's one of your homework assignments."

"And the other?"

"On your way home from school today, you're going to do at least one nice thing for somebody."

He looked at her as if she were crazy. "What I s'pose to do?"

"You figure it out, Miguel. Think about what Maniac Magee would do. And you tell me tomorrow. Don't come to school tomorrow unless you've completed both assignments. Remember, that's the rule."

He rolled his eyes.

Marva said, "And don't roll those eyes at me again. It's offensive, and I don't deserve it. If you do that to someone you work for, you won't get very far. Now you can apologize to me and then go back upstairs and keep working on your class assignments."

When he left, she walked the halls. She looked into the bathroom stalls. She checked the auditorium to make sure no one was hiding there. She went upstairs and made sure Miguel had gone directly back to the library. She came back downstairs and found Mr. Jancek waiting in front of her office. "Can I help you, Milosz?"

He stared at her for several seconds. "I'm sorry to bother you."

"Don't be silly. You're no bother." She smiled.

He continued to stare at her, and then it occurred to her what was about to happen. He had come in here to take a risk—*the* risk. He planned to make the unspoken spoken, right now, and she held her breath and waited.

But just then there was a knock at the door, and Janisa stuck her head in. "Sorry, Ms. Thomas, but Dr. Barton is on the phone for you."

Marva Thomas looked apologetically at Jancek. He ducked out of the office quickly. Marva picked up the phone and said, "This is Marva Thomas."

"Marva, we need to talk," came the familiar deep voice. "I've been thinking about you since this morning."

"You have?"

"I think I've treated you unfairly in all this. I think I've underestimated you."

Marva sat. She didn't know how to respond so she said nothing.

"I always think it's best to admit my mistakes, and you're one of my mistakes. I want to correct it."

"I'm sorry?"

"I should have chosen *you* to run PS 777. I made the wrong decision. What's more, if I'm honest, I knew it was the wrong decision almost immediately. Hector wasn't an effective school leader, and he never would have become one, and you know why?"

"Why?" Marva was too stunned to say any more.

"He didn't have a teacher's sensibilities. He hadn't spent enough time in the classroom. You, on the other hand, you do understand the teacher's perspective. You know the challenges. How many years were you in the classroom, Marva? I've forgotten."

"Fourteen."

"You see? You know how teachers think. Hector only put two years in the classroom before he went for his supervision certification. Yes, he's tougher than you, and he probably could have handled yesterday's crisis better than you did, but you can learn to be tough, whereas he could never have learned your natural empathy. You know what hubris is, Marva? Well, I'm afraid to say that Hector suffered from a lot of hubris. I made the wrong call with him, and I'm sure you suffered as much as everyone else as a result."

Marva was almost too shocked by Barton's words to think straight. "He was a difficult man to please," she managed to say.

"Well, I suspect the teachers won't find you so difficult to please. I am recommending that you be the new principal of PS 777."

CHAPTER 50

The bookshelves in Jane Martin's living room held no books. Instead, they provided the stage for carefully arranged bowls, goblets, vases, and sculptures fired in vibrant textured glazes. The objects looked like luxury merchandise in the display window of a high-end gift shop in Soho. They were so beautiful that Codella almost complimented Martin. Instead, she cut to the chase. "I need answers, and I need them right now, so no more deception. Did you take photos of your partner in front of Sanchez's apartment?"

Jane Martin's eyes registered instantaneous surprise and confusion. "What photos?"

"I'm asking the questions."

"Why would I take photos?"

"Maybe you thought you could bribe him into ending the affair. Maybe you threatened to expose him, ruin his holier-than-thou image."

"Maybe, but it didn't happen that way, Detective." Martin said this matter-of-factly. There was not even a hint of anger in her voice.

"You said you drove to Red Hook on Monday night, but your car never left the garage, so where were you really?"

Martin moved past the bookshelves to the window. She turned her back to Codella and stared down at her view of Broadway and the blocks between Broadway and the river. Did she look out that window and see her old building, her old life with Drew? Had she stood in front of that window and brooded about Drew's infidelity and plotted revenge?

"Where were you?" Codella repeated.

Martin turned back. "The truth? I was looking for answers. And last time I checked, that's not against the law."

"That depends. Where did you go for those answers—and I'm warning you, if you lie this time, I'm going to charge you with obstructing my investigation."

"Save your threats, Detective." Martin slipped her hands into her pockets. Her forearms were thick and veined. Apparently pushing and poking at clay gave your arms definition. "I stood in the Wash and Wear Laundromat from three o'clock on. I saw her driver turn onto his street. I got my answer. I had to know. I had to know so that I could let it go, since she wasn't going to tell me the truth."

Codella took several seconds to process the words. "So you're the face in the laundromat window. You're the one we're looking for, the potential witness to it all."

"That's right."

"Dana Drew left his apartment before five, but you stayed there. You stayed there for almost three more hours. Why?"

Martin shrugged. "Haven't you ever been betrayed by someone? Don't you know how paralyzing that feels?"

"This isn't about me," said Codella. "What were you doing there?"

"Staring into space."

"For three hours?"

"I was thinking about Dana. When I met her. We met in Provincetown." Martin smiled to herself. "On different sides of the aisle at a crappy drag show at this little venue called the Post Office Café." She pulled her hands out of her pockets and combed her fingers through her hair. "The drag queen recognized Dana, and he went after her in that drag-queen way. He asked her who she'd come with, and she said she'd come alone, and he said, 'Oh, but you should never come alone,' which of course made everyone howl with laughter, and then he told her he would help her find some Provincetown pussy, and he pulled me out of the audience and sat me next to her, and said, 'How about her?'"

Codella nodded. She could sense that Martin wanted to tell her the rest of the story.

"Dana was a good sport about it. We shook hands. She bought me a drink. We left the performance together and went to the Mews for a late dinner. Then she took me to the West End condo where she was staying. She had a breathtaking view of the bay and the ocean, and that's where we made love for the first time." Her eyes dropped to the floor and she exhaled a deep sigh.

"I know this must be very hard for you," Codella said, "but—"

"You have no idea," Martin interrupted with unchecked anger. "You want to know what I was doing in that laundromat? I was thinking about how I would never be with her again. I was asking myself if I would ever trust anyone again. And finally I walked home."

Codella gave the woman a moment to calm down. Then she said, "You were staring into your past, but what did you see as you looked out that window? Think! Who passed you? Someone went by that window in a red baseball cap, and he may have killed Hector Sanchez, and whether or not you liked the man, his murder needs to get solved, so help me, please."

"There were so many people," she said. "They were all just a blur."

"You didn't recognize anyone?"

"I might as well have been blindfolded. That's the truth. I'm sorry, Detective."

Codella just nodded. Sometimes you had to accept that people couldn't supply what you needed. "I would very much appreciate your keeping what you've told me to yourself," she said. "Tell no one else you were in that laundromat. As far as the rest of the world goes, we still don't know who was in that window."

CHAPTER 51

Haggerty sipped his Poland Springs. "I still don't understand why you went to his apartment. Is that standard operating procedure when you've got a principal who doesn't like your product?" He stared into the one-way mirror to his left. He wondered what Muñoz, Portino, and Ragavan were thinking on the other side. He stretched his arms over his head. "You want some water or something?"

"I want to get out of here." Dressler looked at his watch. "I have to call the airline. My bags were on that plane."

Haggerty pretended not to have heard. "What were you going to say to him if he'd answered the bell?"

"We already went over this. I was going to show him the research," said Dressler. "I thought if he saw the research, he might open his mind a little. We did a full-year pilot of iAchieve in four schools. An independent, university-based research company certified the pilot results. They were staggeringly positive."

"If they were that good, why do you suppose Sanchez was opposed to the program?"

"I've wondered that myself. I wondered if it was a personality issue."

"You mean between him and Barton?"

He nodded. "I thought maybe I could reason with him man to man."

Haggerty pulled a pack of cigarettes out of his pocket. He took one out and put it in his mouth but didn't light it. "I don't know. I still find it hard to believe you'd go all the way up town like that without knowing he was there."

"Well, you've never had a six-million-dollar sale on the line."

"No, I guess I haven't."

"You know what I think, Detective? I think you and that other detective, the woman, just want to pin this on someone. You don't even care if you have the right person."

Haggerty leaned forward with his eyes narrowed. "That's what you think, huh?"

Dressler looked at his watch again.

"Who else knew you went to his apartment?"

"No one."

"You're telling me you didn't say a word about your plans the whole time you were nailing Barton at the Mandarin?"

"No."

"And you didn't strategize this with anyone at McFlieger-Walsh?"

"No. I told you."

"You just took it upon yourself to try to save the sale?"

"That's right."

"Why?"

"Because it benefits me." Dressler's fists were clenched.

It was the first statement Haggerty actually believed. "Benefits you how?"

"Fifteen percent. My commission on the sale. Nine hundred thousand."

"Not bad."

"And a lot more to come. Once Margery's district buys, so will others."

"Then you could make yourself millions."

"And I've got a son with autism. Care costs a lot of money. My only crime is wanting to take care of my family."

"And fucking around on the side. Don't forget that."

"There's no crime in that," Dressler snapped.

Haggerty crossed his arms. "Did you photograph Sanchez with Dana Drew?"

"Of course not. I live in Dallas. I've only been to his school twice, yesterday and one other time. And as for Dana Drew, the closest I've ever come to her was in a movie theater." Small beads of sweat had formed on Dressler's forehead.

Haggerty stared at those glistening beads of perspiration just below his hairline. "Still, you must not be sad he's dead."

Dressler shrugged. "You said that, not me."

Haggerty watched him carefully. He noted the set of his jaw, the angle of his neck, the tapping of his fingers on the table between them. "I hope you're telling the truth, Mr. Dressler, because we're bound to find that witness in the laundromat. And we're already sifting through all kinds of footage from people who were in that neighborhood Monday night. It's just a matter of time before we put an end to this mystery. And we're not going to look too kindly on anyone who gave us false statements."

"Are we done now?" Dressler asked.

CHAPTER 52

She sat in her car outside Martin's apartment and considered all the crisscrossing lies. Hector Sanchez had pretended to visit truant students in public housing projects when he was really sneaking off campus to crawl into bed with an actress. Drew had disguised her affair with good works and generous donations. Margery Barton had concocted false alibis to cover her affair with a Department of Education vendor, and Jane Martin had stood in a laundromat in a bulky hooded parka for almost three hours to discover the truth. Had Chip Dressler really rung Sanchez's buzzer three times and walked home? And what about all the teachers at PS 777 who had hated Sanchez and Reyes? What lies were they telling? Codella closed her eyes and tried to make the facts adhere into a solid evidence-based conclusion in her brain, but they wouldn't, and so she gave up and followed her instincts.

Ten minutes later, she was back in the closet at MS 174 where Eugene Bosco was sitting at the table correcting multiple-choice tests.

"I see you've moved up a notch from counting toilet paper rolls," she observed.

"Very funny." He set down his red pencil and leaned back. "I don't suppose this is a social call, Detective, so what do you want?"

"Tell me about your friendship with Christine Donohue."

"What friendship? We're colleagues."

Codella shook her head. "You're more than that, and we both know it."

"What makes you so sure?"

236 | Carrie Smith

"You call her Chris. She calls you Gene. You confide in each other. You dine together."

He laughed. "And that's your big tip-off?"

"Tip-offs are rarely big," she said. "Don't waste my time."

"Okay, so we go back. So what?"

"How far?"

"Twenty glorious years at PS 777. We share the same frustrations—like you and your fellow cops must share now that you can't stop and frisk anymore." He smirked.

"Did you share enough frustrations to plan his character assassination?"

"What do you mean?"

"You tell me."

Bosco crossed his arms defiantly. "I never said anything about him that wasn't true—in my humble opinion, anyway. Neither did Chris. We just spoke our minds. We exercised our rights."

"Is that what you were doing when you signed up for the iAchieve sneak preview, even though neither one of you give a flying fuck about technology implementation?"

He grinned. "Chris is on the adoption committee. It's her job to find out as much as she can about the programs she will vote on. She's moving up in the world. She completes her course work for the principal's certification next month. She's got an exit strategy. But you must know that by now since you're such a thorough detective. I Googled you."

Codella registered no surprise at this new piece of information. "And you? What's your exit strategy?"

"Retirement." He shrugged. "As soon as possible."

"So you signed up for the meeting why?"

"I'd do anything to piss off Sanchez."

"No one put you up to it?"

"Like who?"

"Like Barton, maybe, or someone from McFlieger-Walsh who wanted some teachers to embrace the program publicly?"

Bosco shook his head. "I've never talked to Barton in my life, and she's probably just as bad as Sanchez. I spoke my mind because I always speak my mind."

"What else did you do?"

"Nothing—except dream."

"About what?"

"Getting even, what else? All that asshole did was grade us—day in and day out. The slaves always dream about revolt, don't they?"

"Tell me about those dreams."

Bosco put his worn-out sneaker on a chair. "Once in the teacher's lounge, we all fantasized about breaking into his computer and grading him with his own rubric, and e-mailing his report card over to Chancellor Lipsie. What a report card that would be! Symbolic murder—that's all we're capable of."

Was that true? she wondered. Were they incapable of more than puerile pranks, like the students they taught? "What else?" she demanded.

"We thought about lodging a formal complaint against him with our union. I was supposed to look into the procedure, but I never got around to it."

For the same reason he wasn't the murderer, she thought. He was too lazy. "Go on."

"What we really wanted to do was catch him with Drew. Show the world that the 'Savior of PS 777' was just a horny guy lusting after a lesbian."

"What was your plan?"

"Hire someone to follow him around and catch him in the act."

"Did you do it? Did you hire someone?"

He laughed. "I wouldn't waste a dime on that guy. As I said, it was talk. All talk."

She stood and pushed in her chair. "I'll let you get back to those papers."

"Gee, thanks."

She returned to her car, picked up her cell phone, and continued to follow her instincts. "I need to talk to you," she said to the raspy voice that answered.

"Well, I'm not at school right now."

"Where are you?"

"Fairway. It's my shopping day."

Twenty minutes later, Codella was staring at Christine Donohue across a small table against the brick wall at the back of the Fairway Café. On weekends, this café, located on the second floor of the sprawling Upper West Side shopping institution, was packed with talkative brunching couples, but this afternoon, it was nearly empty. Just beyond the café, late-afternoon Fairway shoppers climbed the stairs to the large organic foods department. To Codella's left, tall windows overlooked Broadway. The November sky was already darkening, and through the leafless branches of trees in the mall, she could read the coming attractions scrolling across the digital marquis of the Beacon Theater on the east side of the boulevard.

She sipped her tea. Christine Donohue had ordered lemonade, which now sat in front of her in a mason jar filled with ice and sprigs of fresh, deep-green mint leaves that Codella could smell. Donohue pulled the wrapper off her plastic straw. "You haven't solved the murders yet, I take it." She smirked. "I saw those blurry surveillance blobs you're showing the public. Good luck with that."

Codella ignored her sarcasm. "You and I need to talk about Hector Sanchez."

"I really have nothing more to offer on the subject of that man."

Codella leaned across the narrow table. "I think you do, and we can either talk here or I can take you up to Manhattan North for a little tour. It's your choice."

Donohue pushed loose strands of her artificially red hair behind her ear. "What exactly do you want to talk about?"

"A photograph." Codella stared into the teacher's wary eyes looking for transitory trace evidence: a flash of panic, overdramatized confusion, suspicious.

But Donohue gave nothing away. "What photograph?"

"You know."

"I'm afraid I don't." She met Codella's stare convincingly. "I don't know what you're talking about."

"You and some other teachers talked about taking a photograph of Sanchez and Drew, to ruin his reputation."

Then Donohue laughed. "Oh that. Come on, Detective. That was a joke. That was a bunch of teachers gossiping about their unpopular principal."

"Jokes have a funny way of turning into reality. Is that what happened with your joke?"

"How would I know?"

"When did you have that conversation?"

Donohue looked at her watch. "At the Proud Families photo shoot. Look, I really have to leave. Didn't we go over this already?"

"Pretend we didn't. Tell me about that day."

Donohue picked up her sweating lemonade jar and sipped through the plastic straw. "What do you want to know?"

"Where were you?"

"At a table, watching the spectacle."

"Tell me what you saw."

She squinted at the wall as if the memories were there. Finally, she said, "Imagine a used car dealership at clearance time. That's what it looked like. The day before the shoot, he had the janitors hang streamers and banners and balloons. He'd rented a popcorn machine, and there was music playing. In one corner, Dana Drew's photographer had mounted a green screen, and there were so many lights, you'd think they were shooting the cover of *Vanity Fair*. Parents and children stood in line to have their photos taken, and Sanchez and Drew were pumping their hands and patting their backs, and the sparks were snapping between them. Only a blind person could have missed the chemistry. And I made the comment that someone should snap *their* photo and post it on that parents' blog everyone goes to, and we all had a good laugh and one comment led to another. You know how it is."

"Which teachers were there?"

"Gene. Jenny Bernstein. Anna Masoutis. Some others. I don't remember." She looked Codella in the eye. "Doesn't it shock you when people think they can pull the wool over your eyes so easily?"

Codella couldn't help herself. "Nothing shocks me anymore, Ms. Donohue. Everyone's got an agenda here, and when I figure them all out, then I'll get to the bottom of this. Don't doubt it for a second."

"Am I supposed to be intimidated by you?" Donohue squinted.

"Only if you're hiding the truth."

"What would I be hiding?"

"Your own agenda."

"And what exactly would that be?"

"You know better than I. Maybe you wanted to win Barton her iAchieve adoption by damaging the reputation of her biggest rival."

Donohue laughed. "What's in it for me to take a chance like that?"

"You're getting your principal's certification. Did Barton promise you a choice assignment?"

The right side of Donohue's mouth curled up, half mocking, half in disgust. She shook her head slowly. "Gene was right. You're tilting at windmills. Look, I've got better things to do than stand on a street and snap photographs of people going into a building."

Codella let the teacher's words swing between them for several seconds like a waiting noose. Then she said, "I never mentioned where any photos were snapped or what they showed."

Donohue sipped her lemonade again. "Well, where else would you go to catch them in the act?"

Codella pressed. "You saw that photograph. You know something you're not saying."

"I saw nothing," Donohue retorted angrily. "And I don't want to talk about this anymore. I've told you exactly how I felt about him. I've been honest, but I'm *done*."

"For now, maybe," conceded Codella. "But not for good." She watched Donohue rise, pick up her Fairway bags, and head for the stairs.

Codella drove back to PS 777. Marva Thomas's door was shut when she got to the office, and she knocked as she opened the door. She didn't bother with greetings.

"The day of the murder, Mr. Sanchez returned from his meeting at the district office. According to Janisa, he saw the iAchieve sign-up sheet on the bulletin board out there," Codella pointed, "and he ripped it off the wall. Then he called you into his office. He was angry that you had posted that iAchieve sheet."

Thomas shook her head. "Who told you that? His anger had nothing to do with iAchieve."

"Then what was it about?" Codella asked.

"He was furious with me about Miguel Espina. The minute he got here, he made it perfectly clear I was going to take the fall for that whole thing."

"Why?"

"Because according to him, that's my one and only job— 'keeping heads out of toilets,' as he put it."

"He said those words?"

"He told me I was the least effective AP he'd ever worked with. I've never been insulted quite so bluntly in my life. He pointed to my biblical quote," she indicated the note on her computer, "and told me I was a simple-minded moron, a church lady—he used those words—and that I was in over my head and he wanted me out of his school at the end of the year."

"So he basically fired you."

"Yes, although it's not as easy as that in the New York public school system. And as of two hours ago, I'm now the new principal—pending the official paperwork, of course."

"Margery Barton appointed you?"

She nodded. "As strange as that sounds. I'm still trying to figure out if that conversation was real or if I just imagined it. She actually apologized to me. She told me she had made a mistake choosing Hector over me. She told me she had known for several months that he was a mistake."

"Maybe she has a conscience after all. But you know what it looks like, don't you?"

Marva Thomas sipped her coffee and nodded. "It looks like I benefitted directly from his death. I guess I should move to the top of your suspect list, Detective."

"What did you do on Monday when Hector Sanchez said all those things to you?"

"Nothing. I just let him rant. When people get out of control like that, silence is the best strategy, I find."

"I suspect you're right."

"I have always tried to treat others with kindness," Thomas said. "He would say I'm naïve, but I believe every person has value that transcends their title or status. He didn't appreciate anyone's value. He stripped everyone of their self-esteem. At what point do high standards turn into despotism? I supported him despite my discomfort, but when he lashed out at me on Monday, I knew he was an evil man."

"Why didn't you tell me all this on Tuesday?"

Thomas sighed. "Look, Detective. We all want to preserve some dignity. I have precious little left here. I'm sure everyone got an earful that day. I know they were standing on the other side of the door. I didn't feel like sharing my humiliation with you too."

The AP's sweater sleeves were pushed up to the elbows, and Codella stared at her small wrist bones and thin arms. She was not half as strong as Jane Martin. In a one-on-one battle, she could never subdue Codella, let alone the six-foot-two Sanchez. "Where were you during the Proud Families photo shoot in September?"

"In the cafeteria with everybody else. I was in charge of lining up the families for their big moment."

"Did you know that Sanchez and Drew were having an affair?"

"I'd heard the rumors, but I didn't see how they could be true. I mean, Dana Drew is—" She didn't finish the thought.

"Desire is a complicated thing."

"I suppose so." Thomas lifted her Dunkin' Donuts cup again.

CHAPTER 53

Marva Thomas looked at her wristwatch. It was five forty-five. The detective was gone, thank God, and no children were left to reprimand for running through the halls. No parents were sitting on the benches demanding progress reports. All the teachers had departed, and the school was in sleep mode. This was the time of day Marva liked best, the time after the daily frenzy of the school ended and before the evening of caregiving for her mother began. These were the few precious moments in which she could breathe, and she desperately needed them today. She jumped when Milosz's figure filled her doorway. "Oh!" she said.

"I didn't mean to frighten you."

"I just didn't hear you," she said. "Please, come in. I'm sorry we were interrupted earlier."

He didn't move. "Come out to dinner with me," he said.

"Dinner?"

"We've already had coffee several times." He gestured toward her Dunkin' Donuts cup.

"Oh. Yes. I guess we have." She smiled. She wondered if her face were reddening. "I'd love to," she said, but in the next instant she thought of her mother, her mother's medication schedule, her mother's inevitable shutdown. "But it will have to be quick," she added. "Just let me clear my desk."

He stepped out of her doorway. Her heart pounded as she guided her wireless mouse to shut down the computer. She stared at her fingers. They were shaking. But at least her nails were polished, she thought. Her cuticles were immaculate. Her skin was moisturized. She was wearing the Chanel cologne Carla had given her last Christmas. Had she maintained her appearance, she wondered, out of some vestigial hope that a man would come along and be attracted to her? Was Milosz the man she had unconsciously hoped for? What would people think of her, a principal now, if she became involved with a custodian? Why should she care?

She pulled her purse out of her bottom desk drawer, turned off her desk lamp, and stood. Milosz was waiting near the door. "We're the last ones to leave," he said. "I'll lock up, and we'll go to the Metro Diner. It isn't fancy, but it's quick, and it's nearby."

They walked down Broadway in silence. She could see her breath fog the air in front of her. She felt a moment of panic when they reached 100th Street. What could they possibly talk about over a table? What could she possibly have in common with a Croatian custodian? She stopped. He stopped too. "Something is wrong?" he asked.

She shook her head. He came closer. He put his arms around her. He said, "Don't worry. Now everything will be better. You'll see."

She looked up at him. "He was a terrible person. I feel guilty for saying that, but it's true."

"I hated the way he treated you," said Jancek softly. "Don't think about him anymore."

When they got to the Metro Diner, Marva slipped out of her coat, and Milosz hung it on the hook while she slid into her side of the booth. Marva felt relieved when the waiter appeared with a pot of coffee to pour. They both watched him in silence, and when he was gone, Milosz handed her the cream.

"That's not fair," she said. "You know how I take mine, but I have no idea how you take yours."

"Black." He smiled. "Black and unsweetened. But I like making yours sweet and creamy."

Her face felt hot. Could he see that she was blushing? "It's so good to be out of that place," she said.

"The detective came to see you again."

"She asked me who I thought did it."

"What did you tell her?"

"That I had no idea." She leaned her elbow on the table and rested her chin in her hand. "I've thought about all the teachers who didn't like him, but I don't see how any of them could be the killer, do you?" She watched their waiter carry meals to the booth behind them.

"It's hard to imagine it's any of them," he agreed. "But I suppose you never know."

Marva opened her menu to the specials page. She was starting to feel more relaxed. She leaned forward conspiratorially. The murders were something they shared in common, something they could talk about. "Who do you think could have done it, Milosz?"

He sipped his coffee and considered. "Maybe an angry parent?" he suggested.

"I hadn't thought about that. Like who?"

"Well, like the mother of that boy on Monday. John Chambers."

"Hmmm. Mrs. Chambers is high strung and very protective, but I don't really see her as a killer."

"I know, but then you can't always tell by looking at a person." He leaned across the table. She liked him close to her like that. She liked the smell of his cologne. "Think of that man they caught in Soho last year," he said, "the one who killed a boy twenty some years ago and was working in a bodega all this time with nobody ever suspecting him."

"I remember that, yes, but women don't usually commit murder—unless they've been abused, of course."

"Maybe the father did it. If I were that boy's father, I would be angry over the treatment, very angry. But I'm sure the police are looking into all those possibilities."

Marva stirred some sugar into her coffee and lifted the cup to her lips. "I never met John's father. But why would he kill Sofia Reyes, too? Sofia had nothing to do with what happened to John." She looked around the restaurant and lowered her voice as she said, "I'm thinking maybe it has something to do with Dana Drew. The detective asked me if I knew he was having an affair with her."

"He was?"

"Apparently so. Apparently there are photographs."

"Well, some people know how to fool everyone." He reached his right hand across the table to pat her left one. "Are you ready to order?"

Marva wasn't the least bit hungry. She stared at his big hand covering hers. She closed her eyes and imagined his touch suffusing her pores, entering her bloodstream like a stimulating drug. "You know what I think. I think they're going to find the killer soon."

"What makes you say so?"

"Just the way that detective sounded. They're close. I'm sure of it. And I can't wait for this to be over."

"Me neither," he agreed. "I'm tired of mopping the floors after all those reporters and parents and police trudging through. I can't wait for things to get back to normal. I just want our old routine. Maybe I'm simple, but I like predictability."

"Me, too," said Marva.

CHAPTER 54

Haggerty was smoking a cigarette outside the 171st Precinct when she parked her car.

"You gotta quit those," she told him.

He flicked it into the street. "I was hoping you'd show up."

"You got some news?"

He shook his head. "Not really."

"Where's Muñoz?"

"At the Mandarin. Keeping tabs on Margery Barton's boy toy. Where have you been?"

"All over," she said. "I even got over to Fairway."

"Suddenly had an urge to buy some groceries?"

"No, but Christine Donohue did." The wind was blowing at her back, pushing her toward him. She held her ground and zipped her jacket. "And she knows who took that photo of Sanchez and Drew."

"Who?"

"She's not telling."

"You want me to pick her up and get her in an interview room?"

"Not yet. There's more. Dana Drew's lover, Jane Martin? She's the one in the bulky jacket standing in the corner laundromat."

"Jesus! You've been busy."

"It's cold as hell out here." She stuck her hands in her pockets. "I'm going in there. I'll give Muñoz a call."

"Don't bother," Haggerty said. "I spoke to him ten minutes ago. Dressler hasn't left the hotel. Walk with me. I'll buy you a latté."

"I gave up coffee after the hospital."

"How about some dinner? There's a vegan place on Amsterdam. I've never been in there but I pass it all the time and it's always
crowded."

She frowned. "You're serious? You're going to eat at a vegan
restaurant?"

He smiled. "I'll do anything you want."

She stared at him warily. *Anything but visit me in the hospital*, she
thought. The sky was a heavy charcoal mass pressing down on her,
making it suddenly difficult to breathe. She turned her eyes toward
the curb illuminated by warm light from the street lamps. Pale yellow gingko leaves had fallen to the ground all over the block, and
the crushed, overripened gingko fruit smelled like rotten eggs.

"I'd do anything to take back how I acted that night, Claire,"
he finally said. "I fucked up everything for us."

Her eyes moved from the street to the sidewalk and settled on
a piece of chewing gum ground into the concrete in front of her
boots like an unsightly mole, a melanoma. She shrugged. "You
were an asshole—a big one—and yeah, I was so angry, I took a
promotion just to put some distance between us. But don't worry.
I'm not angry about that anymore. I forgot all about it the day of
my diagnosis. I had bigger issues to think about. So if it makes you
feel better, I forgive you. It's over. It's the past. You should let it go."
She finally worked up the courage to look him in the eye, just for
a moment. "I'm going in now. I've got a couple of calls to make."

She took a step, but he touched her sleeve. "Wait. There's something else. I can feel it. Tell me."

She closed her eyes. She felt her resistance breaking apart like
the fragile crust of ice that occasionally covered the Hudson River
during winter. It wasn't hard or thick enough to contain the strong
current of emotions below it. "I need to go," she said.

But he grabbed her wrist. "No. You need to tell me whatever
you're not telling me."

And then she couldn't hold it back. "You didn't come to me
once in all those months, Brian. You let me go through all that by
myself." She stepped back from him. Her eyes were blurry with
tears. She wiped at them with the sleeve of her jacket. "Shit! You
want to know the truth? Fine. You were the only one I would
have wanted to see, and you didn't come."

"I did come," he said quietly. "But I should have come sooner. I came to see you at three PM on July 12th. You were in bed 602-B. I brought you flowers. What an idiot I was. I didn't know chemo patients can't be around flowers. You were standing next to the bed screaming for morphine, and I stood outside your door for fifteen minutes listening to you in pain until they finally got your drugs and gave you the injection and you fell asleep in the bed."

She looked at him. Now his eyes were glistening with tears that reflected the streetlight. "I was a coward, Claire. I convinced myself you wouldn't want me to see you like that, that it would only make you more angry at me, but the truth is I couldn't take it. I wasn't ready for what I saw. You were holding on with everything you had, and I was standing there falling apart, and I couldn't let you see me like that. I'm so sorry, Claire. I would be so different if we had it to do all over again."

"No thanks." She wiped her eyes again and laughed. "I don't want any do-over. You got that?"

He pulled her into an embrace. She closed her eyes. She felt his stubbled jaw against her cheek. With her nose against his shoulder, she could smell cigarettes and soap. He kissed the top of her head. And then she found herself wanting to kiss him, wanting their lips to find each other, wanting them to dissolve into each other.

She pushed him away instead. "Show me that vegan restaurant. I'll tell you what happened today."

CHAPTER 55

Muñoz pressed his back against the wall of the lobby lounge at the Mandarin Oriental. From his table in the far corner, he could look out on Columbus Circle below and see the steady flow of cars creep east and west across Central Park South, a stream of red taillights like leering eyes. He could also see Chip Dressler perched on an elegant red bar stool to his left. He watched the bartender make Dressler a gin martini. Dressler sipped it slowly, turned, and surveyed the crowded room.

Seated alone at a small table against a long banquette was a deeply tanned blonde woman. The top buttons of her blouse were open so that her ample cleavage was on deliberate display. Dressler's eyes returned to her after each broad sweep of the room. Finally, he turned back to the bartender and a moment later, the bartender set a second drink in front of him. Dressler picked it up, along with his own, and walked to the woman's table. She smiled at him. Dressler smiled back. He set down the drink in front of her. They shook hands. Her eyes scanned the contours of his body. He pointed to the empty chair at her table, and she nodded. Then he sat, pulled in his chair, and they clinked their glasses. Their toast reminded Muñoz of Codella and him clinking their milkshake and tea mug yesterday, but this toast sealed a very different kind of consort.

Muñoz couldn't hear their conversation, but he could see that Dressler did most of the talking. The woman was laughing. She reached out and touched his arm from time to time. He ordered a second round. They clinked glasses again. He moved from the chair across from her to a space next to her on the banquette against the wall, and now her hand lingered on his arm as they spoke.

Had she sat down at the table expressly to become the object of some man's desire for the evening? Was she on a business trip? Was she the bored wife of a hedge fund guy who was on a business trip? The rituals of anonymous heterosexual sex were unfamiliar to him, like the customs of a foreign country he had never been to. But in any sexual encounter, there was the hunter and the prey. Did a woman like that recognize that she was prey at the watering hole? Did she enjoy the experience of being hunted? Did she enjoy the danger of it?

Dressler whispered something into her ear. His lips lingered there, and she closed her eyes. He pressed his hand against her thigh. His other hand went up, and a server, who clearly was used to these scenes, immediately brought Dressler's check. Dressler signed it, and he and the woman slid off their stools and left the bar.

Muñoz took a last swig of seltzer and followed them out at a careful distance. He watched them walk toward the elevator. Dressler's hand was on the small of the woman's back. The elevator doors opened, and they entered. Then the doors closed.

Muñoz pulled out his phone and dialed Codella.

"What's happening?" she asked.

"He picked up a woman in the hotel bar. They just went up in the elevator."

"Stay where you are. Don't let him leave that hotel without you." She hung up.

Muñoz surveyed the hotel lobby. It was going to be a long night. He picked a couch with a view of the elevator bank and sank into it to check his fantasy basketball rankings while Dressler and the woman fulfilled other fantasies.

CHAPTER 56

Marva guided her mother from the bathroom to her bed. A year ago, her mother had walked herself into the bedroom. Now she labored with a walker, and Marva had to help her maneuver the feet of the walker around corners and chests of drawers. Marva had to steer the walker so that her mother could plop onto the mattress. Then Marva had to swing her mother's legs onto the bed. She pulled up the heavy comforter as if her mother were a child. "Sleep well," she said, and the educator in her almost felt compelled to read her mother a bedtime story. Instead, she switched off the lamp next to her mother's bed and turned to go.

"I need some water," said her mother as Marva moved through the doorway. Her mother's tone was not exactly demanding, just matter of fact, as if Marva were a paid caregiver being asked to fulfill her employer's final request of the night.

Marva could have pretended not to hear. She could have crossed the hall quickly and closed her door, but she didn't. She went to the kitchen, poured tap water into a cup, and took it to her mother. Then she held it to her mother's lips rather than force her mother to reach for the cup, because her mother's dyskinesia was pronounced at the moment and she would have undoubtedly spilled it on her pajamas and the sheets.

When her mother stopped drinking and gave a perfunctory head nod, Marva lowered the cup and turned the light back off. "Good night, Ma."

This time, she crossed the hall quickly and closed her bedroom door, turned off her own bedside lamp, and lay on her back staring into the blackness. She remained awake for a long time, but tonight her insomnia was not unpleasant. For the first time in six years of caring for her mother, she felt transcendent. No longer was her sole identity that of indentured servant, and it was as if she had developed a biological immunity to her mother's complaints and criticism. She felt able to look upon her mother with pity and empathy, if not exactly love, because now she was more than her mother's keeper. Now she had something of her own, a secret lifeline, a new identity, a connection to the outside world.

She rolled onto her side and reached her arm around her pillow. She took herself back to the booth at the Metro Diner. She visualized Milosz sitting across from her. She felt his rough hand pressing against hers. She relived their walk home, his arm hooked through hers. She felt the light kiss of his lips against her cheek, only an inch to the right of her lips. If only she had turned her face slightly, their lips would have met. She would have allowed him to kiss her mouth. She would have welcomed his kiss.

She could hear him say, "Next time we don't hurry so much, Marva. I take you to my place and cook for you." One day, she thought, one day soon her mother would be gone, and she would have her life back. She would be happy. Hadn't she earned the right to happiness through sustained unhappiness? Hadn't she more than paid for any joy she might find?

Marva closed her eyes and hugged the pillow tightly, and all her thoughts concentrated on the geography of that light kiss.

CHAPTER 57

The restaurant was no longer busy—they had been here more than two hours and far outlasted the evening rush of vegan diners—and now their tall, disheveled waiter was being more attentive than necessary. Did she want more hot water? She acquiesced in order to get him to stop hovering.

Their meal had started off with Haggerty staring at the menu as if it were written in a foreign language. He stumbled over entrees like quinoa and black beans, chickpea curry, and tofu quiche until he settled on the vegan burger, but she warned, "Don't order that."

"Why not?"

"Because you'll be expecting red meat, and you're going to hate it and complain. Try the chili."

He had obeyed with good humor—in fact, Codella could not remember a time when he had ever been quite so accommodating—and she'd found herself relaxing for the first time in days or weeks or months, and she had watched with open, and slightly fiendish, humor as Haggerty stared down at the bowl of chili the waiter set in front of him. He had sampled the intensely spicy mixture of tomatoes, beans, and vegetables and immediately reached for the gluten-free corn bread she knew he was not going to like. At least one problem had been taken off the table. They'd made their peace. She wasn't sure what she wanted their dynamic to become, but at least he was in her life again, he was someone she could trust.

Her phone lit up as the waiter poured hot water into her stainless teapot and placed a fresh green tea bag on the saucer. She picked up the phone and read the message. "Strange," she said.

"What is it?" Haggerty sipped his coffee.

"A text from Dana Drew. She wants me to come over."

"Now?"

Codella looked at her watch. It was quarter past eleven. "She must have just gotten home from the theater."

"What do you suppose she wants?"

Codella shrugged. "Jane Martin must have told her she spilled the beans to me. Let's hope that means she's ready to be a little more forthcoming about Sanchez. I better go."

"I'll go with you."

He started to rise, but Codella shook her head. "I think she'll open up more if it's just the two of us. Call Muñoz at the Mandarin. If Dressler's still upstairs with the woman, tell him he can call it a night."

She could tell he was disappointed, and she squeezed his arm and said, "Thanks for this," before she turned, ran out into the cold night, hailed the first cab that passed on Broadway, and gave the cabbie Drew's Riverside Drive address.

The doorman waved her past when she flashed her shield, and she got on the elevator. The door to Drew's apartment was ajar, and the message seemed clear: come in. She pushed it open and listened to the silence within. Beyond the spacious entryway, she saw the river-facing windows and the couch where she had sat just yesterday. She peered into the kitchen glistening with stainless appliances, ironclad cookware, and high-gloss marble that reflected the moonlight. She stepped into the vestibule and called out, "Hello?"

There was no answer. "Hello?" she called again, louder this time, as her fingers reached instinctively for the grip of her service revolver. She advanced three more steps, stopped once more, and continued to listen. Every silence had a signature voice, she thought, a personality, a message. It could be soft and soothing like a mother's lullaby. It could be a seductive lover, inviting you to open your mind to secret desires. And it could be a cruel and castigating judge—inducing guilt that could only be absolved through confession.

This silence was different. This was the kind of silence that surrounded your whole body with a high-voltage current of imminent danger. It quickened the pulse and awakened every nerve ending, sharpened the eyesight, and amplified the hearing. It made you into the animal you had forgotten that you were. It made you predator and prey. It warned you to run, to hide, to be ready, to attack.

Codella pulled her gun out of its holster and advanced into the living room. The room was undisturbed. The couch looked as inviting as it had yesterday. A half-filled glass of water on the dining room table suggested recent activity. There were dishes in the kitchen sink, and a bottle of Perrier sat on the granite countertop. She doubled back toward the entry hall and turned into the corridor leading to bedrooms. And then she saw.

They were all sitting in a row on the floor with their hands behind their backs and rags stuffed into their mouths, held there by tape. Drew saw her first, and her eyes flashed panic. Next to her was an attractive Indian woman, a babysitter, Codella guessed. Martin sat next to this woman, and her eyes shifted back and forth between Codella and a part of the room Codella could not see from where she stood. The eyes were a warning. The eyes told her that whoever had tied them up was in that room.

Codella quickly considered her options. Whoever was in the room had already killed two people and now intended to kill everyone here, including her. She had been lured to the apartment. That was clear. It had only taken her five minutes to leave the restaurant and arrive, and five minutes was not enough time for an intruder to have bound and gagged three women and a child. Drew had not texted her phone. Someone else had done that, and he was a violent killer who had snapped a man's neck and sliced so deeply into a woman's carotid artery that she had bled out in minutes.

Codella looked away. She made herself take deep, even breaths. If she gave into panic, she wouldn't be able to think, and she had to think. She had to make a choice, and she had to make it fast. Whoever was in that room knew she was out here. He knew she was debating her next move. She had two options. She could retreat, call for backup, and hope that the women were not dead by the time the backup came, or she could advance and hope to catch the killer off guard.

She stared at her hands gripping the Glock. They were steady. Whoever was in that room would know she had a gun, and he would not have lured her here if he didn't have a gun as well. But would he use his? Would he risk a shot inside the building when his exit depended on stealth? Or would he try to overpower her using physical force, the way he had obviously overwhelmed Drew, Martin, and the babysitter?

She pulled out her phone as quietly as she could and texted four words to Brian. *Come quickly. Bring backup.* She would wait, she told herself. She would stand right here and wait. She slipped the phone back into her pocket and raised her gun with both hands. She looked from Drew to Martin and back again. If the killer made a move, would she see it in their eyes? Would she be able to move fast enough? A minute passed. Two minutes. How much longer was he going to let her stand here before he figured out that she had called for help and that he had to move against her?

When she saw a sudden flicker of panic in Drew's green eyes, she guessed she had bought as much time as she would get. He was coming toward the door—whoever *he* was—and she had to move first. She took a deep breath and then she was all taut muscles and concentration as she rounded the corner in a flash.

Milosz Jancek was sitting on the windowsill, and except for the gun in his hand, he looked exactly as he had the first time she'd laid eyes on him. Ordinary. Unassuming. Slightly unattractive with his crooked smile.

She pointed her gun right between his eyes. "Drop it right now and put your hands up."

He didn't move.

"I said drop it."

He still didn't move. Nor did he raise the gun.

"I'm not going to ask you again. If you don't drop the gun, I'm going to shoot you."

"Go ahead," he said quietly.

Then she felt the gun in her own back and heard a familiar voice. "I think you're the one who needs to drop the gun."

She didn't trust her ears. She turned to see the second face, and in the split second she took her eyes off Jancek, he moved beside her and twisted her arm until she had to release the Glock. Jancek guided her to the floor next to Drew, picked up a spool of white twine, and said, "Put your hands together, Detective. I'm afraid there's no choice."

She stared at his crooked face. Too much was happening. She wanted to freeze time and put everything together in her mind. She watched him take out a pocketknife and cut a long piece of twine. She said, "This isn't going to work. You can't really believe that if you kill us, you'll get away with anything. You'll never even get out of this building."

Jancek tied her wrists without looking at her. Then he pushed a rag into her mouth as if he were feeding her an olive. The gesture was tentative, almost apologetic. But the rag was dry and coarse on her tongue, and the cloth went so far back in her throat that she was gagging. She tried to bring all the seemingly unconnected facts together in her mind and explain how they added up to this, but she couldn't. She looked at Drew. She had no doubt that the terror on the actress's face was the real thing. The babysitter was visibly trembling. Then she turned to Martin, who seemed to be stoically calculating how to react to the situation, but what could she possibly do with her wrists bound behind her? Next to Martin was Drew's daughter. The little girl's eyes were filled with tears, and her arms and knees were trembling. Were all five of them going to become cast members in the killer's reenactment of the passion? Would every one of them bleed out here on Drew's elegant rugs? Would tomorrow's *Post* eulogize them with a darkly clever headline composed by the *Post* headline SWAT team? What would that headline be? Where was Muñoz to help her brainstorm that headline?

Jancek had tied her wrists in front of her, and the twine was wrapped so tightly that her hands were now tingling and her skin was turning pale. Soon her hands would be bloodless the way Sofia Reyes's must have been at the end. She would feel the pinpricks of numbness in her fingertips, and then she would feel nothing. She stared into Chip Dressler's eyes. He was holding a single-action Colt, but she knew now that he wasn't going to squeeze off any rounds that would alarm the sleeping neighbors and send help their way. He didn't have to. She imagined that he was enjoying the fact that the tables had turned so dramatically since Haggerty had interrogated him hours ago. She wanted to ask him if his six-million-dollar sale was really worth all this, but she could hardly breathe let alone speak, and what did it matter? The only question that mattered now was who would be the first victim?

Jancek held the large pocketknife with which he had cut the twine. Codella closed her eyes the way she had closed them in the hospital each time they'd wheeled her into an operating room and inserted a long hollow needle between her bones to inject chemo drugs into her spinal fluid.

Dressler pointed to Martin. "Her," he said. "Do it now."

Jancek looked straight at Martin. So she would be first, Codella thought. Of course it would be her. She was the witness, after all, the witness who had seen nothing.

Jancek took an uncertain step in Martin's direction. He kept looking from Martin to Dressler and back again. If only she could speak. If only she could engage him in conversation. If only she had let Haggerty come with her. She groaned through the rag and the tape holding the rag in place. She sounded like a wild animal, she thought, as Jancek advanced toward Martin. He covered her short hair with one large hand. He was going to pull her chin up and expose her neck for the blade, she thought, and she had to get to her feet and try to stop it. Dressler's gun rotated toward her as she repositioned her legs, and as she froze in place, she saw movement out the corner of her eyes. Dana Drew had struggled to her feet. She launched herself into Jancek knocking him to the ground. Dressler's gun fired, and she went down right on top of Jancek.

"Jesus Christ!" Dressler swore.

Drew's daughter stared at her mother's still body and let out a muffled wail.

Martin sidled closer to the girl.

Jancek extricated himself from the body and looked down at the blood on his shirt. Codella had to do something. It might well be futile, like Drew's effort, but she had to try. She reached out her feet and kicked Jancek hard in the shin. He howled and turned toward her, and she raised her bound wrists and delivered an upper-cut with her fists before Dressler got there and struck the side of her head with the gun. The last thing she heard before she blacked out was another gunshot.

When she came to, Haggerty was pushing the handcuffed custodian out of the room. Muñoz had cuffed Dressler, and he was lying facedown on the carpet the same way Black Eyes had lain on the sidewalk at the Jackie Robinson Village two days ago. She heard the voices of uniforms and paramedics entering the apartment. The static screeches from their radios echoed inside her head. Finally, Haggerty knelt beside her. "Can you sit up?"

She held out her hand and let him lift her. The high whine in her ears made all the other sounds feel faraway. Her brain was throbbing.

"I'll get a paramedic over here."

"I don't need them. How is Drew?"

Haggerty gave her a look that told her everything.

"The daughter?"

"She's okay. In the other room with Martin and the babysitter. Your head is bleeding."

"It hurts like hell, but I'm all right."

He took her face in his hands. "You're sure? Who am I?"

"The asshole who didn't come see me in the hospital."

FRIDAY

CHAPTER 58

"Where is Zoe?"

"She's with a social worker. She's just down the hall. She's safe. Her grandparents have been called."

"I want to see her. She needs to be with someone she knows."

"You can, in just a few moments."

"She needs me now."

"Very soon, Ms. Martin. Jane. Can I call you Jane? I need a statement first. It's very important. I need to hear what happened up there. You're the only other set of eyes and ears I have. You saw much more than I did. I need you to tell us everything you remember."

Martin's words came in fits and starts, some coherent, some not. "I— This is— How can this have happened? I got a message."

"You got a message?"

"A text."

"When?"

"Eleven. A little after."

"You weren't suspicious getting a call so late?"

Martin shook her head. "It's when Dana would have gotten home from the theater." Then she pressed her eyelids together as if she were in excruciating pain, and Codella realized that she *was* in fact in a kind of excruciating pain, but she needed the woman to think right now, to stay with her.

"Jane," she said. "I need you to focus. What did the text message say?"

"I have it." She patted her jacket pockets but couldn't find the phone, and this made her even more distressed.

"Never mind. Just tell me."

"*I need to talk to you.* That's all it said. *Please come. I need to talk to you.* It made me—" She stopped.

"Hope." Codella finished the sentence for her. "It made you hope. I know. Which is what they intended it to do, I'm sure. So you would come. They came for you. They came to kill you. She must have told them you didn't live there anymore. They used her phone to lure you there."

"I went straight over to see her."

"What time was it when you got there?"

"Eleven fifteen, I think. The door was ajar. I pushed it open and went into the vestibule. The lights were all on. I called out to Dana, but she didn't answer. I walked back to the living room, and there they were."

"Who?"

"The two men. The janitor and the other man. Dressler."

"Had you ever seen them before?"

"The janitor, yes. The other man, no."

"Tell me what happened. Describe everything you remember." She felt desperate to have this interview over. The sooner she heard Martin's account, the sooner she could get Jancek and Dressler into the interview rooms, and that's what she wanted to do. She didn't have patience for Martin's shock and confusion and grief, although she realized she was expecting an awful lot from the woman. "Go on," she prodded.

"They came up on either side of me and grabbed my arms."

"Were they carrying weapons? Guns? Knives?"

"I don't think so."

"Did you try to get away?"

"I screamed. Jancek cupped his hand over my mouth, and Dressler tied my arms behind my back. He was holding the rope. He wound it very tightly. Then they dragged me into Zoe's room where Dana and Zoe and Shaffo, our sitter, were already tied up."

"Did they speak to you?"

"No. And they gagged me before I could speak to them."

"Which man gagged you?"

"Dressler."

"And then?"

"Then they left the room for a long time. It felt like a long time, anyway. It probably wasn't, and we just sat there looking at each other, and I tried to sort things out in my mind. I remembered our conversation earlier in the day, and I figured they were there for me, to kill me, because they must have thought I'd seen them that night while I was in the laundromat, and all I could think was that Dana and Zoe and Shaffo were going to die because of me, and I just wanted to have that gag out of my mouth for five seconds so I could tell her one last time that I loved her, that I forgave her."

Codella didn't interrupt. It was only right to let her have this moment. Finally, she said, "Dana did some very self-serving things, Jane, but her last act was selfless. And that's worth a lot. That's what you need to hold on to."

Martin nodded gratefully.

"Where did they go when they left the room?"

"To the living room, I think. We could hear their voices. They were arguing, I think."

"What makes you think that?"

"Their tone. But I couldn't hear any of the words. Then the janitor came back into the room—this time with the gun—and stood there just staring at us for another five minutes until you arrived."

"Can you think of anything else I should know? Anything at all, however insignificant it seems?"

Martin shook her head. "I feel like I'm in a nightmare. I feel like I'm going crazy."

"Someone may be crazy," said Codella. "But I assure you, it isn't you." Then she stood and left the room, closing the door behind her.

Haggerty and Muñoz came out of the adjoining room where they had been watching and listening. She told Muñoz, "Take Martin to see the daughter. Then get Jancek in room A and Dressler in room B." She turned to Haggerty. "You've got Dressler. I'll take Jancek. Let's see what stories they spin."

CHAPTER 59

Jancek's metal folding chair was jammed into the far corner of the interview room next to the one-way glass where he kept eyeing his reflection. Could he feel the stares of Portino, Muñoz, Reilly, and McGowan behind the glass? she wondered. Could he sense Dressler less than ten feet away, in interview room B? His expression was blank. His long-sleeved arms dangled like gangly lynched corpses from each side of his tree-trunk shoulders. Only his eyes moved. They followed her from the door to her chair on the other side of the table. They watched her sit and cross her hands on the table. They watched her lean forward, open her mouth, press the recorder, and announce the date and time of the interview. "Let's start at the beginning, Mr. Jancek. Let's start with the photographs."

His eyes squinted. "Photograph?" he said with no emotion. "What photograph?"

"The one you took of Hector Sanchez and Dana Drew."

She had caught him off guard, she could tell. He had not expected her to start here. His eyebrows furrowed. "How do you know I took a photo of them? What proof do you have?"

She sat back in her chair and smiled. "It's three AM, Mr. Jancek. I'm tired, and I have a splitting headache from the butt of your coconspirator's gun. I'm in here to do *you* a favor. Down at central booking, they're not so nice to criminals who tie up cops and kill A-list movie stars. Do you want to talk to me or not?"

"I didn't kill her. Dressler did."

"And you were right there with him. And I'm telling you now, they won't be in a hurry to set your bail. With your sheet, you're likely to sit in a cell for weeks or months until a grand jury convenes, your court date is set, and your court-appointed lawyer throws together a flimsy defense while the prosecutor rounds up so many witnesses—including me, of course—that it'll make your head spin. There won't be any plea bargaining, I can assure you. I'm trying to offer you an easier path here, but if you're not interested, it's all the same to me." She pushed out her chair. "Shall I have them take you back to your cell?"

Then Jancek came back to life. "I'm not a monster. *He* was the monster." He pounded a fist onto the table. "*Sanchez*. Not me."

Codella felt the force of his fist through her whole body, but she managed to keep her reaction off her face and shrug with bored conviction worthy of Dana Drew. "Tell me something I don't already know. Believe me, I see how it was. He'd been a tyrannical bastard since he came to the school."

Jancek lowered his eyes and resumed a vacant stare.

"He was a big fucking imposter," she continued. "He played up to parents and students so they'd idolize him, isn't that right? But most of the teachers and staff hated him just like you did. And why wouldn't they? He graded them unforgivingly. He humiliated them publically. He barked orders disrespectfully. He was like a sadistic prison warden, wasn't he? Benevolent to the visitors, abusive to the inmates."

She waited. Jancek's eyes locked onto hers but gave no affirmation.

"I'm right, I know it. You all felt abused," she continued, weaving his story for him, building the justification that he would, she hoped, ultimately confess to. "And none of you could stand it anymore when he forced you to take part in that stupid farce called Proud Parents of PS 777. He couldn't have cared less that his photo shoot dredged up a traumatic time in your past. He didn't care if he forced you to relive the terrible abuse of your niece at the hands of Bosnian prison guards. Yes, I know about that, Mr. Jancek. Sanchez was like those prison guards. He thought he could move everyone around like pawns. You remember that day, Mr. Jancek? You remember the balloons and banners and popcorn? You remember how powerless you felt, forced to sit in that cafeteria?"

He nodded ever so slightly.

"And then Chris Donohue had an idea, didn't she? She thought of a way for the inmates to overthrow the prison guard. It was pretty clever, too. You'd hold your own photo shoot. You'd use the camera to tell the *truth* instead of *lies*. You'd expose Sanchez for what he really was. And *you*, Mr. Jancek, *you* would be the photographer."

She paused. She waited. But Jancek said nothing. He wasn't ready to own the story, his story. Should she stop? Should she continue to weave his tale for him? "She asked you to stake out his apartment," she finally said, "and you declined at first—you never intended to do anything wrong or illegal, did you? But in the end, you thought, why not? In a strange way, taking those photos would be an act of public service. You'd be standing up for all the teachers and staff who'd been under his thumb since the day he arrived. You'd finally teach *him* a lesson. You'd give everyone hope. You'd be a hero. And not only that—" She leaned forward. "Not only that, but you would finally compensate for everything you *hadn't* done—hadn't been able to do—to save your niece all those years ago."

Jancek's upper lip twitched, and his eyes had a liquid sheen, but all he said was, "I never said I did it."

"But you *did* do it," she insisted calmly and quietly. "We both know you did." She placed her hand over his and felt it stiffen in her palm, but he didn't pull it away. "And I don't blame you. I get it." And it occurred to her suddenly how ironic it was that she now had to lie in order to coax the truth out of him. "I understand why you did it. You gave him what he had coming." She paused to let her words sink in, to let him feel the permission to confess. And then she asked, "How many days did you have to stand in front of his apartment to get that incriminating photograph of them?"

"Three," he whispered, and his answer was like the blindingly painful needle prick of a poorly executed lumbar puncture. He was in the story with her now. They were dancing through the tangled clues and evidence. Now she had to keep him there.

"You gave that photo to Chris Donohue," she declared rather than asked, "and she told Dressler about it, and that's how this whole thing started."

CHAPTER 60

"This afternoon, you sat in that same chair and told me you had nothing to do with Hector Sanchez's murder. You told me—in a taped statement, let me remind you—that you went to his building, knocked on the door, and then went back to your hotel when he didn't answer. Do you remember saying that?"

Dressler didn't answer.

"Do you remember?" Haggerty repeated. "Or should I play the recording for you?"

"I remember. *Yes*. I remember, all right?"

"Then explain to me why you went to Dana Drew's apartment tonight with Milosz Jancek. Explain to me why you tied up five innocent people and murdered one of them."

"It wasn't murder. It was an accident. I've never had a gun in my hand before. She rushed at me. The gun went off. Your own detective can confirm that."

"What were you doing with a gun in your hand in the first place?"

"It belonged to Jancek. Look, it's a long story."

"I don't like long stories. Just get to the point. If you had nothing to do with the murders of Sanchez and Reyes, why were you in Dana Drew's apartment?"

Perspiration glistened in the hairline of Dressler's tight, black curls as he reached for the water bottle in front of him. He took a sip, set it back down, and let out a deep breath. "I didn't tell you the whole truth this afternoon," he conceded.

"No shit!" said Haggerty. "You lied in a sworn statement."

"Look, I panicked, all right? I have a family. I have a career. I'm on the brink of a big sale. I was afraid to jeopardize all that. But I'll tell you everything now. I'll tell you exactly what happened. You'll see I'm not a murderer."

Haggerty crossed his arms. Dressler was sweating up his expensive dress shirt. He unbuttoned his left cuff to roll it up, and Haggerty noticed it was monogrammed. Who wore monogrammed shirts these days, he wondered, except filthy rich Wall Street types and insecure people trying to look like Wall Street types? "Start talking," said Haggerty. "Unless you want me to draw my own conclusions."

Dressler pressed his palms into the table as if it were a Ouija board and the words he needed would flow up from the wood, through his fingertips, and into his brain. "This afternoon, you asked me if I took a photo of Sanchez, and I said no, and that's true. I didn't take it, but I knew about it. I knew Jancek had taken it. Donohue told me about it. She said if I showed him the photo, he'd have to get behind iAchieve. I didn't want to use it. I didn't want to stoop to threats. But after Monday morning, well, I had second thoughts."

"What happened Monday morning?"

"He hijacked my presentation at Barton's office. The lying son of a bitch stood up and told a room full of principals if they adopted iAchieve, the only winner would be McFlieger-Walsh. He claimed the program wasn't thoroughly tested, which is total bullshit. He looked at every face in that room and said they shouldn't spend millions of dollars to be guinea pigs."

"And you saw your sale going down the tubes."

"The sale I've been working on nonstop for more than a year."

More than a year of fucking Margery Barton, Haggerty thought. "So you decided a little blackmail might be in order after all?"

"Call it whatever you want." Dressler rolled up his other monogrammed sleeve. "He was spreading lies about iAchieve. It was time to confront him on his own stinking lies. But Jancek had the photo, and he wouldn't give it to me unless he came with me. He had his own bones to pick with Sanchez. I said no way, but then he said he'd go there with or without me, so I had no choice."

Haggerty pulled his cigarettes out of his pocket. "People always have a choice." He stared into Dressler's eyes. Dressler looked away first. He picked a loose fiber off his pant leg. Was it a fiber from the twine he had used to tie up Drew? Haggerty wondered. "So you and the janitor went to see him. And how did that go?"

Dressler was biting the inside of his mouth now. "I thought when he saw the photo, he'd be scared shitless."

"But he wasn't."

"He'd already seen it. He told me I was pathetic, and he was going to make sure my iAchieve campaign failed. And then he turned on Jancek. 'What are you?' he said. 'His bodyguard?' and he laughed really hard. He laughed for a long time, and then he got very close to Jancek, and his smile turned to a cold glare. He raised his index finger to Jancek's face and said, 'If I see you bring one more fucking cup of Dunkin' Donuts to my AP, I'm going to pour it down your throat.' And then Jancek jumped on him like a wild animal. It was over almost before it began. He murdered the guy in cold blood. It was terrible."

CHAPTER 61

"I never meant to do it. I wasn't myself. I felt so much rage. I was insane. I only felt that way one other time in my life." Jancek held his hands in front of his face palms up and stared at them as if they didn't belong to him. The hands were large and calloused, the fingers unattractively thick. Codella remembered Margery Barton's perfectly manicured nails shellacked with high-gloss polish. There were always fingers, someone's fingers, at the root of a murder. Jancek's fingers were quivering. "Before I knew what I was doing," he admitted now in a soft, disconsolate voice, "I got behind him and snapped his neck so hard it made a loud noise, like a tree branch, and he crumpled in my arms."

Codella watched tears well up in the custodian's eyes. One of them rolled lackadaisically down his coarse, angular cheek. The tear looked grossly out of place on that face, and she wondered if his display of emotion was an act—a confessed killer's tears often were—but she dismissed the suspicion almost immediately. At his core, she judged, Jancek did not have the equal measures of moral lassitude, cunning, and theatricality required to summon tears at will. He sounded miserable and ashamed of himself as he told her, "I enjoyed it. Just for that one instant. I was glad. I had him in my arms, and he couldn't get away—he had to feel *my* power for a change. I'm not sorry. Not really. I had to do it. For Marva. I did it for her, and I'm glad. Because he had crushed her spirit every day since he took over, and she is too good to be treated that way."

"You were there on Monday morning when he returned from the principal's meeting and took her into his office and screamed at her."

"It wasn't the first time he had disrespected her. I wanted to barge in there and tear his limbs apart."

"But you couldn't, could you? You couldn't help Marva any more than you could help your niece when she was being raped." She spoke in a calm, soothing tone like the hospital chaplain who'd sat at her bedside during her chemotherapies and tried to coax her feelings about cancer out of her.

"Marva needed a protector. I only wanted to be her protector."

"What happened then, Milosz?" She reeled him in from his grandiose thoughts. "What did you do after Sanchez crumpled in your arms?"

"I put him on the floor. He was still alive. He was staring up at me. He was gasping for breath. I will see his terrified eyes in my mind till the day I die. I never killed anyone else in my life. I was out of my mind. I started weeping. I couldn't see straight. I couldn't think. I started looking for a phone to call nine-one-one. I said, 'Oh my God. We have to do something. We have to help him.'"

"But you didn't help him. You took his crumpled body and turned him into a savior."

CHAPTER 62

"I have to use the bathroom," said Dressler. "You can't keep me locked in this little room. You can't keep me from making a phone call."

"Go ahead." Haggerty gestured toward the door. "Walk out of here. Make your fucking phone call. There's a pay phone down on the first floor. Nobody's stopping you. And then we'll get the official wheels in motion. Let me lay it out for you. We read you your rights. We arrest you for murder, attempted murder, and assault with a deadly weapon. We take you down to central in handcuffs, and they put you in a nice cozy cell with a couple of bunkmates who haven't seen a lot of black guys in monogrammed shirts like you, and you get to see what life is like outside the corporate bubble. I wonder if Margery Barton will come visit you." He grinned. "What's your guess?"

Dressler flashed a look of contempt. "I didn't kill or assault anyone. You got that? Now I want to take a leak."

Haggerty rapped on the table between them. "Somebody show this senior vice president of sales where the men's room is."

Seconds later, the door opened and Muñoz signaled for Dressler to follow. When Dressler returned, Haggerty said, "So you want to keep going, or you want to make that phone call and get the wheels turning?"

"What can you do for me?"

Haggerty wanted to say, *I don't make deals. I'm not a sleazy salesman like you.* Instead he said, "Maybe I can keep you from getting fucked up on your very first night in central holding. I can tell a prosecutor you were cooperative. As it stands, I bet we've got enough to put you in a cell at Sing Sing for a nice long stay. Now I need the facts. I need the whole story. Otherwise, I'm out of here."

Dressler nodded grudgingly.

"What happened after Jancek killed Sanchez?"

Dressler shrugged. "I told him, 'What the fuck's wrong with you?' but he didn't even seem to hear me. So I told him, 'This is on you, not me.' And then I walked. I got the hell out of there as fast as I could."

CHAPTER 63

"I didn't turn him into a savior. I didn't do anything," Jancek insisted. "I couldn't move. I couldn't think. I just stood there. Sanchez was moaning. It was loud, so loud. I couldn't stand it. He had tears in his eyes. I had to look away. Dressler told him to shut up, but he didn't. I said, 'We have to call for help,' and Dressler said, 'Shut up, you fucking moron.' Then he left the room. He went in the kitchen. I heard him opening and shutting cupboards and drawers. When he came back, he was wearing gloves—the kind you wear to wash the dishes—and he was holding a dishrag. He stuffed the rag in Sanchez's mouth. That made the moaning a little quieter. And then he dragged the body into the middle of the living room floor. He said, 'Grab his leg and help me!' but I didn't. I didn't go near him. I couldn't believe what I had done. I couldn't believe . . ." He shook his head.

In her mind, Codella visualized the three men in Sanchez's apartment: the temporarily deranged custodian; the quick-witted sales executive; and the once-arrogant, now-paralyzed principal. Was Jancek fabricating, or was he reporting events as they had truly occurred?

"What happened after Dressler dragged Sanchez to the center of the room?" she asked.

"He pulled off his shoes, socks, and jeans. He pulled his shirt over his head. He asked me to help again, but I didn't. He stripped him down to his shorts. And then he stretched his arms out to the sides. He positioned his legs and feet one over the other."

"What about Sanchez? Was he still awake? Was he still alive?"

"He had stopped making noise. He was having trouble breathing. His eyes were starting to roll back in his head. Dressler folded his clothes and took them to his bedroom. He removed the towel from his mouth. He went onto Sanchez's laptop, too. I don't know what he was doing. Looking for something, I guess. And then we left."

She noted the time and paused the recorder. "We'll take a break there," she said and stepped out of the room.

CHAPTER 64

"He claims he did nothing," Haggerty told her. "Says Jancek had a fit and broke Sanchez's neck, and he got out as fast as he could. Didn't want to take the heat."

Codella shook her head. "If he'd left in a hurry like that, we would have found his prints on the inside doorknob. There were no prints on that knob. It was wiped clean, according to Banks. I think he's lying."

"What did Jancek say?" Haggerty stared at the swollen red bump on her forehead. He didn't like the look of that bump.

"He confessed to the murder. Says he went crazy when Sanchez laughed and told him to stay away from Marva Thomas."

"So we've got our man."

"We've got Sanchez's killer. But that doesn't mean he murdered Sofia Reyes, too. He says after he broke Sanchez's neck, he stood there in shock while Dressler arranged the whole crucifixion scene. And if that's true, then maybe Dressler killed Reyes, too."

"You believe him?"

"My gut says he's telling the truth, but it's Dressler's word against his. He described the whole scene, Dressler screaming at him and then taking control of things, figuring out how to erase the evidence. Everything he said aligns with the facts."

"For instance?"

"Dressler put on plastic dishwashing gloves. That explains the lack of prints. He stuffed a dishtowel in Sanchez's mouth, which explains the fibers Gambarin found. He went onto Sanchez's laptop, which explains the website he was looking at."

"Jancek could have done all those things himself."

"True," conceded Codella. "That's true. It's his word against Dressler's."

"Did he mention Sofia Reyes?"

"Not once. How about Dressler?"

"No. But I imagine right now they're in there concocting their stories."

She leaned against the wall. She looked tired, he thought. "At least one of them is," she said.

Haggerty stared into her blue eyes. Her pupils were large, black circles. "How do you feel?"

"Fine. I'm fine."

"Are you still dizzy? You were out for about a minute after we got there. You could have a bad concussion, you know."

"I said I'm fine."

He remembered holding her in his arms on the street hours ago. Something about sitting in that small room with the slippery sales executive made him want to embrace her again now, tenderly, to embrace a different part of himself. "I'm driving you to the hospital as soon as we get done in there."

"Whatever," she said and turned.

CHAPTER 65

The bright lights of the interview room made her squint as she reentered the small windowless space. She did feel dizzy, and a little nauseous, too. She returned to her chair, determined to get the facts and get them quickly. "Look, Mr. Jancek, I want to help you, but there's something about your story that just doesn't make sense. If you felt guilt and remorse about killing Hector Sanchez, if you were so ready to phone nine-one-one the second after you snapped his neck, then why didn't you make the call? Why didn't you turn yourself in? You've had three days to come forward."

She watched him carefully. What explanation would he give to make his actions—and inaction—seem reasonable, justifiable?

Jancek sighed as if to acknowledge the truth in her unspoken thoughts. "Marva," he whispered. "Marva."

"Marva? How does Marva explain anything?"

"I didn't want Marva to know."

"Or is it that you didn't want *anyone* to know, Mr. Jancek—because you're lying? Because you never intended to call nine-one-one?" The words echoed in her brain as she said them. Someone was yelling the words. And then she realized *she* was yelling, and her hearing was defective and her head was pulsing like a ventricle expanding and contracting. Suddenly, she wanted to lie down on a bed, on a couch, on this floor, anywhere, and close her eyes to stop the pulsing. *You could have a bad concussion*, she heard Haggerty's voice in her head. "Quit wasting my time, Mr. Jancek," she said. "Why didn't you make that call? Why didn't you turn yourself in?"

"When I picked up the phone to dial the police, he yanked it out of my hands."

"Dressler?"

"'Don't be an even bigger fool,' he said. 'If you make that call, you'll end up in a prison cell for a long, long time. Do you want that?' and I didn't want that. I wanted to be with Marva. I want to marry Marva. I want to protect Marva forever. And he said no one had to know we'd been there if we just wiped our prints clean and got out without being seen."

Codella pictured Marva Thomas seated in her closet-sized office at PS 777 drinking the Dunkin' Donuts coffee Jancek had faithfully brought her each day. She remembered the Ephesians quote taped to Marva Thomas's computer monitor. *Be kind to one another, tenderhearted, forgiving one another, as God in Christ forgave you.* How far would Thomas's forgiveness extend? Could she rationalize Jancek's act because he had done it for her? Was her Christian moral compass susceptible to the shifting magnetic fields of love and retribution? Would she visit Jancek in prison, where he would most certainly end up? "Tell me what happened next," Codella demanded. "Tell me exactly what happened."

"He went around the apartment, wiping off fingerprints, I guess, while the dog kept nudging Sanchez." Jancek crossed one leg over the other and folded his big hands in his lap. "And then we left."

Now Codella pounded her fist against the table. "No! You're lying, Mr. Jancek. You didn't just walk out of there and go home. Sofia Reyes was dead within two hours of Sanchez, and you and I both know that one of you went to her house and killed her. I know about the Skype call, Mr. Jancek. I know Reyes saw you and Dressler come in, and when you killed Sanchez, her fate was sealed. She was a witness. You couldn't let her live."

Jancek didn't move or speak.

"So one of you killed her, and you had the obvious motive. *You* snapped his neck. *You* had the most to lose. Did you kill Reyes too? Did you cover one murder with another, Mr. Jancek, to keep Marva Thomas and the rest of the world from knowing the truth about you?"

"No!" He rocketed out of his chair so violently that it tipped and crashed against the cinderblock wall below the one-way mirror. Codella stood too. They were faced off now, with just the table between them, and he was almost a foot taller than her. She imagined Portino, Reilly, and Muñoz on their feet now, too, behind that mirror, prepared to rush in and restrain him if he reached out to snap her neck. But he didn't reach out. He gripped his head with both hands as if he intended to crush his own skull. "I didn't kill her. I swear to you. I killed one person in my life. I killed Sanchez. I didn't kill the woman." And then he wept.

"Sit down, Mr. Jancek," she ordered, and he lowered himself like a docile child. "You owe it to everyone to tell me what happened."

He sniffed. He wiped his eyes. She waited. "He wanted me to go and kill her." He rubbed his temples with the heels of his palms. "I told him no. No. I wouldn't do it. He kept at me. 'You want to go to jail? Don't be a fucking moron. If she lives, both of our lives are ruined. You're not ruining my life.' He kept at me. It seemed like forever. And then he gave up. He finally gave up. He could tell I just didn't care what happened. He stuffed the dishrag and plastic gloves in his coat pocket before we went downstairs. When we were outside, he made me swear to say nothing. If I talked, he'd talk too, he said, and he was a better liar than me, and that's how we left it. I went one way and he went another. I've told you everything now."

CHAPTER 66

"You're not telling me everything, Dressler. You want me to think you're the innocent one in all this, but how can I do that when you're sitting there lying to me?"

"What do you mean?"

"I mean Sofia Reyes. What else do you think I mean?"

"Isn't it obvious what happened?"

"Pretend I'm an idiot." Haggerty tapped the tip of his index finger into the table so hard the bone felt bruised. "You've got one shot at the truth. Don't dick me around. Either make me believe you or this interview is over and I process the fuck out of you." He stared into Dressler's green eyes. He could almost hear the calculation behind those green eyes. *What does he already know? Does he know about the Skype call? Does he know Reyes saw us? What did Jancek already tell them?*

Finally Dressler said, "Sofia Reyes was Skyping with Sanchez when we knocked on his door. We walked in and there she was. She saw us there."

"She could have tied you to the murder."

"She couldn't tie me to something I didn't do. I didn't kill Sanchez, and I didn't kill her. She was *his* problem. Isn't it obvious what happened? He went to her apartment and killed her."

"And you didn't think to tell me that until this moment?"

"I told you. I was afraid. I have a lot to lose."

Haggerty lighted a cigarette and blew a stream of smoke across the table. "You'd have a lot less to lose if you'd left Sanchez's apartment Monday night and come straight to the police."

"I realize that now," he said quietly.

Haggerty leaned his elbows on the table as if he were having a casual conversation at a bar. "You're full of bullshit, Dressler." He blew more smoke in his face. "And the smell is getting to me."

"I've told you the truth."

"Then why the fuck were you in Dana Drew's apartment tonight looking for Jane Martin?"

"It's a long story."

"Then you better get started."

"Jancek made me go."

"He *made* you?"

"He had a gun," said Dressler. "He asked to meet me and talk, so I met him in the Time Warner building, and he was all nervous about those surveillance tapes on the news. He told me he'd seen Jane Martin in that laundromat on his way from Sanchez's apartment. He was afraid she'd seen him too. He shoved the gun in my back and said I was coming with him and not to try anything or he would shoot me and then shoot himself, and after what he did in Sanchez's apartment, I didn't doubt he was capable of something like that, so we got in a taxi and he took me to Dana Drew's apartment. I didn't even know it was her apartment until we got upstairs.

"We got up there and Martin wasn't even there. It was just the babysitter and the kid. Jesus! What a fucking mess. Come to find out Martin wasn't even living there. Jancek panicked at that point. He forced them into the bedroom. He made me tie them up."

"Then what?"

"We waited for Drew to get home. He made me tie her up, too. And then he used her phone to text Martin and Codella. He was going to round them up and kill them all. Don't you see that? He was crazy."

"But you had a gun, too."

"He gave it to me, but I wasn't going to use it. He wanted me to slit their throats the way he slit Sofia Reyes's, only I refused. I'm not a murderer. I got my own kid. I love kids. I'm not going to kill a kid or a mother of a kid. That's not who I am. I go to church. I'm the deacon of a church. I count the money every Sunday. I've got a conscience. You're not looking at a killer. Chip Dressler is no killer. I told him I couldn't do that, he'd have to kill me too. So he said he would do it, and I played along. I said I'd guard him, but I never intended to use the gun. I was going to make him stop.

I was planning to save them all. I knew I had to shoot him, but I'd never held a gun before. I've never shot a man in cold blood. I didn't mean to hit the detective on the head. I meant to hit Jancek. Please, I'm telling you the truth here. You've got to believe me. Please don't ruin my life."

Haggerty wasn't listening to Dressler's sales pitch anymore. He was listening to Dressler's voice in his head. *He wanted me to slit their throats the way he slit Sofia Reyes's.*

CHAPTER 67

The story poured out of him now like milk from a pitcher.

"He phoned me two, three times a day after that—to remind me to keep my mouth shut, as if I needed his reminders—and then those surveillance photos were released yesterday, and he went crazy. He wanted me to meet him and talk. We met outside the Time Warner building at nine o'clock last night. I was still in the city because I took Marva to dinner. I had walked her home earlier, and I was sitting in a bar just thinking about her. I met him, and all he could think about was the woman in the laundromat who the police were looking for. Had I seen her? Did I know who she was? And I did know who she was. I knew her from last Friday when I was polishing the floors and she and Dana Drew were meeting with Sanchez and Reyes in the cafeteria. I told him, and I wish I hadn't, because when I did, he said we had to go and see her. We had to find out if she recognized us.

"'Are you crazy?' I said. 'That's not a good idea. We should stay as far away as we can. Maybe she saw nothing. The photos are blurry. The photos can't prove anything.' But he didn't want to take a chance. He didn't want anybody out there who could tie him to Sanchez. I said I wasn't going to go there with him. I wanted no part of it, and that's when he shoved the gun in my side. 'We're both in this,' he said. 'We're both in this mess because of you. And we're going to finish it together.'"

"What did you do?"

Jancek shrugged. "I got in the taxi with him. What else was I supposed to do? He had a gun in my ribs."

"What was the plan?"

"He said Drew would be at the theater. The kid would be asleep. We'd get past the doorman, use the fire stairs, and take care of Martin."

"Kill her?"

"So no one could tie us to the murder."

"And what happened?"

"We got past the doorman, but things went wrong upstairs. Martin wasn't there. A babysitter opened the door. She saw Dressler's gun and panicked. We had to barge in so she wouldn't scream or call for help. I had to restrain her so she wouldn't go to the phone or wake the kid. I didn't hurt her though. I just held my hand over her mouth while Dressler found some twine and tape in a kitchen drawer. We tied her up. She told us Martin didn't live there. She was crying. I taped her mouth. It was terrible. I told him we should never have come there, and he said, 'Shut up. Shut the fuck up and do what I say,' and he tossed me his pocketknife. He had planned for this, you see. 'You're going to wait for a full house,' he said, 'and then you're going to slit their throats.'"

CHAPTER 68

"How do you know Jancek slit Sofia Reyes's throat?"

"What?"

Haggerty tapped his fingers on the table in the small inter-view room. "A minute ago you said Jancek wanted you to slit their throats the way he slit Sofia Reyes's. Those were your words. How do you know he slit her throat?"

"He told me."

"When? When did he tell you?"

"I don't know. I don't remember."

"If somebody told me he'd slit a person's throat, I think I'd remember when. That's not the kind of thing you forget. When did you talk to him?"

"He called me."

"When did he call you?"

"The next day," said Dressler. "Tuesday."

"What time?"

"I don't remember."

"What else did he tell you?"

"Nothing."

"Oh, come on. He tells you he slit her throat, but he doesn't tell you anything else?"

"He said she bled a lot. That's all. I told him I didn't want to know."

"Where were you when he called you?"

"At my office, I think."

"You think?"

"Look, a lot has happened this week. It's all a big jumble in my head. What do you want from me?"

Haggerty smiled. He oozed sympathy. He said, "Sorry. You want another bottle of water?"

"No. I want to get out of here. I've been cooperative."

"We're almost done. Just a few more questions. So Jancek called your cell phone, right?"

"Right. I told you."

"And he said he'd slit Sofia Reyes's throat and she had bled a lot."

"Right."

"But he didn't say anything else?"

"No."

"He didn't tell you the cut was so deep that she never had a chance and she couldn't even raise her hands to try because they were bound so tight?"

"He's a crazy motherfucker."

"And this was sometime on Tuesday?"

"Or Wednesday. I don't know. What's the big deal?"

Haggerty leaned across the table slowly. "The big deal, Mr. Dressler, is that no one except the police and the killer know how she died."

"Jancek knows."

"Does he? Does he really?"

Dressler struggled to keep his face composed, but his tongue wetted his lips, and his teeth bit his lower gum. His nostrils flared on each intake of breath.

"We'll check your cell records, Mr. Dressler. If there's not a call from Jancek, we're going to charge you with the murder of Sofia Reyes. I think this interview is over."

MONDAY

CHAPTER 69

Karen Babb didn't try to stop her from entering the inner sanctum of the district office unannounced. Codella went straight to Margery Barton's office and pushed open the door. Barton was on the phone. "I'll call you back," she said quickly and hung up.

"I assume you've heard about the arrests," said Codella.

"It's all anyone is talking about today," she said. "I can't believe something like this really happened."

Codella almost laughed. She wanted to say, *Don't you mean you can't believe that the man you've been fucking for a year at the Mandarin Oriental was a murderer?* But she refrained. It was satisfaction enough to know that Barton must be thinking it. "Well, it did happen."

"So Chip—Chip Dressler—confessed?"

Codella detected hopefulness in her voice. "If you're asking will you dodge a turn in the witness box under oath, then the answer is yes. Your dirty little secrets are safe for now, Dr. Barton, though I expect your iAchieve sale isn't."

Barton's face relaxed visibly. "I don't know about that," she said with a burst of confidence. "McFlieger-Walsh did nothing wrong."

"Except send a murderer to broker a deal with the biggest school district in the country."

"I spoke to their publisher this morning. John McGreevy. He's offered to equip every school in the district with handheld devices for free, a gesture of goodwill to keep the sale on the table. So actually, the district has every reason to pursue the adoption." She smiled.

Codella felt her outrage surge like a spiking fever. She loathed Margery Barton. She had loathed her, she realized, from the moment they had met. She hated her brittle femininity and her smug condescension. She was the sort of woman who capitalized on every opportunity regardless of the wreck she left in her wake. She offended Codella's sense of honor as deeply as her own father had offended her. "You may well get your program, Dr. Barton," she said slowly, "and you may get to keep your less than ethical infidelity under everyone else's radar, but I will always know the truth about you. And I'll always know—even if no one else does—that you had a hand in this crime."

"That's a preposterous allegation."

"Is it?" She stared into Barton's eyes. "You were played, Dr. Barton, and you know exactly what I mean."

Barton dabbed her lower lip with one manicured forefinger. At least she had the good sense not to protest further.

Codella continued to stare until Barton looked away uncomfortably. "You surrendered your judgment in that hotel bedroom, and when Chip Dressler called you Monday night asking for Sofia Reyes's address, you gave it to him. You made a murder possible when you took that call and failed to question him, when you failed to say that it was not your place to give out that information."

Now Barton's face became an open canvas of panic.

"But you already know all of this. You've known it since Sofia turned up dead. You started to figure it out sometime late Wednesday or Thursday morning, I'm sure, after we left your office and you saw the news reports of Sofia's death. You thought back on Monday and how he had called in his ask-me-no-questions request. You knew then that you were in far deeper than any Roberto Cavalli scarf alibi could dig you out of. You are, after all and despite your poor judgment, an intelligent woman. So what do you have to say for yourself?"

Barton stood erect, struggling to maintain her now porous posture of imperviousness. "I'm not going to say anything," she said evenly.

"I didn't think so." Codella turned to go.

When she double-parked her car in front of the school, Marva Thomas was greeting the children of PS 777 on the steps of the building. As soon as the school bell rang, Codella got out and approached the slender, tired-looking woman. "I'm sorry," she said.

"What for?" Thomas shrugged. "You just did your job."

"At least the school can move on now. Its tyrant is gone. You're all free to shape a new future."

Thomas smiled. "It's a nice thought. But I don't have any illusions when it comes to shaping the future."

"No, I suppose I don't either." Codella thought about her own situation. McGowan certainly wouldn't be able to complain about her handling of this case, but he wouldn't be happy with the national publicity she was getting and would continue to get, given that one of the murder victims was Dana Drew. And her male colleagues at Manhattan North weren't going to make her life easy. But what guarantees did she have that she would even be around to worry about that? Were you really free to shape your future when the next cancer cell might proliferate inside you at any moment? What had Dr. Abrams said at her last exam? "Don't come back for six months." She would be living her life in six-month increments for the foreseeable future. What long-range plans could you make in six-month spans?

"I'm the official principal of PS 777 now." Thomas changed the subject. "Margery Barton had a miraculous change of heart about me. One day I'm not up to the task, and the next, I have her full confidence."

"Yes. I heard. Congratulations. At least she put something right."

"Ironically I'm not going to make big changes. Sanchez was doing many of the right things—raising the quality of teaching, supporting parents and students. He was just doing them in the wrong way and for the wrong reasons. He let things go to his head."

"I wish you the best, Ms. Thomas." Codella began to step away, but then she turned back. "And for what it's worth, I'm sorry about Milosz Jancek. I do believe he cared about you. In his own deluded way, he did want to protect you."

Thomas looked down at the school steps. "I don't want to think about him, Detective. But I appreciate your efforts to console me." And then she went into the building.

Codella drove back to the 171st one last time to thank the team that had helped her. She spoke to Muñoz first, in a loud voice that Blackstone could hear. "You did a good job on this," she told him firmly. "You can have my back any day, Detective."

Portino gave her a fatherly hug. Reilly said, "Don't be a stranger."

Then there was just Haggerty. He was sitting at his desk in the corner of the detectives' squad room as she put on her leather jacket to head back to Manhattan North. They traded a glance, and then she turned away and walked out knowing he would follow. They met on the sidewalk in front of the precinct. "So it's over," he said, "and you're as good as you ever were. You're still the genius."

Martin shook her head. She hadn't been that good, she knew, in so many ways, and she wasn't sure she wanted to resume being who she had been before anyway. The one upside of cancer, it occurred to her, was that it tore you right down to your foundations. If you survived it, you got to rebuild from the ground up, to totally new specifications. From now on, she would follow her instincts, and right now her instincts told her not to close the door on Haggerty. She smiled at him. "You want to get some of that vegan chili with me later?"

He smiled back. "Oh God. You're going to punish me forever."

"Eight o'clock." She turned and got into her car.

ACKNOWLEDGMENTS

To those who have helped me along the way, I am profoundly grateful.

Cynthia Swain, Cameron Swain, and Matthew Swain, for always
    dreaming with me
Kathy Green, my agent
Matthew Martz, my editor
S. J. Rozan, a gifted writer and my insightful teacher
Constance Smith, my sister
Elizabeth Avery
Sue Foster and Sue Lund
Richard Corman

    And from the early days . . .

Warren Jay Hecht, Barbara Grossman, Max Apple
The Hopwood Program at the University of Michigan
The Fine Arts Work Center in Provincetown